STRANGER WORLD

Jack  Castle

Castle Books, Inc.

Jack Castle/Stranger World
www.JackCastlebooks.com
www.JackCastle@aol.com

Publisher's Note: This is a work of fiction. Names, characters, places, and incidents are a product of the author's imagination. Locales and public names are sometimes used for atmospheric purposes. Any resemblance to actual people, living or dead, or to businesses, companies, events, institutions, or locales is completely coincidental.

Book Layout © 2017 BookDesignTemplates.com

Stranger World/ Jack Castle. -- 1st ed.
ISBN **978-1-0878-5760-2**

Praise for

JACK CASTLE

and the #1 best-selling series

Stranger World

"The lines of imagination and reality never have been so blurred as they are in the amazing, yet sinister theme park so creatively envisioned by Jack Castle!"

-Joe Butler, Spokesman Review

"For nearly a decade, Jack Castle has been crafting thrilling adventures for my theme park and guiding millions of guests through them. So, it comes as no surprise his talent as a storyteller has expanded to thrill readers worldwide through his Stranger World book series."

-Gary Norton
Owner of Silverwood Theme Park
(largest Theme Park in the Northwest)

Also by Jack Castle:

Europa Journal
Bedlam Lost
White Death
The Revenants

Stranger World (series):

Stranger Origins
Stranger World
Stranger Realm
Stranger Tides
Stranger Desert
Stranger Dream

For Alexandria
You will always be my baby girl

"You can design and create, and build the most beautiful place in the world, but it takes people to make the dream a reality."

-Walt Disney

Fun Facts:

- **July 17th, 1955:** Walt Disney opens his first theme park (Disneyland) on 160 acres of orange groves and employs less than 900 employees.

- **TODAY...** Disney World has grown to include dozens of major theme parks and resorts all over the world: hundreds of hotels and retail stores, multiple television and media networks, and employs over a (cumulative) billion employees. It now owns a combined acreage to rival the state of Maryland.

- **December 4th, 2014:** The owner of a restaurant in China replaces his waiters with robot servers.

- **March 26th, 2015:** World-renowned geneticists successfully harvest DNA from mammoths preserved in the Arctic and insert it into the genome of an elephant embryo.

- **March 18th, 2016:** In an interview at a technology show, an artificially intelligent, and extremely lifelike robot, told its creators, **"I will destroy all humans."**

What follows isn't merely a flight of fancy. It is a glimpse into a future limited only by our imagination, and by the imagination of those we create.

The Lamppost Man

What's my name? That seems important somehow.

The loud, painful ringing in her ears finally subsided and was slowly replaced with the sound of a gentle, steadily blowing wind. Her body trembled slightly—and for a moment, it was all she could do to just breathe.

Even before her eyes fluttered open, she felt the blistering ice crystals stinging her cheeks. Every bone, joint, and muscle ached, yet somehow, she managed to prop herself up on her elbows.

Surrounded by long blades of bristly prairie grass, she soon realized, if she was going to see anything, she'd have to stand. Rising to her feet, she found herself in the middle of an endless sea of grasslands shrouded by a thin layer of fresh snow as light as a funeral veil.

Shielding her eyes from the departing sun, she stared out over the gently rocking grasses and could almost make out a chain of snowcapped mountains on the horizon. As she stared at them, willing her eyes to focus, she heard a long, ominous howl of a wolf. She would have been more nervous, were it not so far away.

For the life of her, she couldn't remember how she came to be in this place, and as she regained more of her senses, she realized she couldn't even recall her own name. A chill passed through her body. And, as she hugged her shoulders tighter for warmth, she discovered she was wearing a white lab coat, dress pants, and black high-heels.

Hardly the best outfit for hiking through the grasslands, she thought. A harsh wind whipped the scrub brush at her feet and tore at her clothes, forcing her to shield her eyes with her arm and turn to face the other direction.

She wasn't alone.

A short distance away, a bright yellow VW bug was parked haphazardly next to a single-lane of asphalt road. Failing to see any other options she set out for the tiny car.

Drawing closer, she could see the driver's side door had been left open, and the right rear turn indicator was blinking madly at her. *Is this my car?* If so, the New York plate on the rear bumper was her first clue to her possible origins. Peering inside through the open window she found a clean but heavily used interior.

Sliding behind the wheel she thought; *I don't remember ever living in New York. Did I hit my head? And how did I get out in the middle of the grasslands?* She lifted her blond-ish bangs and using the rearview mirror, checked for trauma. *Seems okay.* Finding no obvious signs of damage, she gazed at her reflection further. An attractive blonde woman wearing thick horn-rimmed glasses and a confused look gazed back at her.

Who are you?

She found the keys in the ignition and was slightly amused by the pinkish lucky rabbit's foot dangling from the chain.

Charming. She figured the tiny car was probably out of gas, but to her pleasant surprise, when she turned the key halfway, the needle of the fuel indicator rose to nearly a quarter of a tank. Turning the key the rest of the way she was rewarded with a gentle roar from the teeny-tiny engine that modestly sprung to life.

Checking her surroundings one last time for any other options and finding none, she put the car in gear and drove the VW bug back onto the road.

The petite engine hummed happily along as she kept her speed at a safe and steady forty-five miles per hour. *Was I headed this way in the first place?*

To pass the time, and desperate for some normalcy, she turned the knobby switch on the radio to the on position, but was rewarded with only static. It was the same with all the other stations. She was about to check the glovebox when she saw a distant and unusual shape moving amongst the clouds. It wasn't a plane, helicopter, or balloon. It almost seemed as though it were made of gold and metal, like something Jules Verne might've crafted.

How could something like that even stay afloat?

When it vanished behind some puffy white and pink clouds, she lowered her gaze from the heavens and glimpsed a crossroads directly ahead. At the intersection, on one corner was an oversized solitary lamppost, which made absolutely no sense in the middle of nowhere.

If that wasn't peculiar enough, a strangely-clad man leaned off it. He wore heavy stage makeup, a black top hat, and a circus ringmaster's bright red tailcoat. Presently, he held himself perfectly still, one hand shielding his eyes from the setting sun.

Against her better judgment, she brought the beetle to a stop. She'd decided to keep the motor running for fear it wouldn't start back up again; plus, she didn't want to be stranded with the strange man perched on the lamppost.

Using her open door as a shield, she got out of the car, raised her voice, and said to the Lamppost Man, "Excuse me, uh, *monsieur*?"

Monsieur? Am I French? Her accent certainly sounded French. Whether she came from France, Quebec, or even New Orleans, she hadn't the foggiest.

The Lamppost Man didn't answer. Instead, he continued to remain perfectly still. So still that she actually considered he wasn't a man at all, but rather a very life-like mannequin.

Regardless, she still decided to give it one more try, "Excuse me, *monsieur*, err... sir, hallo?"

This is ridiculous. I'm talking to a signpost.

She moved to climb back into the bug, when she could have sworn the Lamppost Man blinked.

Wait.

Her eyes narrowed as she stared at him for several moments, trying to decide if he had blinked, or if she had simply imagined it. Giving her head a quick shake, she placed one foot back into the VW. At the same time, he slowly turned his head toward her and a giant Cheshire Cat smile spread across his face.

"Oh. Hello there... greetings and salutations!"

"Hello, *monsieur*. I'm sorry, but I seem to have hit my head or something. I woke up beside the road next to this car. I don't even think it is mine."

"That's quite alright, my dear. Quite alright indeed." Still staring down at her from his perch, he asked, "What is your appellation, young lady?"

Her mind still froggy, she had to think about this for a second, and as she did, she asked reflexively, "My what?"

"Your appellation. It means your name."

"I know what it means," she grumped irritably, and then gazing down, she realized she wore a blue lanyard draped around her neck. Attached to the end hung some kind of laminated identification badge.

Studying it, she saw an unflattering picture of herself, and next to the photo was the name: DR. SOPHIA DAVENPORT. *So, my name is Sophia.* She studied the badge a bit further in the hopes of finding another clue to her identity. Unfortunately, all she found was one word in another little box under the category of division, which read: MICROBIOLOGY.

Fighting down the urge to panic, she squared her shoulders back and held up the tag like a small shield toward him. "According to this, my name is Dr. Sophia Davenport, and I am a Microbiologist. Whether this is true or not, I do not know."

The Lamppost Man didn't reply and remained unmoving with that perpetual grin of his, studying her like a bird might take in a worm.

This is getting nowhere. "Where am I? Do you know how I got here?"

"Yes. Yes. I can answer all! But, alas! Where are my manners?" With a mighty leap, he jumped down from his perch, the soles of his shoes smacking the asphalt, and the noise echoing through the air. Bounding over to her, and in a very gleeful voice, he said, "Allow me to introduce myself. My name is..." and using his booming baritone voice here, "THE LAMPOST MAN... Ta-Da!" When she didn't respond immediately, he asked, "Really? Nothing? Na-da? Zip? No cowering in fear? Ohhhh... right. You're newwww around here. You can do all that nonsense of running away in fear later. Besides, I don't know why everyone does that. I mean, to look upon me is to love me. I said... to l-o-o-vvv-eee me! Still nothing? Wow. Tough crowd."

He clasped her small hand in both of his white-gloved hands and began shaking it profusely. "We are so glad to have you. Welcome, welcome. You'll have to forgive me. It's been quite some time since I've been able to greet any guests."

Thinking out loud to himself, he asked, "How long have I been up there anyway? Five days, a month, a year? Oh, that's right. So silly of me--seventy years." He brushed the nonexistent dust off his golden epaulets. "Why, you've certainly picked a most wonderful time to visit. You see, Lady

Wellington has captured the Dauntless and to celebrate, she is planning the most fantastic party. A most-marvelous party indeed."

Sophia, nearly hand-shaken out of her gourd, pulled her hand out of his firm grasp. "Where am I, where is this place?"

"Where are you?" he asked. "Oh, my, my, my." He outstretched both arms to his sides and answered, "Why, silly, you are at the crossroads, of course. Where did you think you were?"

Sophia sighed, fought down her frustration and asked, "Well, can you at least tell me which way to go?"

"Which way to go?" She noticed he had the annoying habit of repeating her questions back to her before answering.

"Why, that's entirely up to you, my dear." Without warning he jumped up onto the bumper and pin-wheeled his arms before pointing out the road to her right and said, "If you go that way, you will certainly meet something large with teeth that is sure to eat you." Pin-wheeling his arms a second time and landing his fingers toward the opposite direction, he then informed, "And this way, many chills, spills, and nightmares await you."

Sophia scanned both directions and didn't see any of those things, only a barren, narrow road leading to the horizon. Staring in the fourth direction she caught sight of a small town in the distance. "What about over there?"

In a move that Sophia would not have thought him capable of the Lamppost Man bounced up off her front bumper, did a back somersault in the air, and landed in front of her. He abruptly put his face next to her cheek and stared off at the town in the distance. When she tried to pull away, he calmly but firmly, pulled her back and explained, "Oh, that is a very satisfying choice indeed. I see many adventures waiting for you there, but..." he checked to see if anyone was listening, and added as though it were a secret, "Beware the butler."

The Lamppost Man then froze and remained perfectly still. Standing that way, with his head cocked to one side, it almost appeared as though he were listening to someone whisper something in his ear.

"Okay," Sophia said in as pacifying tone as she could muster, all the while backing away from him until she stood safely back beside her open door. She was about to climb back in, but feeling a chilly wind, and perhaps feeling a bit sorry for the strange man, she asked, "It's pretty cold out here, and we are in the middle of nowhere. Can I give you a lift somewhere?"

This seemed to snap the Lamppost Man out of his trance. "My, what a lovely invitation," he said, parading over to where she was standing next to her open door. "But there's just one teensy-tiny-little problem."

"What are you doing?" she asked as he pulled her forcefully away from the idling VW. With a great deal of effort Sophia yanked her arm free, but in an impossible fit of speed and strength the Lamppost Man lunged forward, grabbed her again, and flung her roughly to the ground.

Pinning her arms and legs with his own body, and leering down at her he said, "You see, I'm afraid you've arrived a tad bit early. Why, Colonel Stapleton and his daughter haven't even arrived yet." Studying her limbs carefully, he then muttered to himself, "Now, I do hope this goes better than the last time. You bags of flesh can be so fragile." Lifting his eyes back to hers he scoffed, 'Why, the arms and legs just came right off the last one. And all that screaming. My goodness. So loud."

"Let me go. That hurts!"

"That's because I'm breaking your arm." He then paused for a moment, deciding which limb to grab next. "Now I know this hurts, but you can trust me when I say this is all for the greater good."

As he systematically continued to break every bone in her body, Sophia screamed long... loud... and full of anguish.

MISSION TIME 0415hrs

June 22nd, 2012

Afghanistan

"Mayday-Mayday-Mayday!"

Air Force Search and Rescue Helicopter Pilot Lt. Col. George Stapleton had to shout to be heard over the whine of the twin-turboshaft engine, the CHUG-CHUG-CHUG of the door gunner's fifty-caliber, and every klaxon alarm screaming for his attention.

His co-pilot (a fresh-faced kid out of Utah) had a gaping hole where his chest used to be--the round that had killed him had come right up through the floor in front of him.

In the cabin area, flight engineer Dwayne Harkins, and left door gunner, Mike Farro, were more stains on the fuselage than dead human beings. Seated by the chopper's right-side door was the only remaining crew member, twenty-three-old, para-rescue hoist operator, Donald Ozechowski.

To put it mildly, things were not going well.

George clicked the microphone switch mounted on the cyclic control column. "Forward Base, Forward Base, do you read? This is Air Force Search and Rescue, Pedro One. We are inbound with heavy casualties."

The voice of Forward Base came back over the headset built into his helmet. "We read you, Pedro One. We lost you in the canyon but you're Lima-Charlie now."

Ground fire ping-ping-pinged the fuselage again, so George banked hard to get out of the line of fire. "L.Z. was a trap. Everything went south. We are taking on heavy fire!" When he no longer heard the chug-chug of the fifty-caliber machine gun, he knew 'Ozzie,' was gone, most likely hanging lifeless in his sling.

George was alone.

That is, except for the Pavehawk flying ahead of him, overloaded with two pilots, two medics, and exactly seventeen wounded patients.

As if reading his thoughts Forward Base radioed, "Colonel. We can't raise Pedro Two. Do you have a visual?"

Yeah, I do, they're right in front of me.

Staring through the night-vision goggles George had always felt like he was staring through two toilet paper rolls mounted in front of his eyes. But he never argued with the results. Even on the blackest of nights (like this one) he could see perfectly. At the moment, the Pavehawk (a diminutive form of the Blackhawk helicopter modified for search-n-rescue) was hugging the green phosphorous landscape as fast as its badly-smoking engines would allow.

Once George had realized how badly Pedro Two had been hit, he dropped his own helicopter back behind them to draw away the enemy fire. Getting those boys home was all that mattered. If for nothing else, so his entire crew hadn't died for nothing. He clicked his mic again and radioed back, "Be advised, Pedro Two's comm.'s are down. Engines badly damaged. I'm flying rear guard, drawing heavy enemy fire."

"Copy Pedro One. Stand by. We're going to try and get you some support."

When the distress call had first come in, George and his crews were right in the middle of conducting routine training exercises. At the time, he'd been preoccupied with a travel itinerary that would deliver him back stateside in a scant three days. He and the rest of his unit were only reservists, guys with normal jobs back home. For the last decade, eleven months out of the year, he was a college history professor. It was hard to believe that last month his biggest dilemma was writing a new syllabus for the next semester.

But then the distress call came in--the boys on the frontline had been shot down in a CH-47 Chinook troop transport and hostile ground forces were closing in. He and his trainees had diverted from their training exercises without hesitation, landed under the worst possible conditions, and made off with over a dozen survivors.

But, the enemy wasn't about to let them slip away so easily.

"Colonel Stapleton, this is eye in the sky," radioed Captain Marco Phillips, the commander of the AC-130U Specter gun ship currently flying air support twenty thousand feet overhead. "We just picked you up on our radar."

"Glad to have you with us, Spooky," George radioed back with forced cool, using the call sign for the specter gun ship.

But the AC-130 pilot cut him off abruptly. "Colonel be advised, ground forces have locked onto you with a long-range missile launcher. Recommend you launch counter measures."

The cyclic steering column began vibrating even more uncontrollably than before, and he now had to hold on with both hands just to keep his bird on course. *That last volley must've damaged one of the hydraulic lines.* He managed to click his mic anyway.

"All counter measures exhausted."

As the pilot overhead processed the grim news George knew he could peel off and attempt evasive maneuvers, but with Pedro 2 as badly damaged and overloaded as they were, it was all the pilot in front of him could do to keep his bird afloat, let alone maneuver. In the end, it was simple math. He was only one guy left with a plenty of good years under his belt. In the chopper ahead of him were twenty-one young men and women with their whole lives ahead of them.

The AC-130's pilot voice crackled over his headset once more. "Colonel, be advised they have launched missile."

George knew there was nothing else to do. All counter measures had been deployed.

The literal motto of Para Rescue was *SO THAT OTHERS MAY LIVE.*

Darn, so close to retirement. Tessa is going to be so mad.

He clicked his mic one last time. "Understood. I'm holding position." George knew this would be his final transmission-- the last anyone would ever hear from him.

The AC-130 pilot circled overhead, struggling to keep the tears from his voice. "Copy that, Colonel. Missile locked and closing." He counted down the time until impact. "Missile impact in TEN... NINE... EIGHT..."

To increase Pedro Two's chances of survival George throt-tled up the engines to maximum power knowing the additional heat he created would draw the attention of the IR missile's seeker.

Approximately seven thousand miles away, on a beach in Pensacola, Florida, sat a small picturesque house with a wraparound porch and a white picket fence separating it from the Gulf coast. Inside, his lovely wife, Tessa, waited for his return by baking a themed birthday cake. Maddie's ninth birthday party was next weekend, and George planned to attend.

"SEVEN... SIX... FIVE..."

George's gloved hand removed the picture of his adorable daughter taped to the dash. Most other pilots displayed photos of their wives or girlfriends, but George had a special connection to his baby-girl, since the day she was born.

Lifting his eyes to stare through the cracked forward window, George saw the first light of day appearing on the horizon, marking the dawn. He yanked the night-vision goggles off his head and tossed them to the cabin floor. It was a beautiful sunrise, pink and fiery orange, with a splash of purple.

"FOUR-THREE-TWO..."

George smiled. *Not a bad last view.* He tore his gaze from the stunning view and stared at Maddie's picture again. She was a great kid and a real spitfire. His last thought was how sad she was going to be when she found out Daddy wasn't coming home.

Tears in his eyes he said, "Goodbye, baby-girl. I..."

ONE.

Hello Lazarus

"...love you."

George was fairly certain he hadn't been dead for more than a few seconds when a harsh, bright-white light assaulted the backs of his eyelids with a jealous vengeance.

Am I in heaven?

He felt a metallic bed beneath his back. Before opening his eyes, he wiggled his toes and fingers. *All there.* A wave of momentary relief washed over him. *How is that possible? Am I back home? Was it all a bad dream?* That seemed like the only logical conclusion.

He squinted and moaned. "Tessa..."

His voice felt extremely hoarse, as though he had been out for a lot longer than a few seconds--a heck of a lot longer. "C'mon, Tess, turn off the light."

Tessa did not. He fought down the urge to mutter because he loved his wife and had ever since they first met twenty-two years ago at that lousy, grimy bus stop in Amsterdam.

With a great deal of effort, he forced open his eyes.

George was *not* in the master bedroom of their beach-front home in Pensacola, lying in bed next to his beautiful wife. *Nor* was he wearing the incredibly soft flannel pajamas his eight-year-old daughter had bought for him last Christmas with her very own chore money. *Nor* was he in a burning, flailing helicopter about to be blown up by a closing missile.

Instead, he lay naked as a newborn, deposited like a slab of meat on a cold metallic table, and spotlighted in a darkened room.

"Hello?" he croaked. *Why is my throat so dry?* "Tes-sa?"

As he climbed toward consciousness, George had the strange sensation his life was but a dream that he could not quite remember.

George sat up. A cursory examination of his naked body didn't reveal any fresh wounds, bloody bandages or new scars. The unfamiliar surroundings didn't lend any clues either. The room was little more than a concrete box that smelled like dust and cleaning products at the same time.

He reached into the shadowy corners of his memory for some hint as to how he might have relocated from his badly-damaged helicopter to this...place. For a full minute, he came up with nothing. As far as he was concerned, he had little more than blinked and woken up here.

Wherever the heck here is.

With muscles stiff as a corpse, he struggled to sit up with a hefty groan. When he swung his legs off the metallic table, his head swam, and he shivered uncontrollably. Steadying himself with one hand on the frigid steel, he painfully became more aware of his nakedness. Instinctively covering up his unmentionables with one hand, he hopped down from the table and scanned the room. Overhead was a circular domed light, like the kind surgical rooms use--and lining the far wall were a half-dozen storage units. If a broom closet and a surgical O.R. had decided to make a baby, this room would be the offspring.

Nearby, resting atop a short surgical cabinet, he spotted neatly folded clothes--more specifically, *his* clothes. A pair of jeans, a t-shirt, and long-sleeve shirt were all stacked in a tidy pile next to a pair of his old work boots.

What happened to my flight suit?

Seeing his clothes stacked up like that freaked him out a bit. For a moment he actually considered staying in the nude and waiting for the hospital staff to return, but he considered this for only a moment. If the doc told him to undress again, he would certainly obey, but not before getting some damn answers first.

As he reached for his clothes, metal dog-tags jangled about his neck. He grabbed one and held it between thumb and forefinger. The metal was worn and dented. It read, *LT COL. G. STAPLETON.* Serial number *# 593241701.* They were his, alright. *That's weird; I don't usually wear my dog tags when I'm wearing my civies. What's going on?*

With a prickle of growing alarm, he hurriedly began to dress. He pulled on the blue jeans, black t-shirt, and heavy, dark blue collared shirt, which he wore open. Out of habit, he rolled up the sleeves to his elbows, and in doing so, he noted the clothes felt clean and pressed.

Checking the door every few seconds, he dropped down onto a leather-backed chair and began to pull on his thick, tan work boots. It was then he realized these clothes weren't actually *his* clothes. The sizes were spot on, almost felt tailored, but there weren't any labels or name brands of any kind, and even the fabric felt different. It was as though someone had sewn them together from a photograph.

Checking the door again, he spied one of those cheap full length mirrors hanging on the wall. The reflection returning his puzzled gaze was familiar to him. No longer a young man, he liked to think he still had a moderately handsome face;

dark brown eyes and a five o'clock shadow peppering a firm jaw. Despite the equally distributed amount of black and gray hair on his head, he managed to maintain an athletic frame.

So, he wasn't suffering from total memory loss, just short term, specifically how he had gotten here. As far as he was concerned, that was the real question, *How'd I get here? Was I in some sort of accident?*

"Hello?" he called tentatively.

Maybe I should wait.

If Tessa were here, she'd be the first one to remind him that patience was never one of his virtues.

Fighting down anger and frustration, he tried the door and to his surprise, found it unlocked. Shrugging, he eased it open.

Outside the operating room/broom closet was a narrow hallway. Dimly lit bulbs were strung overhead, and thick metal pipes ran along a dirty concrete wall. He got the distinct impression he was underground, like in a bunker.

Was I captured?

But by who? The Taliban? They operate out of caves and hovels. I've never even heard of anything this sophisticated. And why would they want me? I'm a Reserve Search-n-Rescue pilot, not intelligence. And why would they go the extra mile and craft look-a-like clothes.

One end of the narrow hallway was an obvious dead end. In the other direction, he saw bright lights at the end of a long dark corridor. He trotted along on the balls of his feet and kept one hand outstretched, sliding along the smooth walls to guide him.

He was about to enter a massive, wide-open tunnel so large he could've driven a battleship through it. Before rounding the corner completely his training kicked in. He hesitated and listened.

Distant at first, growing louder by the second, was the cadence of at least a dozen military boots marching down the tunnel. Fortunately, a multitude of packing crates lining against the wall afforded ample cover.

Better safe than sorry.

Ducking behind the crates he peeked through a narrow gap at his *would-be* captors. For he was still keeping in mind that maybe the good guys had fished him out of the wreckage and transported him to this secret and very expansive underground base.

Hiding behind the crates he couldn't see much without being spotted. At first all he could see was their uniforms and military precision; which was more than enough for him to know that these guys were not a band of brothers he wanted to trifle with.

They're moving too fast, too fast.

Staying low, he moved covertly down the line of boxes until he found a bigger crack between two stacked crates.

His eyes grew wide.

The steel helmets, bolt-action Mauser rifles riding on their shoulders, the signature potato-masher grenades tucked in their leather belts, spit-shine polished jackboots reaching up to the knee, the Swastika on their red sleeves, all unmistakable—Nazis. "W.W. II Nazis?" He suppressed a laugh somewhere between a chuckle and cry of mental anguish.

Am I on a movie set?

What little he did see, they didn't look like models or movie extras. They were too fierce in their march. These were battle-hardened soldiers.

One of the soldiers must have heard him chuckle because he turned toward him.

George instinctively threw his wrist up in front of his mouth to stifle a scream.

'The Nazi' didn't have a face.

Madhouse

George replayed the memory of the passing Nazi parade in his mind.

Did they really have no faces? He rubbed his hands over his face as though he were washing something off. *Am I going mad? Maybe I'm suffering from some sort of delusion. Heck, I bet they weren't even really there. I probably imagined the whole thing.*

Imagined or not, he did remember the Nazis were escorting a female on a mobile hospital bed. He was certain of it. A blond woman, with thick, horn-rimmed glasses, lying on a gurney, with an IV sticking out of her arm.

Am I in some sort of hospital?

There was something else too; something weird about the gurney that didn't make sense. It took him a second, but he soon realized he hadn't heard any wheels. Gurney coasters sounded the same all over the world, and yet he had heard nothing but the marching boots. Again, he had only managed a quick peek, but the hospital bed seemed to have been floating on the air and moving along by itself.

How is that possible?

George decided to stay out of sight until he acquired a weapon and gathered a bit more intel. He made a mental note of the direction the woman was being taken and promised to go back for her. For all he knew, she was just as much a prisoner as he was.

He slowly rose up from behind the stacks of wooden cargo crates. Before moving into the main tunnel, he hesitated again, only this time, he specifically checked for security cameras. Seeing none, he quietly moved into the massive ovular tunnel and began jogging briskly in the opposite direction of the passing patrol. Hearing his own work boots echo off the walls he slowed down his pace and made more of a mental effort to strike the floor in a heel-toe rolling motion.

He hadn't traveled more than fifty yards when he heard another parade of marching boots in the distance. And this time, from the sound of it, they were an even larger squad than the first.

Spying his only option, George sprinted for an adjoining hallway. Once there, he found three closed doors--two on the right and one on the left. He chose the door on the left. No luck. Locked. The boots were nearly to his hallway. He doubted he had enough time to try even one more door, let alone both.

The second door was also locked. He was screwed. The faceless Nazis were going to find him for sure.

The first of the dozen troopers marched past the hallway opening. All the soldiers had to do was turn their head to the right, and they would be staring right at him, were that possible without eyes and all. In a nimble move, George rolled his body along the wall and tried the last door behind his back.

Success!

He turned the handle the rest of the way and practically fell backward into the room. Once inside the darkened interior, he caught the swinging door and eased it shut.

Backing away from the door he listened as the sound of the marching boots drew closer. A moment of panic overcame him. They must have seen him duck into the room; they must have. The footsteps grew louder. He forced himself to control his breathing. As his eyes adjusted to the dim lighting, he sped a steel pipe in a box of scrap metal against the wall. Moving over to it quickly, on the balls of his feet, he snatched it up and clenched it at the ready. The boots were almost to the door.

Any second now.

Heart pumping furiously in his chest, he raised the pipe ready to swing his impromptu bat at the head of the first faceless person to step through the door. The boots marched closer; he gripped the pipe tighter. *Here we go.* If these bastards wanted a fight, he wasn't going to disappoint.

And then...the sound of their footsteps began to recede...and eventually move off.

George let out a slow calming breath. He backed even farther away from the door, traveling deeper into the room. He wasn't aware of the person standing behind him. Not until she spoke.

The voice was angelic and sweet, and with one vocalized word a lifetime of memories crashed down upon him in an instant.

"Daddy?"

Chapter 4

Maddie

George spun around.

Unlike his own life, which was still nothing more than jumbled pieces of fuzzy memory, he remembered his daughter's life right down to the last detail--starting with the day of her birth. Even though it had been over nine years ago, he recalled it as though it were that very morning.

There had been complications, and Tessa was bleeding out. The situation was so dire, the nurse had practically flung their newborn infant into his hands, so she could assist the doctor with Tessa.

Maddie was a beautiful baby girl from her first breath. She was born with mounds of dark brown hair just like him, and at that moment was crying profusely. And why wouldn't she, she had birth goo all over her face and hair.

A young nurse, or maybe it was the equivalent of a candy striper (George really didn't know) magically appeared beside him.

"My wife?" George asked, hearing the concern in his own voice.

"She's fine," the candy-striper said, holding up a slender hand stopping him. "Here, take this." She handed George the tiniest comb he had ever seen. The nurse then turned on the faucet of a nearby sink, checked the temperature of water with her fingertips and gestured for him to bring baby Madison over to it. "You can wash her hair out under the faucet," she explained. The nurse's aide couldn't have been more than nineteen.

George did as he was instructed and rinsed out Maddie's hair, while the young nurse took another damp washcloth and wiped down her tiny body.

And boy howdy, did Maddie scream.

George had never felt so helpless in his life. He envied the days when dads were forced to wait in smoke-filled waiting rooms for the good news. George had led rescue teams into enemy territory to retrieve downed pilots, but this wailing little banshee was beyond his skill set.

Not sure why, he began singing a lullaby from his childhood in the best baritone he could muster. "Look for the...

bear necessities, the simple bear necessities... forget about your troubles and your strife... yeah, man."

It worked. Maddie stopped crying almost instantly. To the nurse's amazement, Maddie not only opened her eyes for the first time but focused them right on her daddy's face.

"Oh my gawd," the nurse said in a thick Hispanic accent. Popping her gum, she then added, "She's looking right at 'choo. They're not even supposed to do that yet."

"My wife, is she okay?" he asked her again.

"George?" Tessa called over to him.

Tess had her head turned toward them, and the doctors seemed a lot less frantic than before. George heard them say comforting things like, "She stabilized now," and, "Go ahead and stitch her up," but it was Tessa's face he was focused on. Her voice was weak, but she managed, "George, I want to hold her."

The memory of Maddie's birth vanished like a departing mist. Soon other memories washed over him: like the day he and his neighbor built Maddie's first swing set, the time he and Maddie had gone kayaking, the trip to the fair and Maddie had fallen asleep on his shoulder walking all the way back to the car parked over a mile away.

The memories were coming faster now; waiting at the bus stop with her on her first day of school with her yellow raincoat and tiny red umbrella. Her first pony ride, and the time they both nearly barfed on the spinning teacup ride at Disney World.

"Daddy?" her small voice whispered again, snapping him back to the present. Her feet were bare and vulnerable looking. She was wearing a hospital gown, but after scanning the nearly identical broom closet-operating room, he saw she had not been provided with the same courtesy of a set of clean clothes.

"Daddy, I'm scared."

Rapidly crossing over to her, he kneeled down to her level and hugged her fiercely. "It's okay, Maddie-saurus-rex, I've got you."

She hugged him back, and while still holding him tightly about the neck, she asked, "Where's Mommy?"

What to tell her? Maddie was clearly frightened, and he didn't want to frighten her any more. Until now, it hadn't occurred to him that Tessa might have been captured too. The thought of his wife waking up scared and alone in this place, caused him to physically feel ill. *I swear, if someone hurt her, I will turn this place into a glass parking lot.*

He remembered that other woman, the one with the blond hair and glasses on the hovering gurney, which was plenty of proof other civilians had also been captured. If Tessa was here, he'd find her.

Since Maddie's tumultuous birth, theirs had always been a special bond, and honesty was always, *always* the best policy. He pulled his daughter gently away from him so he could watch her face. "I don't know, baby-girl, what do you say we go find her?"

She nodded, sniffed softly and wiped her nose on the back of her arm. "Where are we?"

George shook his head. By his best recollection, not more than twenty minutes ago, he was flying a combat mission in Afghanistan. Fighting back the tsunami waves of shock, mostly for Maddie's sake, he answered, "I don't know, baby-girl. I think we're in some kind of hospital."

A quizzical expression crossed her face, but she simply nodded and didn't ask any more questions.

Other than the steel pipe, Maddie's room really didn't offer anything in the way of weapons, or now that he thought about it, communications devices. Sighing in frustration (and deciding the pipe was better than nothing), he tucked it under his arm and moved back toward the door.

He clasped the handle, was about to open it, but then froze. Turning his head back to her, he whispered, "Now Maddie, I need you to be super quiet, not a sound. Do you understand?"

"You mean like the quiet game?"

George smiled. "Yes, like the quiet game." He was about to exit again when she tugged on his shirt and asked, "What are the stakes?"

At first, he was confused by her question. *The stakes?* Then he remembered they were playing the quiet game. Thinking quickly, he said, "Uh, how about milkshakes?"

Maddie nodded enthusiastically. "Chocolate." When he nodded in agreement, she tilted her head, and thought about her own stakes. "And I'll do dishes for three days."

George cracked the door open and peeked outside. Whispering back over his shoulder, he asked, "Three days of dishes for a milkshake? Yeah, I don't think so. Try again."

She sighed, blew an errant strand of her bangs out of her face, and answered, "Fine, make it five."

George feigned thinking it over for a moment and then replied, "Deal. Now let's go."

Maddie pantomimed locking her mouth up and throwing away the key.

George eased the door the rest of the way open, listened for anymore footfalls, and hearing none, led her quietly out of the room.

Holding the pipe like a sword out in front of him and Maddie by her tiny hand behind him, they moved briskly down the hallway.

"If you can dream it, you can do it."
-Walt Disney

Buttercup

"That's it, that's all I remember."

As George and Maddie navigated the seemingly endless concrete tunnels, he had asked her if she remembered anything, specifically how she arrived, but Maddie didn't know any more than he did, and seemed to be suffering from the same short-term memory loss he was experiencing. The only real difference between them was Maddie seemed far more accepting of their circumstances.

They hadn't run into any more faceless-Nazi patrols. So that was something. And, after hours of walking, they passed through another door that was just like dozens of others that came before. Only this time they were shocked by what they found on the other side.

"Whoah," Maddie breathed.

They found themselves standing on a wide, steel balcony overlooking a gigantic hanger stretching on as far as the eye could see.

The ceiling had to be at least sixteen stories high, and on the expansive floor below was acres upon acres of every-thing imaginable. There were Army tanks, full-sized pirate ships, antique cars and miles-upon-miles of clothes racks from every time period.

"Maddie, stay close."

Maddie blew her bangs out of her eyes again with a comi-cal *phoof* from her lower lip. She smiled, then said, "Okay, dad, but you owe me a chocolate milkshake." She stepped forward, gripped the railing and breathed, "Wow. They really do have everything here. It's like a giant garage sale."

That was as good a description as any.

George spied a nearby set of steel-grated stairs that would take them to the hangar floor below. "This way," he said, keeping his head on a constant swivel and checking for any would be pursuers. Thus far, there were none.

At first, George had thought everything was laid out with-out rhyme or reason, but now that they were on the main floor, it became apparent that massive quadrants were actu-ally sectioned off with purpose.

For example, the pirate ship wasn't amongst the old army tanks; it was surrounded by racks of pirate clothes, swords, treasure chests, and even a small lighthouse on a tiny island. Similarly, the western section had stagecoaches, acres of western wear, and a stable of very realistic-looking horses. Looking past the stable, far in the distance, one section had a fleet of metallic boats that looked like they had been built by ole' Captain Nemo himself.

George was suddenly reminded of his childhood. He used to have this great, big, giant toy box in his room. Much to his mother's chagrin, he would dump out all his miscellaneous toys onto the floor. Lincoln Logs, army men, spaceships, cowboys and Indians, only now it seemed, he and Maddie were about the size of his toy army men.

"Dad, what is this place?"

It took him a moment to realize she'd asked him a question. When he finally answered, he simply said, "I don't know, honey." And when she went to touch one of the fake horses he added quickly, "Don't touch anything."

"Got it. No touchy."

The main aisle was as wide as a four-lane highway. It had taken them several minutes just to walk from the pirate section to the western section.

Past the western area, George finally spotted something familiar. It was an area filled with military helmets, racks of weapons, and scores of uniforms of every branch and every nation. Deep within the military section, he saw the tank they had spied earlier. Parked next to it was an old army jeep, and a deuce and a half.

As he moved closer, he could see the machine guns weren't modern M-16's but the much older, M-1 bolt-action rifles. The grenades weren't modern either, but the size of pineapples. And the Nazi uniforms were a dead giveaway; -all of it, the gear, uniforms and vehicles, were clearly dated to the WW II era.

He reached for one of the rifles on a nearby rack.

Locked.

Where the rifles were dated, the racks holding them were not. No amount of pounding or prying would set them free.

He was about to curse but remembered Maddie was within earshot. Thinking he hadn't checked on her in a while he turned around to make sure she hadn't wandered off.

No surprise, she had done exactly that.

Completing a frantic scan of his immediate surroundings he could see she was no longer in the WW II section. And for a fleeting moment, he actually began to wonder if she had merely been a hallucination.

Who's to say what's real and what isn't in this crazy dream?

Dream or not, he knew he had to find her.

"Maddie!" he shouted, and immediately realized his mistake. Even though they hadn't seen anyone, he suddenly recalled the faceless-Nazi patrol back in the tunnel.

He cried out again for his daughter, only this time in a fevered whisper, "Maddie."

He was about to shout again when he heard her disembodied voice call back to him, "Over here, Dad."

Thankfully, she hadn't gone too far. She was back in the Western section, over by the horse stable, standing on a hay bale and petting one of the fake horses.

Moving over quickly to her, he asked, "Maddie, didn't I tell you not to wander off?"

Seeing her father was genuinely upset with her nearly brought her to tears. "Okay, Dad. I'm sorry."

Feeling like a world class jerk, he said, "Sorry baby-girl." He wiped a tear off her cheek with his thumb. "It's just that I was really worried about you."

"No. I get it. You got scared when you couldn't find me."

George harrumphed. "Scared? Me?" When she nodded, he added, "Is that right?"

She nodded more deliberately the second time.

"When did you get so smart?"

She smirked and said, "Mommy says I get my brains from her."

"Uh-huh," he said, rubbing her head.

"And her looks," she added.

"Keep it up, kiddo."

Maddie giggled. "Oh, oh, and her patience."

"Har, har," he said dryly, and was happy to see she had returned to petting the fake horse. If they were going to get out of this weird place in one piece, he needed to keep Maddie as calm as possible.

The horse was tan in color, Maddie's favorite, and already saddled. "Who's your friend?"

"His name is," she began, then after thinking it over, she answered, "Buttercup."

George's smile dropped when the fake horse blinked its eyes and suddenly moved. George lunged forward, scooped Maddie off the hay bale and jumped backward a few feet.

"It's okay, Dad. He won't hurt you."

"How would you know, you just met him."

"I just know, Dad, okay?"

George looked at Maddie's face and saw she was serious. The horse, seeming to agree with her, nodded its massive head up and down and stamped its front hoof for emphasis.

George slowly lowered Maddie back down to the floor. As Maddie started to approach the animatronic horse again George absentmindedly slowed her approach with one hand.

The horse lowered its head and seemed to delight in Maddie petting his muzzle. "See? He's friendly." And then switching her voice to baby-talk she added, "He's just looking for someone to love him. Isn't that right, Buttercup?"

The horse was so sophisticated that its robotic movements and slight whirring noises were barely noticeable.

As Maddie hugged the horse's muzzle to her chest he said, "Maddie, it's a robot. Robots don't feel love."

A quizzical expression crossed her face as Maddie thought about this. Finally, she asked, "Why not?"

"Because it's a machine, sweetheart, machines don't feel anything."

Maddie tried to speak, couldn't, and only nodded instead.

It was then that George realized she was still wearing only a hospital gown. "You must be cold." Spying a clothes rack back in the military section he said, "C'mon, let's get you something else to wear."

As they made their way back to the main aisle George heard the horse clip-clopping behind them. He turned, part of him ready for a fight, but the horse stopped its advance the moment they stopped walking.

"Awww," Maddie said. "I think he wants to come with us."

"Yeah, I don't think so," George said reflexively.

"Why not? He's lonely." Maddie crossed over to the fake horse again and began petting it once more. Talking to it in the baby voice again she cooed, "Isn't that right, Buttercup, you are just lonely." The animatronic horse nuzzled Maddie back, mimicking a real horse perfectly.

"No way," George explained matter-of-factly, pulling her gently away from the horse.

"But Dad, whyyyyy?"

"For one thing, he'll make too much damn noise."

Maddie's face turned serious. "Dad. You said damn," then explained, "Mommy says we don't use that word."

He apologized and then said, "He still can't come with us."

"It's not an *it*, dad. It's a him. And his name, is Buttercup."

"Doesn't matter, *he*, is staying *here*." Turning to the horse he commanded, "Uh, horse thingy, stay," and immediately mumbled, "now I'm talking to a wind-up horse."

Buttercup whinnied in complaint and took another step forward.

"Buttercup, stay!" Maddie commanded, thrusting her pointer finger to show she meant it.

The horse reared its head, seemingly in understanding, and returned to standing stock still, the light already beginning to fade from its eyes.

George shook his head in amazement. He had never even heard of this level of sophistication before.

As he led Maddie back to the W.W. II section, he heard Maddie whisper softly over her shoulder, "Bye Buttercup."

George was about to say, 'Honey, it's just a stupid robot,' but thought better of it and moved over to the nearest clothes rack instead. He selected a long, drab-green, Army overcoat, draped it over her shoulders, and said, "Here, try this on." Despite it being the smallest size he could find, the coat still looked like she was wearing a tent.

When she lifted her eyes up at him as if to say, 'It's too big', he explained, "Don't worry, I'll adjust it later."

He then selected a similar extra-large coat for himself and slipped it on. As he did, he noticed most of the old army clothes were torn in places, and stained with blood, dirt, and oil. The weapons in the racks also appeared heavily used. Yet everything was laid out as though it had just rolled off an assembly line and smelled clean.

None of this makes sense.

These mysteries would have to wait until he figured out who kidnapped them, if they were friendly, and most importantly, did they have Tessa?

He spotted a drab-green pistol belt fitted with a leather holster, spare mag pouches, bayonet and canteen. He quickly unholstered the pistol. It was an M1 1911. Single-action, as well as semi-automatic, the .45 caliber pistol was a real classic with lots of stopping power. A quick inspection revealed it to be surprisingly clean. He slammed home a full magazine and chambered the first round, the sound instantly reassuring. Now that they had a weapon, clothes and some gear, he felt ready to go.

But where?

From the upper balcony the hangar had seemed endless. Plus, they still had no food, and his canteen was empty. Given the size of the place, what they really needed was transportation.

Spotting the WW II Jeep in front of him, he got the idea.

Yeah, it could work.

The aisles between sections were certainly wide enough. It might take time to move everything blocking the jeep in, but once they did, they could make a lot better time.

As he walked around to the driver's seat, George ran a hand over the bright white star on the Jeep's hood. He was about to slide in behind the wheel when he realized Maddie wasn't wearing her jacket. "Hey, what happened to your coat?"

"It's too big, so I took it off. It's okay, I'm not cold."

She definitely should have been. Maddie was still in her bare feet. There was a pretty good chill in the air and the concrete floor was borderline frigid. By all accounts, she should've been freezing.

"You're not?" He picked her up, sat her on the jeep's hood and felt her forehead. She was neither hot nor cold. Palm still on her forehead he asked, "You feeling okay?"

"Uh-huh," she said. "Why?"

"Well, because I would've thought you would've felt cold or maybe even hot from a fever, but you're neither."

Before Maddie could respond, loud alarm klaxons suddenly sounded and red spinning emergency lights dropped from hidden panels in the ceiling.

Oh, no.

That's when George knew in an instant; their luck had finally run out.

Chapter 6

Hover Drone

"Maddie, grab your coat. We are leaving."

He had to shout to be heard over the deafening alarms, but Maddie wasn't listening. Instead her eyes had gone wide and she was leaning over so she could stare at something... at something behind him.

Picking up on her cue, George spun around and saw it for the first time. The hovering drone was ceramic white in color and about the size and shape of a VW bug. It also had extremely thin and elongated forelimbs dangling from its body giving it the appearance of a flying insect.

It was still about seventy feet away, floating next to an enormous ventilation shaft near the ceiling. Its propulsion was a complete mystery to him, but he could just make out vapors below the craft indicating some sort of exhaust.

Instead of a cockpit, the hover drone had a black-paneled face with a single yellow eye darting about like a ping-pong ball in a pool of black liquid. Several panels opened on its outer shell and an array of search lights, each moving independently of one another, began searching for something... searching for them.

Instinctively, George crouched behind the Army Jeep. He soon realized Maddie was still sitting on the hood, out in the open, her eyes transfixed. Just as one of the search lights was about to detect her, he yanked her down off the hood.

Maddie leaned over and whispered in his ear, "Maybe it's friendly, you know, like Buttercup."

As if on cue, Maddie's robotic horse whinnied out loud.

The drone's yellow eye turned crimson. More panels flipped over to reveal numerous sleek-looking laser pistols.

George felt his eyes widen and said, "Yeah... I don't think that thing's like Buttercup."

In a deft flying move, the hover drone descended sharply and began hovering in a slow circle around Buttercup, all its weapons trained on the robotic horse. Like before, the horse stomped its foot at the ground and bobbed its head.

They heard a strange computer sound from the hover drone. At this the horse abruptly picked up its head, its eyes flashed the same red as the drones, and then Buttercup stood stock still.

"Buttercup!" Maddie cried.

The hover drone had started moving off but the moment it heard Maddie's cry, it spun around with uncanny speed and turned all of its search lights on her. George heard the laser pistols warming up as if preparing to fire.

In the split second allowed to him, George tackled Maddie to the ground. As they fell to the hard-concrete floor, George flipped over in midair onto his back and took the brunt of the blow, allowing Maddie to land on his chest.

Beams of white-hot laser energy zinged overhead and melted the metal of the tank behind them into slag. Maddie, covering her ears, screamed, and tried to get up.

George, desperately trying to reclaim air into his pan-caked lungs, pulled her back down to the ground and moved them both under the big army truck.

Seconds later, more laser fire erupted all around them, but the beams were unable to pierce the truck's thick engine block.

As the hover drone circled the truck, either to locate them or get a better angle, George lunged out from hiding, grabbed one of the pineapple-sized grenades from one of the weapon racks, then quickly dove back underneath the truck. Facing Maddie, now on her knees and holding her palms to her ears, he motioned with his finger and a stern face, 'Stay here.'

When she nodded back, George waited for the drone to fly past and counted how long it took to circle the truck. Getting its timing down, he rolled out from beneath the truck, pulled the pin, and threw the grenade like a football. He aimed at a place in the air near the back of the truck where he calculated the drone would circle around to again.

As the grenade hurtled through the air, George dove back beneath the truck, covering Maddie's body with his own. The grenade didn't hit the hover drone, but it was close enough when it detonated. The explosion was so massive it completely engulfed the hover drone sending it streaking toward the fake western buildings like a falling star.

After crawling out from underneath the big truck, George could see where several fires had sprung up where the hover drone had crashed into the building labeled *Funeral Parlor*.

"Baby-girl, are you okay?"

Maddie, crawling out, nodded that she was. No sooner had George helped her to her feet, they heard a commotion coming from across the aisle.

Heavily damaged, struggling to maintain altitude, the drone rose from the ashes. Its hull was badly scorched and the housing above the eye-plate was so badly dented, it gave the appearance its single red eye was now scowling at them.

George wasn't confident they'd be so lucky a second time.

He felt tugging on his jacket. "Dad, over there. A door!"

Maddie was right; about twenty yards away he spotted a metal door to a steel bunker. *Where did that come from?* He didn't remember seeing it before.

It didn't seem possible, but the hover drone turned toward the door, held it long enough to puzzle out their plan, and then faced them once more.

George knew they'd never make it. The twenty yards might as well have been twenty thousand. The hover drone would easily cut them in half long before they reached it.

Buttercup must have thought so too. For the robotic horse reactivated itself, lowered its head down, and plowed right into the back of the low-flying hover drone. In its weakened state, the hover drone spun out of control several times before careening into the hull of the pirate ship.

George wasn't confident that a head butt from a horse, even a robotic one, would keep the drone down for long, but at least now they had a fighting chance to sprint for the door.

"Run, baby-girl, RUN!"

"What about Buttercup?" she started to ask.

"I said run!" he shot back in a voice that cut off any further argument.

They ran. Every few feet, George risked a glance over his shoulder at the hole in the pirate ship. It wasn't long before the red eye reappeared in the hull's darkened interior.

The moment they reached the door, Maddie turned the knob. "It's locked!"

George scooted her out of the way. "Let me try." Two good turns only confirmed Maddie's original assessment.

"Dad, it's coming back!"

George didn't waste time looking, instead he drew the 1911, yanked Maddie behind him, aimed at the lock on the door, and fired three times. All three bullets struck their mark and the battered lock fell to the floor allowing the door to glide open in an almost welcoming manner.

Still not looking back, George grabbed Maddie by the arm and dove through the doorway.

They hadn't even hit the floor inside when the hover drone crashed into the bunker's steel entrance like a hateful missile. Refusing to give up its prey, it kept slamming into the doorway over and over again.

They quickly backpedaled on the floor on their butts and moved as far away from the entrance as possible. Instinctively he reached for his pistol only to realize he must've dropped it as they leapt through the door.

How could I have been so careless?

Thankfully he didn't need it, the bunker's solid steel held, and the doorway was too narrow for the angry drone to enter or line up a shot. No matter how much it tried, the hover drone could not follow.

After a time, it ceased its relentless attack.

Lowering itself down in front of the open doorway, it trained its narrowed blood-red eye on George. The huge dent over its faceplate giving the appearance of it glowering at them more than ever.

George swore he could feel actual hate coming off the thing and had to remind himself it was just a machine.

On the other side of the room, he spied a hatch on the floor, like on a submarine. He wasn't sure where it led to, but anywhere was better than here. He got to his feet and helped Maddie to hers.

"C'mon, baby-girl, down the hatch we go."

Maddie didn't have to be told twice. She spun the wheel and yanked open the lid. George peeked down and saw a ladder well leading to a narrow tunnel. "You go first. I'll be right behind you."

Before climbing down, Maddie gazed up at him and said, "Buttercup saved us, did you see that, Dad?"

He nodded and gently guided her down the hatch.

George had seen Buttercup save them… as had the hover drone. Before following Maddie, George turned and saw the angry drone had returned to the robotic horse. It opened all its panels and trained its weapons on poor Buttercup. Before firing, the hover drone spun to face him one last time, as if to say, 'See? This is your fault.' It then turned back toward Buttercup and fired all its weapons at once.

As the horse wailed in pain, Maddie screamed, "Buttercup, no!" She then scrambled back out of the hatch and started running for the door.

Before she could exit the bunker, George caught her up by her waist and carried her back to the hatch. He gently prodded her back down the ladder, then climbed down himself, taking the time to seal the hatch behind them.

After a short climb down, he saw Maddie standing in the middle of the narrow concrete tunnel. She had her hands held high, waiting to be lifted, which he immediately did.

Burying her face in his neck she sobbed, "He killed him. Buttercup saved us, and that stupid flying egg killed him for it."

"I know, baby-girl, I know." He stroked her hair, rocking her gently as he carried her down the new passageway.

But Maddie was right.

One murderous robot tried to kill them while the other gave its life so they could escape.

Where the heck are we?

Chapter 7

The Tunnel

"We've been walking for hours."

"I know, baby-girl."

"I'm thirsty."

"I know."

"I'm hungry."

"I know, baby-girl."

"I'm going to have to go to the bathroom soon."

He was glad she was finally talking again. Maddie hadn't said anything since watching her fake horse get vaporized right in front of her.

As they plodded down the seemingly endless concrete tunnel, she held his hand; something she had been doing less and less as she grew older.

For the moment, they seemed to have eluded the angry hover drone, and the faceless Nazis. This was especially good because the tunnel offered nothing in the way of cover; nor did they have any weapons. He silently cursed himself again for dropping the pistol back in the hangar. But, it wasn't like he had much of a choice. In all his years in the military, he had never witnessed the hover drone's equal.

Focusing on something he could understand, he calculated their average foot speed at about three mph. Guessing the amount of time that had transpired since they entered the dimly lit tunnel, he estimated they were nearing the five-mile mark. In that distance, they hadn't spotted so much as a door, window, or even a piece of garbage.

Shuffling alongside him, Maddie asked, "Do you think we'll ever find Mom?"

George thought about this before answering. He could tell by her tone she was feeling downcast and melancholy. As a survival instructor, he knew the number one rule of survival was never-ever lose hope, so he said, "We don't even know if she's here. But if she is, you can bet we'll find her."

And the Academy Award goes to...

"I worry about her, ya know."

George tousled Maddie's hair, much to her displeasure. "I know you do, kiddo."

"Dad..." she complained, immediately fixing her hair.

This seemed to placate her for now. The reality was the underground complex was so huge, it was beyond comprehension. George knew what Tessa would want him to do first. She would want him to get their daughter out alive. They had discussed it once before while hiking the Alaskan interior, and another time while navigating the streets of New York. If they ever got separated or one of them went missing, Maddie's survival always came first. All other concerns were secondary.

Maddie stumbled and George kept her from falling. "You want me to carry you?"

She shook her head. "No, I'm alright. I can go on a little longer."

George wasn't so sure. The canteen on his belt was still empty, and they still hadn't found any food. It was getting harder and harder not to lose what little hope they did have. An image of their clothed skeletons sitting side-by-side with their backs to the tunnel wall flashed through his mind.

"Dad, is it alright that I'm a little scared?"

He nearly said, 'Of what', but then remembered the angry hover drone back in the hangar and didn't want to bring it up again. No. He needed to bolster her confidence somehow.

"Do you remember what my job was in the Air Force?"

"You were an instructor at the academy, right?"

George nodded. "Uh-huh, but before that, long before you were born, I was a P.J."

She gave him a quizzical look, followed by a knowing smile. "You were pajamas?"

George smiled. "No honey, I was a Search-n-Rescue pilot with the Para Rescue Rangers. It means my job was to fly into the worst combat situations and hostile environments and bring back people alive. We were trained how to fight, scuba dive, treat all manner of injuries, and survive under the worst possible conditions."

Maddie sniffed, wiped away a tear on the back of her forearm, and asked, "Were you good at your job?"

George grinned. "Well, they made me a captain, and after dozens of missions, I got promoted and taught others how to do the job. So yeah, I'd guess you could say I was pretty good at my job."

"Mommy once told me you got a medal for saving a whole bunch of people in," she thought a moment, "... in Acka-bara-stand."

George squinted as he smiled. "I think you mean Afghani-stan."

Maddie pursed out her bottom lip in thought. "No... I'm pretty sure she said Acka-bara-stand. I remember because it's the same place some Genie named Aladdin comes from."

George suppressed a laugh, failed miserably. When he saw Maddie didn't appreciate this, he quickly added, "My point is, if I can rescue all those people, do you think I'm going to let anything happen to my baby-girl?"

Maddie shook her head.

"So, what do you say we get out of this stupid tunnel and go find Mom?"

"Okay, Dad."

With that said, he draped his arm over her shoulders, careful to keep his weight off her tiny body, and they walked onward in silence.

After a time, she asked, "Dad? Did you rescue Aladdin?"

He didn't respond because he spied something up ahead. Something wonderful.

A door.

In a shallow alcove to the left stood a lone steel door.

The moment they approached; the door cracked open with a pneumatic hiss. The bottom half slid easily into the threshold, but the top half only rose a quarter of the way before getting stuck. Unseen motors whined in protest. Several sparks popped around the frame, and the struggling motors soon became silent.

George shielded his eyes from the sparks while keeping Maddie safely behind. The fire was over before it began, leaving behind only minor scorch marks on the door.

"C'mon, let's go."

They ducked quickly under the top half of the door. As they passed under, George noted the steel door was a lot thicker than he first realized. "Keep moving," he said firmly.

Before George could even scan the room's interior, he heard Maddie say behind him, "Uh, Dad? I'm stuck."

George turned and saw part of Maddie's hospital gown was stretched between her waist and the doorframe. He immediately identified the culprit as a gear sprung loose from the defunct door.

"Hang on, baby-girl, I'll get you out," he started to say, but he never got the chance, as the door immediately began to fall.

Maddie screamed.

Break Room

Maddie knew her dad would never save her in time.

Her father lurched forward with uncanny speed, but Maddie quickly calculated the distance and knew he would never reach her, so she simply closed her eyes.

When the top half of the heavy door fell, she waited for the terrible crushing blow that would end her mayfly existence. Oddly enough, her last thought was how sad he was going to be after she was gone.

A tearing sound.

Strong hands grabbed around her waist.

Her spine curved backward as she was violently pulled forward from the hips.

A deafening THUD sounded behind her.

When Maddie opened her eyes, she was surprised to find herself amongst the living and lying on her dad's chest. She could feel his heart pumping furiously beneath her.

"Holy cats, that was close," he exclaimed. As they both sat up, he asked, "Are you alright?"

She could only nod in answer. Maddie wanted to say thank you, she wanted to tell her dad how much she loved him, but the first thing she blurted out was, "You ripped my gown."

Her dad stared where she was clutching the torn cloth in her hand. He raised his eyebrows, rolled his eyes, and shook his head.

Maddie gazed back to where the top half of the steel door had crashed to the floor and should have crushed her. She accessed her memory and said aloud, "You know, we studied guillotines in school. I never thought I'd actually see one."

"Very funny."

Maddie thought it odd her dad thought this funny. She was being totally serious.

Inside the room, long rectangular tables sat rotting from leaky pipes overhead. On the floor, water pooled in many places, and at least two dozen chairs littered the floor like children's forgotten toys.

"What *is* this place?" she asked.

George spied brightly colored vending machines standing against the walls were like stalwart sentinels.

"Hhhmmm. Some kind of break room, maybe?"

Her dad took a step forward and heard something crunch underfoot.

"Wait." he said, holding her back with an outstretched hand. Maddie immediately froze. He pointed to the floor. "Glass."

Maddie nodded solemnly. He knelt down so she could scramble up onto his back. They crossed the large open room. Nodding at the stalwart sentinels, he asked, "What do you say we break open those snack machines and see if any food pops out?"

"Oh yes, please," she replied enthusiastically, but when he moved toward them, they both heard it at the same time.

A woman's voice.

They both cocked their heads to listen more intently. George gave her a questioning look and pointed to the breakroom's exit as if to say, 'I think it's coming from down the hall.'

It was definitely a human voice, but the one thing that bothered her the most was she couldn't make out the language.

It might as well have been an alien from another world.

Costuming

"Qing mai chu di yi bu."

They followed the sound of the woman's voice down a darkened corridor. Here, most of the bulbs were flickering or had already burned out. As they entered another expansive open area, they heard a warm humming noise.

"Hello?" George called out tentatively.

In answer, a fluorescent neon-green pedestal rose up from the floor in front of them.

The pleasant female voice they heard earlier continued, in a tone akin to a request, "Qing mai chu di yi bu." When neither of them moved the voice repeated, "Qing mai chu di yi bu."

After hearing it the second time George said, "I think she's speaking Chinese."

"Where's it coming from?" Maddie asked. "I don't see any speakers."

She was right.

The glowing platform gently blinked on and off and was accompanied by a soft chime as though urging Maddie to step forward. "BLING... BLING... BLING," it emitted softly.

Maddie must've been thinking the same, for she said, "I think she wants me to stand on this green step-up thingy."

Before he could tell his impulsive daughter not to step on the glowing green, step-up thingy, Maddie did just that.

A half dozen, neon-green, laser-light beams appeared from nowhere. After a few seconds of searching, they converged on Maddie. The beams began scanning her body and paid special attention to the details of her face. Maddie must have seen his body tense up because, she said, "Dad, it's okay. It doesn't hurt. If anything, it kinda tickles a little." In a matter of seconds, the lasers had created a computer rendering of her in hologram form, which was now presented itself by floating in front of her.

"Cool," Maddie breathed. "Just like *Star Trek*."

Again, George was amazed at the level of technology.

Several free-floating screens winked into existence and floated around Maddie in a semi-circle. Each panel began flashing hundreds of wardrobe selections across their frameless screens in rapid succession. At first, the fashions blitzed through far too fast for the eye to discern any real detail. All George could tell was some of the clothes were brightly colored and others weren't. After his brain and eyes finally began to keep up, he realized the wardrobe wasn't so much clothes as they were costumes: pirate, superhero, animals, and more. The abundant choices reminded him of all the numerous antiques back in the giant hangar.

As the scanning continued, the pleasant female Chinese voice returned. "Qing xuanze."

When Maddie didn't make a choice, the computer program seemed to be narrowing down the selections for her.

After several more seconds, only five selections remained, one for each hovering screen. Two of the choices resembled princess dresses, one a cowgirl, one a zombie, and another of a pirate theme. All had constructed an image of Maddie inside each design. The constructs smiled back with lifeless eyes as they modeled their respective costumes for her.

After a few more moments of indecision, Maddie selected the simplest of the bunch--the blue knee-length Princess dress, with a dark blue ribbon for her hair, white socks that went up to her knees, and black ankle-strap shoes.

"This one." She leaned forward slightly, touching one of the floating screens in front of her with her forefinger.

In an instant, the other four screens vanished, and the screen with her selection slowly followed suit.

Silence.

Finally, Maddie said, "What now?"

In answer, a half-dozen laser thin elongated robotic arms descended smoothly out of the ceiling. As George and Maddie stared up at them, they didn't notice the four solid walls silently rising up out of the floor around Maddie until it was too late.

"Maddie," George said. "Maddie, get out of there right now!"

George bounded forward, but the smooth walls rose up around her, cutting him off from her and encasing her within. Just before she had vanished from his sight completely, she had turned her chin over her shoulder to gaze back at him, with wide, frightened eyes.

"Daddy," she said softly, "Daddy, I'm scared."

Maddie's pleas became muffled as the four rising walls melded with the ceiling.

"Let her go!" George shouted, but no amount of pounding, kicking, or cursing did any bit of good. He ran around Maddie's cylindrical tomb and found nothing in the way of a handle or window. Putting an ear to one of the walls he could barely hear the muffled whirring noises within as the lasers did their work.

"Maddie, if you can hear me, I want you to get down on the floor, as close to the ground as possible."

No response.

Finding nothing to help batter the wall down with, George took a few steps back and prepared to charge Maddie's enclosure. A loud hissing sound from the ceiling interrupted his plan, and the four walls dropped back down into the floor. As they did, he glimpsed the robot lasers in the mist as they vanished back up into the ceiling.

Waving the dense fog away, he shouted, "Mad-die!"

Whirring fans in the floor sucked away the steam and he could see Maddie still standing on the pedestal.

"Oh, thank God," he said, as they ran into each other's arms. "You okay? Let me look at you."

Maddie's eyes were wide, but she seemed unharmed. When she spoke it was with a sense of wonderment. "That...was...so...COOL."

She no longer wore a hospital gown with bare feet. Instead, she now wore a light blue dress, white knee socks and black shoes. Miraculously, the machine had even styled her hair and tied it up over her shoulders with a pretty blue ribbon.

"Seriously, Dad, you should try it."

As though sensing Maddie's request, the disembodied voice returned, this time in a lovely British accent. "Please step forward."

George shook his head. "Yeah, I don't think so." The closest he would ever come to playing dress up was the military uniform he wore for twenty years.

Even though he hadn't stepped on the pedestal the lasers did a quick scan of him anyway, and soon a mirror image of him appeared. Within seconds this time, several floating screens displayed pictures of him wearing various costumes. One was a cowboy sheriff, another was a space pirate, and another some kind of jungle explorer.

Maddie clapped with glee a few times and pointed. "Oh, I like the cowboy one."

George shook his head again, grabbed her by the hand and pulled her along after him.

"Awww, man," she complained. "But Dad, you would've made a great cowboy. Look, he even has a shiny badge on his vest."

"Please step forward," the voice wailed after them.

"Maybe some other time," he said, still trying to wrap his mind around the costuming machine back there. It had not only undressed Maddie, but put her in a costume, styled her hair, and did it all so quickly.

This technology is all so unbelievable. This has to be a dream. It has to be.

Clamoring for the Surface

The long corridor eventually ended in a series of stairs leading upward, which in turn led to a large room with several
sets of doors that reminded George of elevators in a hotel
lobby.

Maddie ran over to one set of doors near the center and
quickly depressed the oversized square button to one side.

The doors parted (sans ding), and a bright white light
beckoned them to enter.

"C'mon, Dad, maybe we can take this to the surface,"
Maddie called and vanished within.

Fearful the doors would close before he got there, George
jogged to catch up and stepped inside.

"The indicator says -104. Does that mean we are 104
floors underground?"

"That'd be my guess," George said, and before he found any buttons, the elevator jerked upward with a steady hum.

"Why are the numbers counting down when it feels like we are going up?" she asked.

He smiled down at her. "Because we're moving toward the surface."

"101, 94, 85, 64, 55," Maddie continued to read off the numbers aloud.

When they passed the number 3 the elevator came to a violent stop nearly tossing them to the floor.

There weren't any buttons to push, but George did notice a maintenance hatch in the ceiling. "Don't move." He stood on the elevator's handrail and easily popped the hatch.

Peeking out of the roof he called down to her, "There's a ladder. I think we can climb the rest of the way out."

Lying on the roof of the elevator he reached down to her. She jumped up and he caught her hand easily and hoisted her up.

"Wheee!"

Standing on top of the elevator, he said, "Now don't be scared."

"I'm not scared," she replied immediately.

"You're not?"

"No. I think this is neat."

George thought this odd since Maddie had always been a little scared of heights. It was never paralyzing, it usually only took a little coaxing, and she'd get moving again, but now, she tackled the ladder like a rock climber. He had to hustle just to keep up.

When they had climbed about twenty feet, she called down to him. "I kinda like climbing ladders. This is fun."

As they continued their ascent, George had to force down thoughts of not finding his wife. How could they in a labyrinth so large? And, what would they find on the surface? A foreign country, a military base, some sort of secret testing facility? These thoughts occupied his mind like swirling poltergeists, which was why he practically ran into Maddie before realizing she had stopped her ascent.

"Why'd you stop?" he asked irritably.

Her small face glanced back down at him. He thought it odd she wasn't perspiring from the climb, until he remembered the ballet lessons, she took five times a week. It was the advanced class, and they were grueling enough to make a Marine barf up his lunch. A simple three-story ladder climb was nothing.

"Just keep going," he said impatiently.

She let go of the ladder with one hand and pointed above her. "I can't. It's a dead end."

Staring past her, he saw she was right.

"If you don't know where you are going
any road can take you there."

-Lewis Carroll

Author of Alice in Wonderland

Fairy Maze

The statue of a winged-angel boy peed into a magnificent stone fountain.

Nearby, a three-foot long creature--one resembling a caracal cat with oversized tufted ears, short tail, and yellow phosphorous eyes--sniffed the base of the ornate fountain. It was searching for a morsel of food and was fairly certain it had seen a family of rodents here earlier this morning just begging to be eaten.

The feline's ears flicked wildly at the sound of stone grinding upon stone. Body frozen, the creature heard the muffled cursing of a human voice coming from inside the fountain.

This was new.

The little angel boy of stone began turning on its pedestal (never stopping its urination as it did so) and eventually peed right on the cat.

The cat wailed loudly in surprise and bounded nimbly away. The mice would have to wait to be eaten another day.

Meanwhile the little angel-boy statue continued to corkscrew in place several more times before falling over and smashing into several pieces on the rich blue grass.

******

George Stapleton popped his head out of the newly made shaft like a gopher, frowned slightly at the sight of the broken statue, and then climbed out. He then reached back down into the hole and pulled Maddie out with one hand.

"Wee!" she yelled as he lifted her up and out of a hole for the second time in the last hour.

After being underground for what felt like days, it took a moment for George's eyes to adjust to the daylight.

The ornate fountain they had just climbed out of was surrounded by tall, square-shaped hedges, like one might find in a hedge maze.

Checking their surroundings Maddie breathed, "Kewl. Now this is more like it."

Jumping down from the fountain's base Maddie wasted little time examining the maze and quickly found an exit. "Over here, I think this is the way out."

Leaving the broken fountain behind, they ventured down a dirt trodden footpath flanked by neatly trimmed hedges.

"This is not what I expected," George said.

"Are you kidding," Maddie said, practically skipping, "I love this!"

After navigating the maze for a few minutes longer they found themselves at a crossroads with four pathways to choose from.

A small wooden sign near one of them read, *GO THIS WAY,* but when they followed the sign's arrow they soon found a dead end with a second wooden sign that read, *FOOLED YOU!*

They double backed to the crossroad and before selecting another path George said, "Hang on a sec." He broke off several branches from the hedges, stripped them of their leaves and placed them on the ground in the form of an X. "This way we'll know not to go this way again."

"Good idea," Maddie said.

He raised an eyebrow and said satirically, "Oh, I'm glad you approve."

After a second dead end, they were soon making good time down a third path when George heard a rapid humming sound.

Before he could ask Maddie if she heard the same brisk flapping noise too, a winged creature flew over the hedges and flitted about his face. At first, he thought it to be a colorful hummingbird. Then, to his surprise, he noticed the winged creature had a tiny human face, and he wasn't certain, but he thought he heard it giggle.

"Dad!" Maddie exclaimed. "*Fairies!*"

"So, you see them too?"

Well at least I'm not delusional...or we both are.

Maddie nodded enthusiastically. The fairy was the same size as Maddie's Barbie dolls back home, only insanely thin, and with a crazy blue hairdo.

I am losing my mind.

The giant underground complex, the futuristic costume changer, the robot horse, and the angry hover drone--all of those he could explain, but fairies? This demanded a whole new level of disbelief.

I must be in some sort of coma. Yeah, that's it. I bonked my head when I crashed.

A second fairy, this one draped in light green feathers and an acorn for a hat, dropped down in front of them and whispered to the first. The few sentences he managed to catch were bizarre and exotic.

In an excited whisper Maddie asked him, "What are they saying?"

George shrugged his shoulders. "I dunno."

"Dad, I thought you spoke seven languages?"

"I do, but I've never heard anything close to what they are saying."

"Do you think they are," she hesitated before finishing, "real?"

"Can't be. Gotta be some kind of hologram of something," he muttered. He tried waving his hand through one of the Fairies, but the winged nymph dodged nimbly out of the way and bit him on the thumb.

"Son-of-a..." he began indignantly.

His loud swearing startled the two fairies and they whizzed backward a few feet before zipping away.

When he saw Maddie glaring at him with a look of disapproval, he held up his thumb at her and said, "She bit me!"

Maddie pulled his thumb close so she could examine it. And in a way that reminded him of her mother, she said, "It didn't even break the skin."

George yanked his hand back and said grumpily, "C'mon, let's follow them, maybe they'll lead us out of this crazy maze."

They jogged after the two fairies and soon caught up with them. George was pretty sure the two flying nymphs could've easily outdistanced them. It was almost as though they were leading them on. Regardless, not far up ahead of them, George spied a decayed stone wall blocking their path. The fairies hesitated a second as if to confirm they were still following, and then darted through a large crack in one of the thick stones.

"Wait," Maddie yelled after them, but they were already gone. "Awwww," she complained. "We'll never catch up with them now."

She bent down, closed one eye, and peered through the hole in the wall.

"Can you see anything," he asked.

"Not really, it definitely opens up into a big field on the other side, but all I can see is a big tree and more hedges."

George examined the height of the wall. Even if Maddie stood on his shoulders, she couldn't reach the top. And, when he attempted to part the hedges, he discovered they were filled with vicious spikey thorns.

"I guess we'll have to go back to where we started," he finally told Maddie.

"But we've come so far," Maddie whined.

He was about to agree when they heard that familiar sound of stone grinding upon stone.

It wasn't coming from the rock wall though. No. Instead it was a pedestal rising up in the center of the footpath.

"Maddie, get back," George ordered, fearing it might be some sort of trap.

The short obelisk finished rising and stopped with a loud KER-CHUNK. They both stepped closer and could see four symbols on one side.

Maddie extended one finger toward it. "I think we have to push some of these buttons," and before George could stop her she began pressing them at random.

Drunk tuba notes sounded out with each pressing. As soon as Maddie stopped pushing buttons they ceased. This was followed by a rapid clicking sound. After the clicking stopped, a rectangular door sprang open in the wall and a tiny crossbow fired an arrow right at Maddie's head.

George, having seen the tiny trap door snap open, tackled her to the ground just as the bow fired. He could hear the tiny whooshing sound as the bolt zipped by overhead.

"How about we don't push any more buttons?"

Wide-eyed, Maddie agreed, "Okay, Dad."

They got to their feet and George examined the buttons once more. "These are symbols for the elements," he pointed to one drawing that depicted wavy lines. "This one is water, the leaf represents earth, the tornado air, and the triangle is fire."

"How does that help us?"

"I think we have to push the buttons in a certain order." Seeing Maddie was clearly becoming despondent he added, "Hey, I thought you were the video game expert."

This seemed to brighten her up a bit and she started to look around. "Okay, if that's true, there should be a clue around here somewhere."

They began searching but after a full frustrating ten minutes they had found nothing.

"There's nothing here," he said, trying to keep his own frustration out of his voice, and failing miserably.

"Wait a second, Dad. Do you remember the first Fairy we saw?"

George thought about the fairy with the blue hair that he thought was a humming bird. "Yeah, she was blue, what about it?"

"Blue like water," she said mockingly, then when she saw he wasn't following, "And the second Fairy, I think she had an acorn for a hat and her fur was green."

George snapped his fingers and pointed at her. "Representing the Earth."

She moved back over to the obelisk. "Okay, so what do we have then, Water, Earth and..."

Sensing her thoughts, he joined her and said, "We're going to have to guess the next one. We've got a fifty-fifty chance of being wrong. And that's assuming we're not sup-posed to repeat water and earth."

Maddie began reaching for the buttons.

Stopping her, George said, "No, wait. I'll push the buttons this time."

"That's not fair, what am I supposed to do?"

He pointed to a distant corner. "Crouch over there nice and low, and be ready to run."

George took a deep breath and exhaled sharply to calm his nerves. If something happened to him, Maddie would be all alone. He rubbed his hands together, checked one last time to see if she was a safe distance away, and then pushed the first button (water). So far, nothing happened. He stayed on his toes, ready to move out of the way, and pushed the second button (earth). Still, nothing happened.

"Okay, here goes number three," he said, and was about to push the third button.

"Wait," Maddie cried, nearly causing him to choke.

"What?" he asked angrily, but not facing her.

"Which one are you going to push, Wind or Fire?"

George shrugged. It was six of one or half-a-dozen of the other. "Well, I'd rather get blown by wind than burned by fire so, here goes."

He pushed wind. And nothing happened. He then pushed Fire. And still nothing happened.

After waiting a few seconds more Maddie ventured, "Maybe you're doing it wrong, or maybe you need to push Wind last?"

"I pushed it in the exact order of the clues," George began, but then they both heard the grinding noises as the stone wall dropped slowly into the ground.

Maddie stepped up to join him, and without even realizing she was doing it, grabbed him by the hand.

What lay beyond was something right out of Lewis Carroll's classic literary tale. Now Maddie's *Alice in Wonderland* costume had made perfect sense.

And that's when George knew, he really had gone mad.

Chapter 12

Brunch

They stepped over the threshold and the hedge wall rose silently and efficiently behind them.

Maddie knew her dad was frightened for her, frightened she was going to get hurt. He needn't have worried. Still, it was nice having someone care so fiercely about her well-being. Maddie had always felt safe around her father; she *remembered* that.

"I must be cracking up," she heard him say. Maddie knew George wasn't talking to her, but more to himself. She noted he often did that when he was trying to puzzle something out. She decided to give him more time to take it all in. He was one of the brighter ones. She knew he'd be alright.

As for her, she thought their little adventure was going simply marvelous. Nothing like she'd ever experienced before. It was so exciting not knowing what was around the next corner. It literally could be anything.

The field before them was expansive, but still enclosed by hedges. Because of this, it felt as though they had reached the center of the maze and not the way out.

Fat trunked trees provided a canopy of shade, and at the base of each trunk were small doors, most of which were so tiny she doubted even she could squeeze through them, even on her hands and knees. Further, clocks of every sort hung from the tree branches like apples, all ticking loudly, as though counting down to something.

A large, rectangular table was set up in the middle of the field. Her dad must've seen it too because he ushered her toward it with a gentle push. They walked closer and saw four ladies having afternoon tea, with at least a dozen manservants waiting on them.

The ladies wore wide brimmed hats trimmed with flowers and summer dresses decorated with frills and lace. A parasol, matching in color, was next to each chair.

The small army of servants stood at attention around the table or were in the process of serving. Each of them wore simple frock coats, long trousers, buckled shoes, and powdered wigs. Their stoic faces were painted in white makeup and red rosy cheeks.

They walked toward the tea party in silence, but when they were about a dozen feet away, they stopped. Maddie could only guess that her dad didn't want to scare them by accident and was waiting for them to be seen.

Pretty clever, my dad.

Now that they were closer, Maddie could see one tiny lady in particular. She was sitting at the end of the table in a high-backed chair. It was higher than the others. Where the other ladies' hats were adorned with brightly colored flowers, hers was adorned with the plumage of an exotic bird. It was so well-preserved, Maddie thought it might spring to life at any moment. The miniature woman at the end of the table wore a dress with puffy sleeves and had waves of brightly colored hair frothing around her forehead. But oddest of all, strange painters armed with tiny paint brushes were painting her face in an almost theatrical ballet performance. *No. That wasn't quite right.* It wasn't her face they were painting. The tiny woman was wearing the most beautifully delicate-looking porcelain mask.

The plump painter finished up with a few final swishing touches and Maddie heard him say (in what she was pretty sure was an Italian accent) "Lovely, simply, ah-lovely."

One of the other guests at the table clapped wildly and exclaimed, "Yes, wonderful. Never better. Truly."

Staring at her reflection in the ornate mirror another servant was holding before her, the woman behind the mask asked in a voice that betrayed her advanced age, "Really? You really think so?"

The other ladies nodded in vigorous agreement.

Her Ladyship's eye suddenly fell upon Maddie watching them. Startled by new arrivals, she checked herself over quickly and shooed the painter away with a dismissive wave. Satisfied she was ready to receive guests, she called out to them in a thick British accent that was almost cockney, "Hello dearie, please, please, won't you join us for brunch?"

Maddie and her dad exchanged a questioning look. She heard her dad's tummy rumble and knew he was too polite to say how hungry he was.

Although correctly proportioned, the tiny woman wasn't much bigger than her. This, of course, did not affect the volume of her voice in the least. "PLEASE, WON'T YOU SIT DOWN?"

Maddie jumped slightly, but then spying the abundance of food, she began to drool and blurted out, "I'm so hungry." Without further ado, she went over to the table and plopped herself down in a chair that a manservant had pulled out for her.

Not wasting any time, she immediately grabbed the nearest sliced apples and began shoving them into her mouth.

"So good," she managed with a mouth full of food, both hands reaching for a delicious baked treat with whipped cream and a cherry.

"Manners," her dad said in a scolding tone.

"Hmmpfff, sowey," she replied, whip cream now smeared on her cheeks and nose.

"Sorry about that," her dad said as he circled the table and slowly took a seat offered to him across from her. He jumped slightly in alarm when the manservant dropped a linen napkin in his lap. He gave the manservant a hard stare for scaring him, but the manservant was oblivious and wore an expression as blank as the rest of the servants.

"NOT AT ALL, DEARIE... You two have certainly worked up quite the appetite navigating my little maze. I am Lady Wellington of the Paradise Isles, and these," she waved the other ladies away with another dismissive wave, "my royal courtiers."

"Pleased to meet you..." one of the consorts began, but at this Lady Wellington pounded the table with her fist and glared at the woman from beneath her porcelain mask. The woman immediately fell silent, especially when one of the larger manservants stepped forward in a threatening manner.

Maddie stopped chewing and waited to see what would happen. Also, she wasn't sure of this--but she thought her dad was holding a butter knife a few seconds ago, but now it was gone from the table.

A tense moment of silence passed and then Lady Wellington gave a slight bow with her head. "It has been so long since we've had guests," then with clenched teeth she added, "I'm afraid some of us have forgotten the proper conduct in such situations."

The woman who had spoken looked aghast. Maddie had to swallow hard to get down her last bite of un-chewed food.

Her dad simply said, "Think nothing of it." He reached for a slice of bread and began smearing butter on it with a spoon. As he did so, he asked, "We, uh, seem to have gotten lost. Can you tell us what this place is exactly? Can you tell us where we are?"

Lady Wellington simply smiled drunkenly at them for a moment.

One of her consorts pantomimed to her that one of their guests had asked a question. "Oh," her Ladyship said, obviously embarrassed. Receiving only a slight nod, one of the manservants rushed forward with a giant cone-shaped horn and held it up to the Lady's ear. "WHUAATTT DID YOU SAY?!" she asked in a voice reserved for the not-so-recently deaf.

Her father concealed a smile, but Maddie knew her dad well enough that she saw it. He was careful not to shout back but instead raised his voice only a little and asked, "Do... you... know... where... we... are?"

Lady Wellington, listening intently, nodded curtly, indicating she had heard him, and replied, "OF COURSE I DO, DEARIE."

Her dad raised a questioning eyebrow.

"Why, you're in the middle of a maze!" At this, Lady Wellington pounded the table with the palms of both hands and brayed in the most obnoxious laughter.

For Maddie, this confirmed her theory that they were actually in the middle of a maze, and nowhere near out of it.

When the Lady Wellington was able to, she checked to make sure all her friends were also laughing, and they were, and at this, she laughed even louder. "BWAH-HAH-HAH!!!"

Maddie could tell the consorts' laughter was forced, but they made a good show of it.

Her Ladyship wiped a non-existent tear from her porcelain mask by dabbing it delicately with a napkin. She then added, "I mean, I would've thought that was *obvious*." And this brought another round of garish laughter.

Two of the other consorts also laughed along, while the third swatted at the fairies they had seen earlier.

Maddie wasn't sure why, but she didn't feel like laughing at all.

Chapter 13

Off with their Heads!

"CRUMPET CART!"

Lady Wellington said this last command with such abruptness that both Maddie and George jumped in their seats.

A loud squeal was heard, and a pig pulling a two-wheeled wooden cart appeared. The pig's tusks chugged black smoke as its robotic legs carried it across the glen and over to the table. Upon closer inspection George could see the cart was overflowing with baked goods and a giant teapot.

"Ahhhh, the crumpets have arrived," Lady Wellington announced magnanimously.

When the pig cart passed Maddie, his daughter selected a cupcake with whipped cream and a cherry on top. "That's not a pig," she said politely.

"Figured that out all by yourself, did you, dearie?" Her Ladyship asked, then more of her boisterous laughter ensued.

George was beginning to tire of Lady Wellington's bitter comments, lewd laughter, and the way she evaded his questions. These people were obviously insane. He doubted Maddie was aware of just how whack-a-doodle they really were, and the very real danger they were in. On the plus side, they were getting a badly needed meal, and a chance to get off their feet and catch their breath.

Mostly out of habit, he took a more detailed glance at the manservants; their movements seemed stiff, and their faces expressionless.

That's when he realized what they actually were.

Robots?

If so, they were the most advanced he'd ever seen. For sanity sake, he decided they couldn't possibly be robots, but only men wearing clever Halloween masks. Either way, most of them were broad shouldered and athletic and George noted each of them wore a dagger on their belts. Even on his best day (and maybe twenty years younger), he doubted he could take them all on.

Then George noted one particular manservant. Unlike the others, he had a particularly fat face, thin mustache and sagging jowls. Even though the morning air was still cool, his only job seemed to be holding a giant feather that was most likely used to fan her Ladyship.

As they dined on tea and crumpets in silence, with only the occasional clinking of silverware, one of the royal courtiers leaned over and whispered to Maddie, "Isn't she beautiful?"

Maddie took a minute or two to think about it, and then said, "Who? Lady Wellington?"

The royal consort's eyes went wide, and she nodded enthusiastically, almost madly.

George held his breath. It wouldn't take much to tip their crazy meter over.

Maddie studied Lady Wellington thoughtfully for a moment. "I guess so. It's kinda hard to tell with the mask on."

George exhaled with a controlled breath. *That wasn't so bad.*

Maddie dipped her crumpet in some more jam and added innocently, "I mean, you should have seen my mom. Now she is what you would call beautiful."

Maddie realized everyone at the table was now staring at her. "What?" she asked. "What did I say?"

And, here we go. Pack your bags, next stop, crazy train.

"Did she just say what I think she just said?" another royal consort asked in a hoarse growl.

Lady Wellington, looking aghast, hopped down from her chair, (yes, she was that short), stomped over to where Maddie sat and yanked her chair around to face her. Putting her face close to Maddie's and lifting her opera glasses to her eyes, she cackled. "Well answer the woman. Did you?"

Maddie shrank in her chair. "All I said was, my mother was beautiful too," she replied meekly. "That is, I didn't mean to imply you're not beautiful as well."

Under the table George gripped the butter knife he had palmed earlier back into his hand.

There was a dead silence almost immediately and everyone seemed to be wondering what the Lady was going to do or say next, but no one would make eye contact with her.

When the shock was finally beginning to wear off Lady Wellington stammered, head shaking. "I beg your pardon," she said crossly, rearing herself upright as she spoke. "Am I not beautiful as well? Why, the propensity of it all." Then, after realizing she wasn't sure of the definition, George overheard her as she asked one of the consorts in a calmer, more inquisitive tone, "Is that right? Propensity of it all?"

The royal court woman's mouth opened widely. She finally managed, "If you say it is, my Lady. If you say it is."

Maybe we'll get out of this without a fight after all, George thought.

Maddie, obviously trying very hard not to offend Lady Wellington again, began very cautiously, "My Lady, if I offended you," she began, but one of her consorts whispered something in her Ladyship's ear.

"Really?" Lady Wellington asked the consort, and her body immediately turned rigid as though she had just been kicked in the gut. The consort nodded and whispered in her ear again, and when he pulled away, her Ladyship looked directly at Maddie. "Well this changes everything."

"You sir," the Lady said loudly, addressing George. "You can go about your merry way, but I'm afraid your daughter, the young lady, Margie, wasn't it?"

"Maddie," his daughter said, correcting her.

"Yes, in any case, Marsha will have to stay here with me."

George got to his feet so fast his chair toppled over behind him. He growled, "Yeah, I don't think so."

Lady Wellington seemed incredulous, but it was difficult to say with her mask on. "You do realize what you have there? What I mean to say is, *you do realize what she really is?*" She raised her hands over her head and shook her head, as if in disbelief. "Ah well, nonetheless..." and with surprising speed the Lady lunged forward and grabbed Maddie roughly by the arm. "Come with me, young Margarine."

"Let me go! You're hurting me," Maddie cried.

"Now first you are going to have to learn some manners, young lady."

Before George could circumnavigate the table, Lady Wellington backhanded Maddie in the face. As Maddie fell backward her hands pin-wheeled and her fingers somehow clasped the woman's porcelain mask, ripping it from her face.

Everyone heard ceramic glass breaking as the mask hit the ground. This was soon followed by a wailing shriek, "My face, my beautiful face! What have you done?"

George finished circling the table and had nearly reached Maddie's side when the sobbing Lady lifted her head for the first time without her mask.

Seeing her real face George unintentionally blurted out, "Blecch."

It was as though her face had been boiled in acid. Except for her eyes Lady Wellington's face was a red, festering mess. "What have you done?" she cried. After glaring at Maddie for a moment she adjusted her wig and began screaming, "GUARDS! Take this little brat at once."

Anticipating this command, two of the robotic manservants scooped Maddie up by her arms.

"Dad!" she cried, her cheek turning red where her Ladyship had whacked her.

Time to go.

The guard on Maddie's left snapped back his head. He crossed his eyes and seemed surprised by the sight of the butter knife now sticking in his forehead. A trickle of clear liquid (that wasn't blood) trickled down his face.

The second guard holding Maddie watched his comrade release his hold on Maddie's arm, drop to his knees and topple over. When the guard lifted his eyes from the ground, he saw a large round serving platter swinging toward his face.

TWANG!!!

The second guard's head recoiled from the blow, and he too fell to the ground with a nose that was pressed into his face.

Still holding the silver platter he had stolen from the table, George asked Maddie if she was okay. When she nodded that she was, he then asked her irritably, "You couldn't zip it for one meal?"

Maddie stamped her foot. "I was sticking up for Mom!" she shot back. And then, seeing another manservant coming up behind him, she yelled, "Dad, look out!"

George swung two more times and two more manservants went sprawling (one over the table, sending tea and goodies flying everywhere, and the other taking the platter with him). Lady Wellington and her royal courtiers fled the scene, and the other six manservants took their fallen comrades place.

Here we go.

George found himself wishing he still had the pistol he had found belowground.

The first manservant took him by surprise and swiped at his belly with a dagger.

George grabbed his stomach. When he pulled his hand away, he saw his palm covered in blood. A hair slower and they would have disemboweled him, but fortunately it was only a superficial cut. As ludicrous as all this was, the danger was very real.

Lady Wellington, now watching the combatants from the edge of the field, clapped rapidly with gleeful approval. "Wonderful, wonderful." Raising a palm to the side of her mouth she shouted, "Kill the man, but bring me the girl alive."

"Maddie, stay behind me."

He needn't have bothered; Maddie was already diving under the table.

When the knife-wielding manservant came in swinging a second time, George stepped into the man's inside and gripped him by the wrist. A second guard charged forward and George, still holding the knife-wielder by his wrist, lunged forward and stabbed the charging manservant in the heart.

The manservant stumbled backward a few steps with the knife buried to the hilt in his chest.

George then violently reared the back of his head into the man's face behind him, breaking bone (or whatever it had for bone, it was crunchy all the same). For good measure, he elbowed him once and flipped him expertly to the ground.

Two down, four to go.

Three of the remaining four charged him at him all at once. With Maddie defenseless under the table retreat was not an option.

George grabbed a teapot from the table and hurled it like a baseball. The first attacker ducked out of the way, but the unguided missile hit his buddy behind him in the face, and he went down.

And then there were three.

Two of the three manservants plowed into George and they all went tumbling onto the table like felled bowling pins. As they rolled over the table to the other side, George felt a searing pain in his thigh. When he landed in a heap on the other side, he discovered a dagger protruding from his leg.

Getting to one knee, he gritted his teeth and removed the dagger from his thigh. Before even regaining his feet, one manservant jumped onto his back, threw an arm around his neck and started choking the life out of him, while the other charged toward him.

In that split-second, George knew these men (who weren't real) had to die. He had hoped to spare at least some of them, but Maddie would be defenseless in this strange and deadly world without him.

With a quick uppercut, he thrust the knife up and into the manservant's lower jaw, killing him instantly. George then reached behind his back and drove both thumbs into the ears of the manservant clinging to his back, stunning him into letting go. Two left jabs and a hammer-fist to the temple, and he was down for the count.

Okay, last one.

The last manservant seemed much more hesitant to at-tack than his compatriots. George realized it was the funny-looking one with the fat face and thin mustache.

Nonetheless, George balled his fists and was about to step forward and strike him, when the last manservant held up his palms in surrender and said, "Wait, don't hit me! I'm just an accountant!"

This caused George to hesitate. "What?"

The man nodded, jostling his jowls comically. He glanced quickly over his shoulder as he spoke, and whispered, "Yeah, I'm an accountant out of Butler, Pennsylvania. I got captured by this crazy witch and pressed into servitude."

Infuriated by this interruption, the Lady Wellington roared, "What are you waiting for, slave? Kill him!"

George noted for such a tiny woman she certainly had a powerful pair of lungs.

The fat-faced man jumped at the sound of her voice. Obviously not really wanting to, he drew a jeweled dagger from his belt and held it high over his head. "Sorry about this, pal," he whispered. "I don't have a choice." And then, loud enough for the Lady Wellington to hear him, he shouted a battle cry and ran forward as fast as his fat stubby legs would carry him.

The attack was crude and clumsy.

George easily blocked the fat man's downward strike, wrist-locked the knife out of his hand and flipped him to the ground. As he pinned the man's head with his knee and was about to plunge the knife into him, he heard the man sobbing rapidly, "Please don't kill me, please don't kill me."

When George lifted his eyes to scan for any immediate threats, he saw Maddie in the shadows, staring at him from underneath the table. She was watching him with eyes wide. Tears streaming down her cheeks, she shook her head, begging him not to hurt the man beneath his knee.

George sighed and whispered to the fat-faced man, "Congratulations, buddy, you owe your life to a nine-year-old girl. You better just stay down." He pantomimed striking the fat-faced man in the head with the handle of the blade. The accountant wouldn't have won an academy award or anything, but he feigned being knocked out well enough.

When George looked back at Maddie her jaw was hanging open. "What?" When she didn't answer him right away, he asked quickly, "Are you okay? Are you hurt?" He checked her over for any signs of wounds.

"No, Dad, it's just…"

George didn't find anything physically wrong with her. "It's just what?"

"It's just," she exclaimed, "I've never seen you fight like that."

George frowned in a way that said, 'Is that all?' but settled for actually saying, "C'mon, let's get out of here."

As Maddie crawled out from underneath the table, George snatched a folded cloth napkin from the table and tied it over his leg wound. He then used the table to pull himself to his feet and then pulled up Maddie up after him.

He was about to stomp over to Lady Wellington and throttle some answers out of her, when she pulled on a long brown lever on a nearby tree and dropped through a hatch in the ground. George wasn't surprised by this, especially after seeing the massive complex below.

As George and Maddie dusted themselves off, he gazed down at his daughter and said, "Baby-girl, you've got more lives than a cat."

"I know," Maddie heartily agreed. She tilted her head to the side, counted on her fingers, and mumbled to herself, "Let's see--the hover drone, the guillotine door, the cross-bow bolt, and now this." Confident she had the right numbers, she added, "I think this is my fifth life. I really need to be more careful."

"Uh-huh."

Seeing that he was hurt, Maddie lifted his arm and draped it around her small shoulders.

"C'mon, let's get out of this stupid maze."

As they hobbled out of the field toward what appeared to be an exit, Maddie said, "Still, I think it was pretty cool the way you beat up all those guys back there."

"Yep," he answered, wincing with each step, but doing his best not to show it.

"I mean, you like totally punched all those guys right in the face."

"Maddie!" he said, using his Daddy voice.

"Okay, okay." Then, after thinking about it for a second longer she asked slyly, "Can you teach me how to punch people in the face?"

Chapter 14

Barnaby Hornbuckle

"Dad, you're bleeding again!"

Although painful, the slash across his belly was mostly superficial. The hole in his thigh was another matter, as the puncture wound was deep. After they had left the grassy meadow, he used one of the manservant's daggers to cut bandages from a tunic and make a more suitable field dressing. Now that the bizarre glen was far behind them, it was beginning to really hurt.

Despite this, he managed with some semblance of believability, "I'm okay, baby-girl."

Seeing him wince with each step, Maddie grabbed his hand and draped his arm over her shoulders once more. "Here, keep leaning on me, Dad."

He smiled weakly and didn't argue. This time, he actually did lean on her a bit.

"Hey, can I come with you?"

George spun around. Realizing the request came from the stupid accountant, he said, "No. Get lost."

"My name..." he began meekly, "my name is Barnaby Hornbuckle,"

A huge smile had spread across Maddie's face and she waved enthusiastically back at him. "Hi, Barnaby. Nice to meet you."

"Beat it," George said. This man wasn't his responsibility, and he most likely would get them all killed.

"Look, I'm really sorry about back there. I'm just an accountant out of..."

"I know," George cut him off and finished for him, "an accountant out of Butler, Pennsylvania, I heard you the first time when you came at me with a knife."

Barnaby stammered, "You think I had a choice? That crazy witch would've had me killed if I hadn't."

"Oh c'mon, Dad. Let him come with us."

This was the smelly cat all over again. What was that stupid cat's name again? He was always forgetting. *Oh yeah, Lucy.* Maddie had found this half-dead cat in the road one afternoon. The poor thing must've been hit by a car. Anyway, Maddie nursed it back to health, but the accident screwed up the feline's bowels so bad that the thing always smelled like a skunk. But it didn't matter to Maddie, because like her mother, Maddie was the patron saint of lost causes. And that was the first time he realized, when he and his wife had first met, he was the smelly cat.

Barnaby, refusing to give up, removed the makeshift bag from his shoulder and said, "Look, I brought food. I remembered you hadn't finished your meal."

"Food?" Maddie repeated hungrily. She carefully undraped his arm and ran back to Barnaby Hornbuckle and peeked into his bag.

George watched the man's body language warily, but Barnaby seemed non-threatening. The portly fellow opened the bag for Maddie to see the contents inside and said, "It's not much, just what I could grab off the table before they came back."

As Maddie dove into the goodie bag and brought out an apple, Barnaby continued with a hundred-yard stare, "You don't know what it was like. I was a *slave*, emptying her honey bucket, painting her nails, standing for hours upon hours on end holding that stupid fan, even on the coolest of days. I thought because I was the only survivor out of my group that I was one of the lucky ones. Now I know better."

What did he just say?

George interrupted, "Wait a minute, did you say, a group?"

Barnaby nodded his head. "Yeah, you guys didn't wake up with a group?"

George and Maddie exchanged a look and then he answered, "No, it was just the two of us."

"Wow, you guys are more screwed up than I thought." When George gave him a hard stare Barnaby quickly continued, "Anyway, like I was saying, my group and I got separated, most of us got captured by that witch's soldiers back there. Eight long years, that's one more than being an indentured servant in the Bible, ya know? I'm pretty sure I'm the only one left."

"What were those manservant things back there anyway, some kind of robots?"

"Sort of, I don't really know. All I can tell you is..." he gestured wildly with his arms, "this is all real. Those fairies, the manservants? Fake or not, they'll kill you just the same."

George shook his head. "Gotta be some sort of trick, an illusion or something."

"That's what I thought at first, too. For years I tried to figure it all out, find a logical reason to explain everything. But you know what? There isn't one. All I remember is, about eight years ago, I woke up in the suit I was buried in. I know, because I remember picking it out. Anyway, I wake up in this field of prairie grass. I mean, we're talking about a field of grass the size of Wisconsin. It just goes on forever, and it isn't long before I realize I'm not the only one. There are like, dozens of us, and all of us seemed to be from different time periods."

George was wondering what Barnaby meant by different time periods, when Maddie asked, "What were their names?"

Barnaby shook his head, his jowls bouncing again. "I don't remember. It was so long ago, and we didn't exactly have time to exchange names or anything before we all got captured. It was like they knew where we were going to arrive because they were waiting for us. As soon as they attacked, everyone scattered. I think I was in shock or something, because I just stood there and let them take me. It's all just a blur, but I distinctly remember a market or something. Yeah, it was like this big auction. I remember that was when Lady Wellington bought me, and I've been wearing this stupid costume ever since."

Barnaby tried to hold back the tears, looked away in shame, and managed to stifle most of his sobbing. To George's surprise, Maddie grabbed Barnaby's hand and said, "It's okay, Barnaby, you don't have to be scared anymore. You're with us now."

Barnaby tried to answer, but could only manage to nod down to her.

George sighed. "Great," he muttered, then turned around and started walking down the path again. Behind him he heard Maddie say, "Don't worry about my dad. Mom says he's what you call an acquired taste."

About an hour later, they came to a fork in the path. Both paths appeared identical.

"No, not that way," Barnaby called after him. "That leads to the Zombie-Pirate swamp. Trust me, you do not want to go in there. Even Lady Wellington steers clear of the Zombie-Pirate King."

George stopped, sighed, and decided Barnaby was probably telling the truth. He backed up and hiking his thumb down the path to the left, said, "I don't suppose you know what's down this way?"

Barnaby closed his eyes in concentration. After a time, he opened them. "Sorry, I'm not sure. Lady Wellington doesn't normally travel on foot. We usually just sail overhead on her hover barge. The thing is massive."

Barnaby scanned the two paths ahead, and then the one behind. "Hang on a second. If there's a fork in the road, there's usually a backstage door nearby."

George didn't see even the remotest sign of a door, only more of the impassable hedges lining the path.

Barnaby walked up to the fork in the path, stopped for a second, and then marched right into the hedges and vanished, as if by magic.

"Wow, Dad! Did you see that? He walked right through!" Maddie exclaimed.

George refused to be impressed, even though he really was.

"This way!" Barnaby's disembodied voice called after them. "Now that the door is open, you can just walk right on in."

"I think we should go with him, Dad."

Before Maddie could dart after Barnaby, George put a restraining hand on her shoulder. Lowering his voice, he whispered, "Look, I'll let him stick with us until morning, but after that, we go our separate ways."

"Fine by me," Barnaby said, sticking his head back through the hedges so he looked like a floating head.

"I think he heard you," Maddie whispered back.

Barnaby nodded vigorously in a way that made his jowls bounce again, then vanished back into the bushes.

Maddie stifled a laugh, but George gave her a hard stare, trying to keep down his own smirk.

Without even thinking about it, Maddie grabbed his hand and called after Barnaby, "Don't worry, Barnaby. We're coming!"

Chapter 15

Canyon

"Can we stop now?" Barnaby asked. "I can't walk another step."

The colors of dusk started to paint the sky. George knew it would be getting dark soon. As much as he didn't want to, he had to lean more and more of his weight onto Maddie. They were both exhausted, and understandably so. Spending most of last night below ground, this morning at the bizarre tea party, and hiking for most of the day had really begun to take its toll. If they didn't find someplace to rest soon, they were going to drop from sheer exhaustion.

George was just about ready to call it quits and build some sort of campsite, when they arrived at the mouth of a canyon. The moment they approached its threshold a wooden torch mounted on a cliff wall suddenly flickered to life.

"Must be on a sensor or something," George said aloud.

In succession, more torches sprang to life down the canyon, as if beckoning them within. George could see the canyon meander back and forth, but he couldn't quite see all the way to the other end.

"What do you think?" George asked.

It took a moment before Barnaby realized George was talking to him. His face was aghast (as it normally was when he wasn't pouting), when Barnaby finally turned and asked, "What do you mean?"

George sighed, swept a hand toward the canyon, "The canyon, Barnaby. Have you been this way before or not?"

"Dad," Maddie spoke under his arm. "Be nice to Barnaby, he's just as scared as we are."

Barnaby lifted his eyes from Maddie and back to him. He shook his jowls and stammered, "I can't tell you. Er... what I mean to say is... I've never gone this way before."

George grunted as he released his hold on Maddie and hobbled over to the torch mounted on the cliff wall. With some effort, he removed the wooden torch from the metal clasp bolted into granite.

The moment George raised the torch and better lit the canyon's interior, a stiff wind arose from within and fanned the flames.

At least now we not only have more light, but a weapon.

"C'mon, Maddie," George said, but before she resumed her post beneath his arm, Maddie called over to Barnaby in the most reassuring voice she could muster, "Don't worry, Barnaby. My dad will protect you."

One glance over his shoulder and George could see Barnaby wasn't convinced.

George rolled his eyes, but relented, "C'mon."

They were deep into the rock canyon when Maddie first noticed the odd protrusions in the wall for what they really were.

"Dad, look! A fossil," Maddie exclaimed, "I think he used to be a dinosaur."

George guided his torchlight onto the wall and discovered she was right; the skeleton of a dinosaur he couldn't quite place was emerging from the wall.

"I'm pretty sure he's a Euoplocephalus," Maddie said.

Impressed, George asked, "A Euco...plo...ce...phallus? What are you, a paleontologist now?"

Ignoring her dad's jibe Maddie replied, "We studied them in school. You can tell by the hard shell on their backs and the way their tail looks like a big mallet. See?"

George resisted the urge to tousle Maddie's hair and led them onwards. Leaving the dinosaur bones behind, George noticed a dark recess in the canyon coming up.

He held up a hand and ordered in his no-nonsense voice, "Wait here."

"What's a matter?" Barnaby asked, obviously alarmed.

"There's a blind spot coming up, and I want to make sure nothing's hiding inside it."

"Alright," Barnaby quickly agreed. "I'll, uh, stay back here and uh, guard Maddie."

You do that, George thought.

"Be careful, Dad," Maddie said after him.

Holding the torch out in front of him as both light and defense, George found the nook was little more than just that, a nook.

"There's nothing here." He waved Maddie and Barnaby quickly past it.

As Barnaby passed him George asked out of Maddie's earshot, "You sure you've never been this way before?"

Barnaby squinted as he thought about this. "I might have, but it would've been over eight years ago. I can't remember. I'm sorry."

George nodded that he understood, but the reality was he didn't trust the man. Barnaby wasn't telling them everything, of that he was certain. George suspected there was more to the story of how he and the rest of his "group" had been captured.

The canyon twisted as they came upon the head of a giant dinosaur waiting for them. The monster's jaws were open appearing ready to devour them. Startled, Maddie's eyes widened. "Whoa, what's that?"

Suddenly, they both heard rapid footfalls retreating behind them. When they turned, they glimpsed Barnaby vanishing back into the canyon.

George lifted his torch and the light revealed that the giant mouth belonged to the head of a fossilized Tyrannosaurs Rex. To exit the canyon, everyone was required to step into the monster's open, sharp-toothed maw.

"At least he's not alive," Maddie said quietly, and then giggled nervously. Realizing Barnaby had fled, Maddie turned around, cupped her hands to her mouth and shouted, "Barnaby, it's okay, it's just another fossil!"

They both listened to see if Barnaby had heard her, but Barnaby was as good as gone.

Maddie raised her cupped hand to her mouth once more, but George worried someone *or something else* might hear them and stopped her. "Don't worry, I'm sure he'll figure it out... eventually."

With slumped shoulders, Maddie nodded feebly, and shuffled toward the exit.

As soon as they reached the giant skull Maddie touched one of the massive teeth.

George, instantly alarmed, barked, "What are you doing? Don't touch that."

"But Dad, it's a fossil. It is dead," she responded dryly. "It has been dead for e-ons."

"Yeah, what if it's booby-trapped?"

She gave him a quizzical look. Clearly this had not crossed her mind, and she slowly brought her hand to her chest.

"Yeah, that's what I thought," he said lightly. In truth, he had already scanned the path for tripwires and everywhere else for sensors. But in this place, it never hurt to be extra careful.

They exited out the back of the T-rex's skull and onto a precipice overlooking a dark forest. Now that they were out of the canyon, they could see that dusk had been replaced with full on nightfall. Adding to the darkness, an overcast sky made it so no moon or stars were visible. Everything beyond the reach of the torchlight was bathed in total blackness.

"Hey, Dad, look over there... lights."

Maddie was right, staring over the treetops, in the distance, about a mile or two away, was what appeared to be a brightly lit parking lot. Raising the torch a bit higher, George saw a narrow path leading down a gentle slope into the forest. Before he could mention it, they both heard the shuffling of footsteps rushing up behind them. He didn't need to turn around to know it was Barnaby.

Huffing loudly, Barnaby gasped, "Sorry about that... I sorta... I sorta lost it back there."

George shook his head at this, but Maddie took Barnaby's hand in hers. "Don't worry about it, Barnaby. It scared me and my dad a little too."

Hearing this, George flashed Maddie a *faux* stern look. She giggled.

If he was being truthful with himself (but not out loud with Barnaby), the distant parking lot did seem more inviting than the skeletal maw and canyon they had just negotiated.

Barnaby was studying the dark forest when he asked, "What do you think?" Should we wait here until morning?"

Maddie shook her head briskly and answered for him. "No way." Tugging at the obese accountant behind him, she added in a voice much like her father's, "Let's go."

Chapter 16

Dino-Town

"Fine-nuh-ley," Maddie sighed.

The distant parking lot turned out to be a distant gas station.

Leading down to it, both sides of the path were shrouded in dense jungle with thick ferns and tall trees. Maybe the feeling was because of all the dinosaur fossils they saw back in the canyon, but George felt as though they were heading toward a tiny settlement that had been dropped in some sort of primordial world.

As they drew closer, George instinctively reached for a pistol that was not there. He felt naked out in the open like this, and he couldn't shake the feeling that they were being watched. Deciding he didn't want to be seen as they approached, he doused his torch in a nearby puddle.

Barnaby flashed him a puzzled look over this.

In answer, George put a finger to his lips and pointed in the direction of the lit parking lot.

Barnaby shrugged, his face indifferent. Clearly, he saw no reason to worry... yet.

The path ended in a small, dimly lit parking lot. Across the street lay the gas station.

As they crossed the two-lane asphalt road, Maddie pointed to a tall, rectangular shaped box.

"What's that?"

George smiled. Of course, she wouldn't know what that was. They were becoming less-and-less available these days, gone the same way as the typewriter, glass milk bottles, and rolodex-card system. "It's a phone booth."

Maddie shook her head. "Never seen one. What's it do?"

"That's how people used to make phone calls, ya know, before cell phones."

Barnaby gave him a perplexing look. "A cell phone, what's that?"

Tired from lack of sleep, George walked a few more steps before he realized what Barnaby had asked. "How can you not know what a cell phone is?"

Barnaby shrugged his shoulders. "What? You mean like a walkie-talkie?"

Are you kidding me? Who doesn't know what a cell phone is? The irony was not lost on him. *I'm trapped between a guy who doesn't know what a cell phone is, and a little girl who has never seen a phone booth.*

Before he could elaborate further the telephone in the phone booth began to ring... at full volume.

"Maddie, wait!" George called after her, but it was too late, she was already sprinting for the phone.

George gritted his teeth and hobbled after her. When he arrived at the phone booth Maddie was already inside, tentatively picking up the phone off its cradle. Not knowing which end to put to her ear, she held the receiver sideways, "Hello?"

George entered the booth. He could just make out a voice on the other end; it sounded familiar.

Hearing this too, Maddie instinctively put the receiver up to her ear. Her eyes went wide with alarm. "Mom! Mom, is that you?"

"Maddie, hand me the phone," George said, then snatched it from her hands.

"Tessa? Tessa? Where are you?" He yelled into the phone, but only a busy signal answered in reply.

A million questions ran through George's mind, but the paramount issue was whether or not Maddie had heard her mother's voice. He solemnly replaced the phone to its cradle, and gazed down at his daughter. "Maddie, listen to me very carefully. What exactly did you hear?"

Maddie's eyes began welling up with tears. "It was Mom. At least I think it was. She kept saying, 'Hello? Hello', over and over again, like she couldn't hear me at all."

First, wiping away his daughter's tears with his thumb, George pulled Maddie closer to him and gave her a hug. "It's okay, baby-girl. Don't worry. We'll find her."

"Hey guys!" called Barnaby. He was standing near the edge of the road and gesturing to a wooden sign next to him that read...

Welcome to...
DINO-TOWN!!!
Your Gateway to the Past!
2 mi ahead

As they joined him by the sign, Barnaby said, "It's got to be some kind of joke, right?"

"Dad, Dinosaurs! Can we go?"

George furrowed his brow as he looked over at Maddie. "You want to go to a place called Dino Town after we just left a place with fairies in it?"

Barnaby pointed to an additional, smaller sign. "It does say they're the friendliest dinosaurs on the planet."

Maddie laughed a bit too enthusiastically, her sense of relief at finding a town burst forth. They all felt it. Where there was a town, there were people. Where there were people, there was food, and first aid. As for the dinosaurs, it was most likely just a bus ride past a bunch of life-sized plastic dinosaurs.

George gazed past the sign and down the road. He didn't see any town, only eternal darkness.

Interrupting these thoughts Maddie walked past him and shouted out a loud and proud... "Hello!"

George stopped her before she could cry out again, and in a tense whisper, he said, "Hey Maddie, how about we don't start announcing our presence just yet?"

Maddie shrugged, obviously a little disappointed, then asked, "Okay, what's the plan then?"

In answer, George lifted a hand to shield his eyes from the station's bright lights and studied the gas station again. He couldn't remember the last time he had seen gas pumps without digital displays. Beyond them he saw a large one-story building. The sign above the entrance read...

FRED & MARTHA'S DINO-MYTE
Gas Station & Souvenir Store

"I don't know about you but I'm so hungry I could eat a dinosaur named Barnaby."

Maddie laughed so hard she snorted.

A quick glance at the overweight and sweating Barnaby told him middle-aged accountant didn't appreciate the joke.

Focusing back on Maddie, he slung his arm over her narrow shoulders and said, "What do you say we go inside that gift shop and see if they have some real food?"

"Alright. But if we don't find any food, you still can't eat Barnaby."

"Agreed," Barnaby seconded.

"I make no promises," George said.

"Dad..."

Chapter 17

Fred and Martha's Gift Shop

George, Maddie and Barnaby closed on the gift shop's main entrance.

As they approached a pair of antique gas pumps with clear bubbles of gasoline on top, George tried to recall the last time he had seen a gas pump that wasn't digital. Curious, he grabbed one of the handles and squirted a little gas onto the ground. As the fuel hit the pavement the numbered dial rotated and there was a distantly familiar DING!

It's like we went back in time.

Adding to this theory, George noticed a colorful calendar taped to the side of one of the pumps. The year listed was 1951, and the August picture on top was a Norman Rockwell knock-off featuring a little boy wearing a striped shirt and peach fuzz crewcut. The boy sat delighted at the counter of a good ole' American diner, eating a slice of apple pie with a scoop of vanilla ice cream piled on top.

"C'mon, dad," Maddie said, tugging on his hand, pulling him toward the front door of *Fred and Martha's Gift Shop*. "I'm sooo... hungry."

Leaving the archaic gas pumps behind, they saw an equally antique safari truck parked near the main entrance.

A sandwich board sign had been set up in front of the truck...

*"Our Dinosaur Tours are
the Safest Guaranteed!"*

George was forced to wonder how somebody could get their money back after getting eaten by a dinosaur. Of course, that was assuming they didn't have living-breathing dinosaurs as in that dino movie that came out a few years back. Most likely they were just like the animatronics at the theme parks down in Orlando.

On the other hand, those fairies back in the maze had seemed real enough; their bite marks on his knuckles still itched like crazy.

George gave the old safari truck a closer inspection. The tires were flat and the windshield was badly cracked, and yet the cargo rack on the roof was jam-packed with expedition gear.

Standing on the running boards, and peering inside the cab, George mumbled aloud, "Yeah, I don't think this truck has been run for a *long* time."

"Can we go inside the store now?" Barnaby asked, "I'm starving."

"I second that!" Maddie intoned.

The bell over the doors jingled as Maddie yanked open the door to the main entrance.

"Maddie..."

His daughter cut him off. "I know, I know," and mimicking his deeper register she said, "Stay close and stay behind me."

George smiled, then scanned the interior. A walk-up snack counter was situated just inside the door and waited for passing motorists to buy a refreshing snack or beverage.

The cash register (similar to the gas pumps) looked as though it belonged to an age gone by. Spotting a pack of Lucky Strike cigarettes for sale (same brand our boys smoked in World War II) he thought, *Whoever built this 1951 replica was meticulous right down to even the smallest details. Even the old-style rotary phone on the wall seems genuine.*

A phone! George lifted the receiver to his ear.

Of course, it didn't work. That would've been too easy.

The dead phone wasn't what was really bothering him. What really caused him the most concern was how everything belonged in the 1950's. And yet, the place didn't look like an antique. It seemed as if it were built only yesterday. Adding to the mystery further, why was everything inside covered in at least a decade's worth of dust?

Where are we?

George's eyes fell on a framed, black-and-white photograph next to the phone. Wiping the dust from the glass with the palm of his hand he saw it depicted various paleontologists unearthing a new discovery at a dig site. A few of the other pictures on the wall were of smiling tourists taking safaris in a vehicle that strongly resembled the truck out front.

This alleviated his fear somewhat that any moment a meat-eating dinosaur might smash through the front windows, leap inside and gobble them up. This place was obviously a tourist trap offering food and merchandise for tours of the various dinosaur dig sites. The grant-starving paleontologists probably even got a little kick-back for waving at the tourists and answering their questions.

Realizing he hadn't checked on his daughter in the last few minutes, he quickly scanned the store.

Surprisingly, Maddie wasn't tearing into the bags of food on the layers of display racks. Instead, something else had captured her attention entirely.

"Really? You're starving, but instead you're digging through a pile of toys?"

"What? I like toys." Out of a wire mesh bin filled with stuffed animals, she snagged a tan, German shepherd stuffie and held it up to him. "Look Dad, it's just like Apollo back home." Hopping up and down, she asked repeatedly, "Can I have it, can I have it?"

George scanned the store's interior once more. Every surface was covered in a layer of thick dust. It was becoming more-and-more apparent that the place had been abandoned for a *very* long time.

"I don't see why not. There doesn't seem to be anybody here."

Maddie shook and patted the dust out of the stuffed animal causing them both to cough.

Once he could breathe again, George said, "I'm going to check behind the counter and see if I can find a phone that actually works. Don't wander off."

Maddie offered him a crisp, sarcastic salute. Spying racks of candy bars, she made off for the back of the store.

She wasn't gone for long, however, before briskly walking back, clutching her newfound toy to her chest.

Lowering her stuffie's head away from her lips, "Uh, Dad, I think I found something."

Still searching beneath the clerk's counter for a phone he asked, "Yeah, what'd you find?"

"A guy."

George froze. "A guy? What kind of guy?" Maybe it was someone who could help them, or at the very least offer up some answers, like where they were, exactly. Realizing he was still rummaging beneath the counter a sudden feeling of guilt swept over him. "How's he dressed? Like an employee?"

Maddie lowered her stuffie from her lips again before answering. "I don't think so... but I'm pretty sure he's dead."

Chapter 18

Bunk Down

"Stay here," George said sternly. "Got it?" He was only talk-ing to Maddie, but behind her, Barnaby nodded fervently in understanding.

George removed the stolen dagger he kept tucked in his belt and moved toward the back of the store. Of course, Maddie didn't listen, but at least she stayed behind him.

Glancing over his shoulder at her, Maddie seemed to take keen interest in how he carried his blade (concealed behind his wrist, hidden but ready for action). Before today she had never really seen her old man in action.

Rounding the aisle's endcap, he found Maddie's dead guy sitting on the floor with his back against the far wall of the shop. He was wearing cargo shorts, white knee-high socks, and brown lace up boots. George couldn't see the dead man's face as he was wearing a bush hat and his head was slumped down.

Maintaining a safe distance, George was about to call out to the man when he crouched to get a better angle on the man's face.

Although *extremely* lifelike, the frozen, somewhat artificial-looking face was an immediate giveaway.

"A robot?" George asked aloud.

"Really? Kewl," Maddie cooed, tentatively walking up the aisle behind him, clutching her stuffie to her chest. "I've never seen a robot before." Tilting her head to one side, she added, "Why is he dressed like a jungle explorer?"

Still standing safely behind Maddie, Barnaby offered, "Maybe he's one of the tour guides we saw in the photos?"

George was about to respond, but seeing Maddie's face, and the way her tiny hands tightened their grip on her newfound toy, he said, "Maddie, why don't you and Barnaby go back and wait for me by the front counter?"

His daughter overrode him hastily. "I'm okay, Dad. It's not like he's a real person. I can totally handle it."

George turned toward her and scrutinized her face. "You can totally handle it?"

Maddie nodded, exaggerating the movement when she did so, and whispered determinedly, "Yeah... I'm not scared."

Normally George would put his foot down. He wasn't sure this very-lifelike robot (who appeared very dead) was anything a nine-year-old girl should be seeing. But, if his suspicions were correct, this little adventure was far from over. In fact, this might be only the beginning. After nearly getting killed several times in the last twenty-four hours, he needed to consider the fact he might not be around to see her all the way through it to the end. So, he needed to start training her... and fast.

"Alright, kiddo. You can stay. But, the moment you feel sick or just want to walk away, you just do it. Understand?"

Again, the exaggerated head nod.

George knelt next to the lifeless robot and thought, *His face looks like the man servants we saw back in the Fairy Maze.*

Pointing to the robot, he asked Barnaby, "Do you know about this?"

Barnaby shook his head. Seeing George was waiting for more of a response, the accountant explained, "I've never seen this exact guy before, but I can tell you he's only a low-level stuff, ya know, only designed to do basic chores. But, I've seen others where you can't even tell the difference."

George pursed his lips as he thought about this. "What about Lady Wellington? She a robot too?"

Barnaby immediately shook his head. "No, she and the other women at her table weren't robots… but they ain't exactly human either. Truth is, I don't know what they are."

"Dad! Do you think he'll come back to life? You know, like a zombie?"

George couldn't help but laugh. Despite the dire circumstances, he answered, "Sure, why not? We've already seen fairies today. Why not zombies?"

When he saw Maddie's face go serious, he quickly added, "I'm only teasing, he's not a zombie, he's just a dead robot." He lifted the robot's safari vest and checked for damage. In doing so, even he had to admit, a small part of him was waiting for the inert automaton to spring to life.

Thankfully, it didn't budge.

"If I were to guess, he probably just ran out of power."

Barnaby was the first to speak. "What now?"

George knew what the overweight accountant was really asking, stay here or take their chances walking to the town down the road. He wasn't fond of the idea of traipsing down the highway in the dark. Plus, if there were robot people, maybe there were robot other things.

Barnaby must have been thinking the same thing, because he volunteered, "Ya know, I saw some sleeping bags and cots over in the camping supplies section. We could bunk down here for the night, maybe hike to the town in the morning."

"Seems safe enough," Maddie agreed quickly. Judging by her face, clearly this idea appealed to her as well.

Knees aching, George stood up. When he did, a wave of exhaustion swept over him and his knees buckled slightly.

Whoa, I am way more tired than I thought.

Instead of mentioning it, he said, "Yeah, that's probably for the best."

It didn't take them long to stage a little campsite in the camping section of the store: 3 cots with sleeping bags on top and lanterns surrounding them like night watchmen.

Maddie had insisted they cover the robot man's face with a jacket. When she wasn't looking, George did one better and tied the robot's hands and ankles together using some rope from the camping section. He also planted empty glass bottles around its legs; if it moved, they'd know about it.

Despite all the dust, the food was surprisingly still fresh. After they gorged down on everything they could find, Maddie allowed him to tuck her into her sleeping bag. However, she refused to let go of her stuffie while he was doing it. He could see she was barely holding it together. The stress of the day was really beginning to wear on her. So, he sat down on her cot next to her and asked, "Hey kiddo, you doing okay?"

A single tear rolled down her cheek and her voice croaked when she answered, "Okey-dokey." It was something her mother used to say when she wasn't fine, but would never admit it. George lifted her slightly and hugged her fiercely. It went without saying, but he'd die before he let anything happen to her.

Maddie sobbed quietly into the area between his neck and shoulder.

Feeling helpless, he said, "Hey, I almost forgot, I found you something."

Hearing this, she pulled away, wiped the tears from her cheek, sniffled, and asked, "You found something? What'd you find?"

George reached down into the bug-out backpack he had been preparing. It was an old Army issue L-shaped flashlight; the kind designed to clip on your belt or vest.

"I found you a flashlight."

Wiping more tears from her eyes with the palms of her hands she asked, "Does it work?"

In answer, he clicked it on, and the red flashlight bulb bathed the store's interior in a crimson haze.

"Ohhhh, that's kewl," Maddie breathed, taking it into her small hands. She then proceeded to shine the red beam at her surroundings.

"Here, let me see it for a second."

Maddie instinctively tightened her hold on the flashlight and was half-serious when she said, "Uh-uh, this one's mine."

George shook his head and laughed. "Okay, okay. I just want to show you something."

Reluctantly, she handed it over. He clicked the flashlight's button a second time, and the red beam changed to white.

Maddie's eyes went wide.

"That's not all, watch this." George clipped the L-shaped flashlight to his front pants pocket so he didn't have to hold it and yet it still lit the way like a headlamp on a car.

"That's neat! Now, give it back."

Nodding in acquiescence, he unclipped the flashlight and gave it back to her.

As he did so, Barnaby plopped down on his own cot. The cot's wood-frame groaned as he began unlacing his shoes. "Boy are my dogs barking."

George smiled as he saw Maddie's look of confusion; her eyes darting about for the dogs. "What dogs?"

Also seeing her confusion Barnaby explained, "Um, not literally. It's just an old expression about tired feet."

George and Tessa never did understand why Maddie always delighted in making friends with people other than her own age. Sometimes she visited the elderly woman as she gardened in her yard. Other times, she played with the preschoolers across the street. But, she never seemed to gravitate toward kids her own age.

When asked about this, she explained that she pretty much knew what all the kids her own age were thinking. She was more curious about what the grownups thought, or she delighted in sharing what she knew with the younger kids.

George kissed Maddie on her forehead and said, "Good night baby girl, sweet dreams."

Maddie responded with her customary good night in Italian, "Buona notte, Dad. Sogni d'oro," which meant good night and sweet dreams.

When she saw he wasn't climbing into his own sleeping bag, Maddie asked, "Dad, where are you going?"

"It's okay kiddo, I'm not going far. I just want to double check the store and make sure everything's locked up tight?"

Maddie's hand shot out and grabbed him by the hand. On the verge of tears, she said, "Please don't go, Dad. I'm scared."

Hearing this too, Barnaby offered, "Hey, why don't you let me go?" and rose to his feet.

"Sure," George said with a little more fervor than he intended. To soften the blow he added, "Just be careful," but Barnaby had already padded off in his socked feet.

Watching him go, Maddie signaled George with her finger to lean in closer. When he did, she checked to see if Barnaby was listening. Certain that he wasn't, she whispered, "Dad, please be nice to Barnaby. He's our friend."

George managed a weak smile, but what he really thought was... *Stupid, stupid smelly cat all over again.*

On the other hand, he and Maddie had only lived in this strange and terrifying world for about a day-and-a-half. He couldn't fathom what it must have been like for Barnaby trying to survive for nearly a decade.

George laid down on his own cot and hadn't even closed his eyes before Maddie dragged her own sleeping bag on top of them. She snuggled up into the crook of his shoulder, let out a terrific yawn and drifted off in seconds.

George fondly recalled all the times Maddie had crawled into their bed at night when she was scared from a nightmare or a television show she probably shouldn't have been watching. His thoughts naturally turned to Tessa. His stomach turned at the thought of not knowing where she was. What if she was still down in the underground tunnels? Should they go back and search instead of pressing onwards?

Maddie rustled beside him, and then snuggled closer. No. They had barely escaped the tunnels last time. The first thing tomorrow, he'd get Maddie out of this weird and strange place and home safe. That's what he'd want Tessa to do if their roles were reversed. He just had to keep reminding himself of that.

Barnaby soon returned. Quietly as he was able (which wasn't quiet at all) he climbed into his own cot. When he saw George watching him, Barnaby gave him a thumbs up.

George responded with only a slight nod. He still didn't trust the man and was fairly certain he wasn't telling them everything.

Within seconds after pulling the sleeping bag on top of him, the accountant from Butler, Pennsylvania was already fast asleep and beginning to snore.

As George began to drift off to join Maddie in deep slumber, and Barnaby began to snore even louder, none of them heard the bushes rustling heavily, just outside the store.

Chapter 19

Dinosaur

Buzzing noises.

That's what George heard as he climbed the long flight of stairs toward consciousness. Eventually, the insanely loud buzzing noises in his ears finally ceased.

When he opened his eyes, he found himself still lying on the cot in the gift shop. Part of him had secretly hoped he would have awakened in the master bedroom of his beach-front home in Pensacola, with Tess sleeping delicately beside him.

Instead, the obese accountant slept in an adjacent cot, his snoring so loud it was ridiculous.

George sat up, albeit slowly. His muscles were so stiff and sore, he felt as though a professional boxer had worked him over while he slept. His cheek ached where one of Lady Wellington's henchmen thumped him good, and when he swung his legs over the side of his cot, the stabbing pain in his thigh reminded him of the knife wound in his leg.

Why does it always feel worse the next morning?

With a groan he rose to his feet, but in the process, he banged the back of his head on a nearby shelf. He fought down a curse and rubbed his scalp profusely.

As the sting began to slowly wear off, he scanned the interior of the giftshop. Barnaby was still out cold, but Maddie was nowhere to be found. George could see where his daughter had been sleeping in the cot beside him, and for a moment he began to question whether she had been but a dream. *Take it easy, most likely she's in the bathroom or exploring the toy section; she's a good kid and would never wander off outside.*

At least that's what he told himself.

He was about to shout for her when the bright sunlight in the front windows beckoned him to look outside. Moving over to them, he could see a great deal more details than he could last night, such as the alien-looking fauna encroaching on the tiny gas station.

Tessa's voice suddenly popped into his head, her tone sweet and soothing, 'George, you need to find our daughter. You promised to keep her safe.' He could almost imagine her standing at the window beside him. Heeding her advice, he leaned his forehead to the window and checked the front parking lot. What he saw caused a wave of panic strong enough to seize him.

Maddie!

Over by the safari truck, George barely glimpsed his daughter, as she vanished into the jungle with stuffy clutched in hand.

Even though it had only been two minutes since awakening, he cursed himself for not thinking about her sooner.

"Maddie!" He shouted through the window after her, but he wasn't really expecting an answer; he was still inside. Knowing how his daughter had inherited her mother's curiosity and his recklessness in equal measure, Maddie was probably headed into the jungle to do a bit of exploring.

Turning his chin over his shoulder, he shouted to the back of the store, "Barnaby, get up!"

As George ran back to his cot to pull on his boots, the slothful accountant mumbled something about wanting to sleep for five more minutes, smiled, and drifted back to sleep.

"Barnaby, I said… wake up!" George threw a pillow at Barnaby's head to emphasize his point. The pillow bounced off the accountant's face, and he woke up sputtering on his own saliva.

Not wasting a second longer, George raced for the exit as fast as his sore and broken body would allow.

Stepping outside, George called out again, "Maddie!" This time he was louder with more urgency in his voice.

He ran across the parking lot and stopped at the back of the truck. There was a narrow dirt path that meandered back and forth into the jungle. Not seeing her, he cried out once more, "Maddie!" *If anything happened to that little girl,* and with the same thought, *I don't care how old she is, I am going to spank her little behind for running off without me.*

"Maddie," he shouted again, hobbling down the path.

Still nowhere to be seen, he heard, "Over here, Daddy." It was his daughter's teeny-tiny voice, coming from just up ahead.

George rounded another bend and saw her standing at the end of the path on a muddy embankment of a wide stream. The moment he saw her, a tidal wave of relief rushed into him. Shielding his eyes from the rising sun, he began with a sigh of relief, "Maddie, you shouldn't have run off like that. You scared the bajeezus out of me."

Wide-eyed, Maddie turned back to him and said, "Dad, I know you're not going to believe this, but I think... I saw... a dinosaur."

He was about to say something akin to, 'That's crazy,' or 'Get back inside,' but then he saw the oversized tracks in the sand of the shore. Kneeling next to them, George studied the large three-toed footprints in the muddy embankment. They were at least twice the size of bear prints he had seen once on Kodiak Island--better known as 'Bear Island'--in Alaska.

"I think I've seen this movie," he mused under his breath.

George was about to turn back to his daughter when a glimpse of movement caught his eye. Maddie saw it too.

"See, I told you. I told you I saw a dinosaur."

Not daring to move, George stood motionless. In the stream, not thirty feet away, was a living, breathing dinosaur. It was standing near the opposite shore, in about three feet of water, on two thick hind legs. George wasn't sure how they had missed him. Perhaps it had something to do with how the dinosaur's skin blended right in with the forest. The creature had to be at least ten feet tall, had tiny forelimbs, and sported a tall, fan-shaped crest on its head that reminded George of an Elvis pompadour. The fin continued down the length of its back and ended along its long tail.

Tapping a large book with colored pictures Maddie said, "I think it's a Corythosaurus."

"Where'd you find that book?" George asked incredulously.

"It was in the gift shop. I started reading it while you guys were sleeping, like for-ever."

If the dinosaur was a fake, it was a good one. George could see the rib cage flex as the creature breathed. The way it chewed river grass in its duck-billed mouth reminded George of the way a cow incessantly chews its cud.

Not willing to push their luck any further, he said quietly, "We need to go."

"Why?" Maddie asked, using that whiney voice, the one she reserved only for him and knew better than to try with her mom.

"Safety issue," he said curtly. Who knew what was lurking beneath the surface of the river, or beyond the shadows of the trees? George imagined an enormous water creature lunging out of the river and snatching up Maddie in its array of multi-toothed jaws before wriggling itself back into the depths of the stream. *After everything they had seen so far? Sure. Why not?*

"Dad, It's okay," pointing to a picture of the creature in her book, she added, "See? It's a leaf eater. It doesn't eat meat."

"Yeah? Who's to say there isn't a hungry meat eater lurking around, looking to eat a leaf-eater."

As though for emphasis, a distant crash rose from the jungle. It was so thunderous, a flock of iguana-looking birds erupted from a canopy of trees and took flight.

Yep. Time to grab Maddie and drag her butt back to the safety of the gas station. Maybe he and Barnaby could get that old safari truck running and drive it the heck out of here. Down the road, they could find some real help, call the cops, the military; somebody with back up needed to be told about this freak show.

The sound of a tree being pushed over echoed amongst the trees. It sounded a lot closer this time and served as a harsh reminder that they were still out in the open.

"C'mon, honey," George said trying to keep the fear out of his voice while taking Maddie by the hand. He turned to lead her quickly back toward the gift shop when...

"Oh, thank God you found her!" Barnaby breathed, huffing and puffing from running a scant fifty feet.

George was about to say something snarky in response when his old instincts kicked in, and he realized the jungle had gone quiet. Barnaby started to say something else, but George shushed him.

Suddenly from downriver, they all heard an eerie sound, like the bleating of a drowning elephant. This time, even the Corythosaurus picked up its head nervously. The wading dino quickly swallowed his leafy breakfast and dashed off into the woods.

Feeling the adrenaline surge through his veins, George watched as a second dinosaur crashed through the jungle on the opposite side of the river. This new arrival had a broad beak and armored head. Its heavily armored back had thick plates and bony horns all the way down to its clubbed tail.

George guessed the length to be at least twenty feet, and about the size and width of a large truck. Without tearing his gaze from the new arrival, he asked Maddie in a harsh whisper, "Your book say anything about that guy?"

"Let me check," Maddie said, already flipping pages. "I think it's a Euoplocephalus, you can tell by the club-shaped tail. It's just like the fossil we saw back in the canyon."

"How did you," Barnaby started to ask, but then saw Maddie holding an open book of Dinosaur identification. "Does it say whether or not those things eat meat?"

Smiling broadly, Maddie answered, "Says he's an herbivore."

Barnaby wiped some more sweat from his forehead and muttered, "Well, that's a relief."

A sly grin slid across Maddie's face. "That doesn't necessarily mean it doesn't eat meat."

Barnaby's face fell. Then, realizing she was just teasing him, he replied dryly, "Oh. Hah-hah."

George felt uneasy, vulnerable. He had seen this movie before. Everyone's laughing and joking, and then something terrible shows up and starts eating everyone. "Alright, fun time's over. Let's head back to the gift shop and get some breakfast."

Before they could, an extremely strange and loud trumpeting sound was heard in the distance. George had never heard the Arc Angel Gabriel's horn but if he did, he imagined it would sound like this. Two more mighty blasts were heard, and before the echo of the last one died out completely, the frantic beating of insanely loud drums flooded the air.

Laughter ceased at once. Barnaby's face went ashen. "Wait. I know that sound. No... no... no..." he kept repeating in a panic.

"What is it, Barnaby, what's wrong?" George asked.

"We have to get out of here. We have to hide."

"Why?" George yelled out after him.

"The Gatherers!" Barnaby shouted back over his shoulder. "The Gatherers!"

Running far faster than George would've thought Barnaby capable of, George watched the man sprint off through the trees. "Barnaby, where are you going? The gift shop's the other way!"

But it was too late. Barnaby was gone, and so was the club-tailed dinosaur, as if he too knew better.

The bleating trumpets sounded again and this time they took on a more musical note allaying any fears that it was some ginormous monster ready to devour them. *So why did it scare Barnaby so badly? Just where exactly was it coming from?* It sounded like it was... everywhere.

As though wondering this too, Maddie pointed her tiny forefinger toward the heavens and breathed, "Dad, look up."

When George lifted his gaze skyward, the source of the bleating trumpets and booming drums immediately became apparent.

Whatever it was, it was so large, it blocked out the sun.

Chapter 20

Gatherers

The hovering barge was massive.

At first glance, George thought his eyes were deceiving him, but the craft floating about seventy feet above them had to be about the size of a football stadium.

Floating wasn't the right word either, at least not to George. Whether in water or air, a *floating* craft would bob up and down. Yet this thing was moving across the sky perfectly level, like a fixed object—with no motor noise or wind from rotor blades.

Mirroring his own thoughts, Maddie asked, "Is that a blimp?

"I don't know, baby-girl. I've never seen anything like it." Remembering how Barnaby had fled at the first sign of the thing, George urged Maddie back toward the trail.

As soon as they arrived back to the gas station, Maddie cried, "Hey Dad, what are those funny-looking *people*?"

It was the way Maddie said the word 'people' that concerned him. As if she wasn't entirely sure they were human.

To block the early morning sun, George cupped his hands around his eyes and focused on the edges of the barge.

Powerful-looking men stepped onto short diving boards, and after a quick prep, dove off headfirst into a perilous descent. Screeching noises accompanied them as they plummeted to their deaths.

Maddie gasped.

Hearing their death cries too, George reflexively put a hand on her shoulder and pulled her closer to him.

It soon became apparent the men had bungee cords attached to their ankles and trailing behind them. The bungee cords (which now that they were closer looked more like vines) lowered them all the way to the surface. Each time they did, there was a slight hesitation before they rose back up. Still upside down, the powerful men would snatch things from the surface: tools, foodstuffs, anything of value and within easy reach, before they sprung back up again with bounty in hand.

As one of them seized a sleeping bag off the roof of the safari truck, George and Maddie could see the powerful-looking gatherers weren't really men at all.

They were monsters.

Each gatherer was half the width of a normal man but had to be at least seven feet tall. And despite their skinny bodies and sinewy limbs, they seemed impossibly strong. George saw one pick up a barrel of oil and pull it back up with him with ease.

Dozens more began dropping all around them, each of them painted a different color, with some sort of clay. One was forest green, another ocean blue, and still another fiery orange. But when one bungeed down next to them and grabbed a discarded wheelbarrow George could see the clay was their skin.

Maddie screamed when one dropped down beside her. Hearing his daughter's cry, the creature turned its hairless head toward them. The thing had no mouth or nose, only a large v-shaped hole for what he assumed were its eyes.

George grabbed Maddie's hand and pulled her toward the gift shop. However, outrunning dozens of repelling gatherers proved problematic. Now that they they'd found new prey, they seemed to be concentrating their efforts on capturing Maddie.

Dodging their elongated grasps, George weaved his daughter around the gas pumps, past the safari truck, and headed toward the gift shop. George could only hope the building might provide some protection. He steered Maddie around one upside down gatherer snatching for her legs and kicked another's two-fingered hands away.

Nearing the gift shop's main entrance, several gatherers dropped down in front of them and waited, as though sensing where they were headed.

Glancing skyward, George noted the hover barge was still in motion. They only needed to outlast them for another few minutes or so and the ship would be past.

Cut off from the gift shop, he shouted, "C'mon!" and pulled her toward the safari truck,

"Daddy, I'm scared," she cried, running after him.

Dodging dropping gatherers and their stretched-out limbs, they somehow reached the cab of the truck. George turned his back on his daughter only for the one second it took to open the truck's heavy metal door.

One second was all they needed.

"Daddy!" she cried as her small hand was ripped from his grasp and she flew up into the sky, her arms and legs outstretched toward him.

George's heart sank into his stomach. "Please, God. No."

He dodged out of the way as a second Gatherer tried to snatch him up too. Missing him entirely, the Gatherer, didn't go back up. Instead, the grotesque monster curled up in a most unnatural way and gave his vine a quick tug, locking it into place. Bungee cord secured, it flipped over to land on its feet. George noted that the bungee cord was actually tied around only ankle allowing it to walk. The Gatherer, this one a burgundy color towering over him by at least two feet, stretched out its arms toward him like Frankenstein's monster.

Remembering he still had the knife, George ducked under the elongated monster's grasp and stabbed his blade into the creature's thigh.

The gatherer howled in pain as George pulled out his knife.

So, they can be hurt.

George didn't see any blood, in fact, he equated the attack to stabbing a giant piece of licorice.

The gatherer didn't fall though; instead it hobbled on his one good leg, grabbed his bungee cord, and gave it two deliberate tugs. Within a second, the injured gatherer's legs were whisked out from under him and it rose skyward, feet first.

As George watched the injured creature lift to its mothership, another fiery-red gatherer dropped toward him, hands outstretched.

Before it arrived, George used the bumper of the safari truck to quickly climb onto the hood.

As the red gatherer rocketed past him to the pavement, George grabbed the vine in one hand and gave it a swift tug.

As predicted, the vine locked into place, and instead of rising back up the gatherer went face first into the pavement with a sickening CRUNCH. Before the gatherer could recover, George looped the vine around his left hand and used his knife to slice the vine below.

Now that the gatherer was cut loose, George gave the vine two deliberate tugs and... WHOOSSHHH! He was off like Superman taking flight.

The ascent was terrifying, but as a Para Rescue Ranger, George was no stranger to jumping out of airplanes, and in a way, the rise was kind of fun.

The ride was over in seconds and the bungee cord soft-landed him on a wide platform running around the edge of the barge and seemingly built for that purpose. Unfortunately, the take-off had been so abrupt, he'd dropped the knife.

Only a moment after George had landed, an earth-tone gatherer stepped up to the platform next to him. It had its hands above his head like an Olympic diver making ready to dive. Spotting George, it dropped its hands and turned toward him. Before the Gatherer could seize him, George jumped up, grabbed a railing overhead, and planted both feet in the gatherer's face. Instead of a beautiful swan dive the gatherer intended, it pin-wheeled its arms before falling off the ledge.

George turned back toward the ship and scanned the deck. The ship wasn't a ship at all. It was more like a floating land mass. He spied a narrow passage through some boulders and trees. He was about to go through it when he heard Maddie's voice.

"Dad! Over here!"

George saw two more gatherers, both forest green, leading Maddie down the length of the platform. The gatherers swiveled their heads all the way around and saw him too. Suddenly, an alarm klaxon that would've been more at home on a German U-boat began blaring loudly. In answer several more gatherers exited from within the woods and cut him off from Maddie.

George glanced over his shoulder and saw an equal amount racing up behind. Spotting a hatchet in a pile of recovered bounty, George lunged for it and snatched it up in his hand.

Spitting the words out venomously to the nearest of them, he growled, "Buddy, that's my daughter you're holding. I will kill every last one of you before I let you have her."

In answer, the Gatherer removed a wooden peg from the bandolier he wore across his chest. The peg was about the size and shape of a bowling pin. And in the blink of an eye the wooden peg flew out of the creature's hand, tumbled end-over-end, and struck George in the back of his hand.

With a cry of anguish George dropped the hatchet and cradled his injured hand.

George's eyes darted for the weapon, but the gatherers surrounded him in an instant. George punched the first in the throat causing it to stumble back, then front kicked another's knee, so it bent sideways, but three more took their wounded comrades place. Instead of grabbing him, they began pushing him instead.

That's when he realized they had no intention of subduing him. They were pushing him back toward the ledge.

"No, no, no," he kept repeating, his foot precariously near the edge. It wasn't so much that he cared about dying, that ship had sailed the moment he joined the military and became a Para Rescue Jumper. No, if they killed him now, Maddie would be their helpless captive.

George grunted, and with every ounce of strength he pushed back.

With a collective sigh, the Gatherers pushed him over the side.

And George fell to his death.

Chapter 21

Hello Dearie...

"Let me... go!"

As her strength waned, Maddie gave up fighting against the two towering golems escorting her. She even attempted passive resistance by dropping all her weight, but they simply carried her into the bowels of the ship without missing a step.

The below decks were unimpressive--grimy steel-riveted walls, and an endless line of pipes, many of which seemed to be leaking steam.

As they led her down another steely corridor Maddie told them, "My dad is going to come for me, ya know. And when he does, you two are going to be really, really sorry." If the two golems had heard her, they made no indication. They simply marched her onward.

"I'm serious. My dad is a soldier. He's killed like a million bad guys. And you should see him when he hasn't had his coffee. Oh, you're going to get it, alright. I bet he's on his way here right now, and when he gets here, he's going to kick your ugly, green butts."

Her captors continued to say nothing.

They came to a set of stairs, one set going up and the other down. Thinking the steel-riveted barge was going to be laid out like a medieval castle, she was certain they were going to go downstairs. Afterall, isn't that where the dungeon is kept? Which was why she was surprised when they marched her upward.

The top deck wasn't laid out like a castle at all. It was more like the most luxurious resort Maddie had ever seen.

For starters, each swimming pool was designed to look like a lake, and each lake was encircled by the most beautiful landscaping, well-manicured lawns, and animal-shaped topiaries ever created. At one end of the clear blue waters was a towering Grecian temple made of white stone.

And the people; there were hundreds of them. They were everywhere--lounging on the shores, sitting beneath shaded trees, and conversing on the wide terraces in front of the temple. The entire scene reminded Maddie of a painting her mom kept in her study. It depicted happy picnickers at a park by the lake at the turn of the nineteenth century.

Like in her mom's painting, the men and women wore colorful clothes that were as eclectic as they were eccentric.

The men conversing in front of the temple were wearing tunics and funny cone-shaped hats with bells on them. One of the beautiful women lounging on the lake's shore with her friends had a Saber-tooth tiger on a leash.

All of them seemed happy and content, laughing and talking with one another, some in languages Maddie had never heard before. The one thing they all the happy picnickers had in common was none of them seemed concerned with the chaos and broken lands below.

The clip-clopping sound of a horse drew Maddie's attention to a horse-drawn carriage crossing a cobblestone bridge. Upon closer inspection, Maddie saw the horse was actually some kind of Wooly-Rhinoceros. In addition to the rhino being shaggy, he had a Y-shaped horn at the end of his snout and seemed domesticated.

As Maddie's captors still held her, the carriage finished crossing the bridge and stopped before them. Several servants, all dressed in rags, leapt from the carriage, got down on their hands and knees and formed a human staircase for the occupants to disembark. They were interlocked so perfectly, if Maddie hadn't seen it for herself, she would have never known the stairs were people.

Another slave reached up a hand to escort a single occupant down them. It was a woman who wore white gloves, and a dress far more beautiful and elaborate than any Maddie had seen so far.

Two more slaves, holding long bamboo rods with palm fronds at the ends, ran forward, and shielded their mistress from the sun. When the palm leaves parted like a curtain, Maddie could finally see the woman's face for the first time.

She was wearing a porcelain mask.

"Well, hello there, Dearie!" she bawled, in an elderly woman's voice and Scottish accent.

When Maddie didn't answer Lady Wellington screeched, "Are you well? I thought we'd lost you. I bet you're surprised to see me. I thought we'd have a picnic. The weather's just perfect for it, don't you think?"

Several of her well-dressed entourage, most of them being the women Maddie had seen earlier back in the glen, all sounded off in rapid agreement, "Oh yes, perfect indeed."

Lady Wellington raised her hands like a conductor about to begin a performance, nodding in acquiescence. When her Ladyship realized Maddie wasn't agreeing with her too, she asked in a less than musical tone, "What's the matter dearie, don't ya like picnics?"

Maddie shook at her captors embrace to no avail. Lady Wellington gave a slight nod of her head and they released her at once. The moment they did, Maddie shouted, "You better let me go or my dad will..."

"Your dad will what?" she asked, cutting her off mid-sentence. And before Maddie could answer she said, "Save you? I don't think so, dearie. Dinnae fash yerself. Your dad can't save you, my dear child, because your dad, you see... well let's see, how do I put this delicately... your dad wasn't able to save himself. He's dead."

Maddie refused to believe this. The last time she had seen her dad he was fighting with the tall men who had abducted her. He was a good fighter. No, a great one. She imagined that, just like in the movies, he was probably sneaking around the ship in some sort of disguise and was going to rescue her at any moment. "You're lying. My dad's not dead. And, he will come for me. And when he does, you'll be sorry."

Everyone had gone silent at this. The musicians stopped strumming their instruments, the servers stopped serving food and drink. After a time of shock-and-awe, Lady Wellington let out a long explosion of bellicose laughter. The crowd, hesitant at first, soon joined in with her.

When her Ladyship was finally able to get her merriment under control she managed, "Tsk, tsk, tsk. Oh trust me, dearie." Raising her hands majestically once more toward her entourage, "We were all watching, and we all saw him fall to his death." For emphasis she plucked a succulent fruit from a nearby serving platter and tossed it to the stone steps where it went splat.

Maddie still refused to believe this. She swore she wouldn't cry. Her heart would break before she'd let Lady Wellington and her friends see her cry. "I don't believe you!" she roared back.

Lady Wellington made an impatient scathing sound and with a wave of her hand she commanded, "Och, haud yer wheesht. I weary of this, silly girl. Remove this little brat from my sight at once."

The two green golems behind her stepped forward once again and clasped her arms in their hands.

"No, not you. You'll only scare the wee thing out of her wits." Staring at Maddie evenly, "*And* we can't have that, now can we?" Searching the throngs of her entourage she asked, "Now where's that confounded Lieutenant?" (she pronounced the word *Leftenant.)* Raising a gloved hand to her mouth she called out into thin air, practically singing the words, "Oh. Leftenant.... Leftenant..."

A young woman with a pretty face suddenly stepped up beside Maddie. As Maddie lifted her gaze, she saw the woman wore black knee-high boots, off-white trousers, and a nautical jacket. The royal-blue coat was adorned with ornate gold buttons, a sharp notched collar, and gold epaulets.

A black leather pistol belt with spare pouches ensnared her small waist and she spoke with a crisp British accent when she said, "Right here, m'lady."

That's weird. There was no one standing beside me a second ago, Maddie thought. *Where did she come from?*

"Earn your keep for once and take this wee brat to her quarters."

The British Officer clicked the heels of her shiny black boots and gave Lady Wellington a quick salute that looked nothing like the way her dad saluted, and she said, "Right away, Your Ladyship."

Gazing down at her, the blond-haired woman softened her gaze before introducing herself. "Hello there, little miss. My name is *The Leftenant*, formerly 2nd in Command of Her Majesty's Airship, the *Dauntless*." She removed one of her white gloves and held her hand open toward her in a way that suggested shaking hands.

Once Maddie took her offered hand, the Leftenant shook it briskly, all the while, saying, "It is a genuine, genuine pleasure to meet you. Would you be so kind as to allow me to accompany you to your chambers?"

When Maddie hesitated Lady Wellington screeched so loud it caused her to jump, "Oh ye don't have to be so polite about it as all that, just grab the wee brat already, and drag her out of my sight."

The two green golems stepped forward, but the Leftenant stepped in front of Maddie. In a commanding voice she said, "Hold your place, you brutes. Her Ladyship gave me the task of escorting the young miss and I shall do so, post-haste."

The golems, unsure of what to do, looked over at Lady Wellington for guidance.

Her Ladyship, however, was already involved in a discussion with several of her handmaidens. Once she saw the golems gazing over at her, she dismissed them with a wave of her hand. "Go on now. Shoo, shoo, away with you. I have much more important matters to attend to before our arrival to Portlandia." Her Ladyship then signaled for another servant to join her.

In answer, a flamboyantly dressed man quickly ran up to her Ladyship, set up his paints, and kneeled before her with paintbrushes in hand. Maddie recognized the man immediately, it was the same portly, makeup artist she had seen in the glen earlier.

The pretty *Leftenant* turned back around and gazed down her petite nose at her. She was about to say something but took a moment to blow an errant strand of blond hair out of her face first, but it promptly fell back down. Raising one eyebrow, she exhaled, "Right then."

First, taking the time to don her white glove once more, she bent awkwardly at the waist, leaned in close, and whispered in Maddie's ear, "Let's go, little one. I promise you, I'm not so bad as all that."

Unsure of what else to do and wondering if what Lady Wellington said about her dad was true, Maddie clasped the Leftenant's outstretched hand and allowed herself to be led away.

"Right this way, little miss."

The Leftenant

The Leftenant arrived outside young Maddie's quarters.

For a time, the young captive had been inconsolable, refusing to eat or drink. But the Leftenant had monitored her very closely and waited patiently for the most opportune time to make further contact.

At first, she thought the poor girl was just another simple captive, one who would live out her existence in servitude to Lady Wellington as so many other shanghaied captives had. But no. This one was different. According to her sources, which even she had to admit were rather questionable, the young girl's father might not be as deceased as her Ladyship thought. If he did indeed survive, his love for his daughter might prove useful toward her own motives.

Very useful indeed.

The Leftenant knocked lightly upon the young girl's door, which given the circumstances, was ridiculous. However, even after all this time of being pressed into her Ladyship's service, she still considered herself an Officer first, and that dictated at least some modicum of decorum. "Little Miss... Maddie... it's me, The Leftenant. May I come in?"

No answer.

The Leftenant had no idea how to proceed. Despite her hundreds of years of existence, comforting prepubescent children was far beyond her skill set. She had served as 2nd in command of an exploration-class airship after all, not as a bloody nursemaid.

The Leftenant was about to knock a second time when she heard a child's small voice say, "Come in."

Steeling her nerves, the Leftenant gave her coat a stiff yank, smoothed out the non-existent creases and entered young Maddie's bedchambers. The young girl certainly had not been granted the most luxurious accommodations on board Lady Wellington's pleasure barge, but the room wasn't quite as bad as say, the crew quarters. Spotting a tray of un-eaten food on the nightstand the Leftenant straightened her jacket once more. "Right. Now Miss Maddie, it is quite essential that you eat your food and regain your strength."

As though she hadn't heard a single word she had said, the young girl asked, "Why do you say Leftenant and not Lieutenant?"

How irritating. A ground-dweller questioning an officer.

Practically blurting the answer out, she answered, "Because Leftenant is the way it is properly pronounced." She thought about this some more and then asked, "Don't they have schools where you originate from?"

Spot on work, Leftenant, she admonished herself silently. *Way to earn the young girl's trust. Scare her and insult her, all in the first few minutes of meeting her. Smashing.*

The young girl surprised her when answering the query. "Yes, ma'am. I'm in third grade but my teacher says I read at an eighth-grade level."

"Yes. Quite. Long live the American school system," she replied, pumping a fist in the air sardonically. Then thinking more about Maddie's answer, "Furthermore, in the future, you may address me as Leftenant, not ma'am."

"Yes ma'am," Maddie began reflexively, then quickly correcting herself, "Yes, *Leftenant.*"

"Right." The Leftenant brushed non-existent dirt off her uniform and straightened her jacket once more. "Perhaps there's hope for you yet, little Miss."

The Leftenant held her breath (which was ridiculous of course, given her make-up) while the young girl tentatively reached for an apple slice on the platter.

"There's a good girl, eat, keep up your strength and all that."

Maddie slowly crunched down on the apple, and after a few more bites began eating with a bit more fervor.

Mission accomplished, Leftenant. You got a nine-year old girl to eat some apples. Congratulations and bravo! But as she turned to leave, Maddie's fragile voice hindered her escape. "Where are you going?"

The Leftenant froze in her tracks. *Is there something wrong with me? Why would an irritating pre-adolescent girl give me so much pause? Perhaps I need a checkup?*

Turning slowly, for the first time in a long while, she wasn't quite sure what she was going to say. "I'm sorry. I'm afraid I have other duties to tend to."

This was a lie of course seeing how she was perfectly capable of fulfilling hundreds of tasks all at the same time.

Maddie, watching her, slowly crunched another apple slice. Mouth full, she asked, "Can't you stay with me? Not long. Maybe we could just talk with me for a little while?"

The nerve. As though a first officer of the Queen's navy had nothing better to do than to play nursemaid to a snivel-

ing child. Not even a very impressive specimen if I'm being totally honest.

The Leftenant tucked an errant strand of blond hair behind her ear once more. "Of course, young miss. I'd be happy to make your further acquaintance."

Tears welling up in her eyes, lips trembling slightly, the young girl sniffled, and gave a slow nod of her head overflowing with unkempt curls.

Seeing this, the Leftenant began, "There-there... No need for all that. Rest assured I shall allow no harm to come to you, little miss."

In a fit of blinding speed, far faster than she would have thought the child capable of, Maddie lunged forward, and encircled her miniscule arms around the Leftenant's narrow waist.

Stroking the young Maddie's mounds of dark hair, as she held her, the Leftenant thought...

Yes. I am definitely in dire need of a checkup.

Chapter 23

Graveside

George stood over the open grave.

The sky became overcast and threatened to rain at any moment. The wind gusted so hard the dozens of black umbrellas threatened to turn inside out. The crowd of mourners dressed in black struggled to hold on to them, along with their hats and veil coverings. Feeling the wet cold himself, George clutched his own thick trench coat closed.

The sermon was over, and yet nobody moved. George didn't recognize a single person. And on second glance they all now appeared to be men. *Wasn't there a bunch of women a second ago?* And now all the men were wearing black suits and dark fedoras that had reached their heyday in the fifties.

I don't even know any of these people.

Wait. Standing on the other side of the open grave, he spotted one person he did recognize.

His wife... Tessa.

She was doing her very best to hold back her tears. He attempted to rush over to her side, but his legs were rooted in place. He called out to her, but his voice sounded as though it were underwater, and she did not hear him. In fact, no one seemed to hear him.

This is what a ghost must feel like. I should've known that place wasn't real. Maddie, the Fairies, Lady Wellington, everything, -it all makes sense now. I wasn't dreaming. I hadn't been transported to some magical place.

I'm just dead.

But if he was dead, why was the coffin sitting next to the grave so small?

No, not possible. The gravestone... it didn't belong to him... it belonged to...

George involuntarily choked as he read the fresh marker:

MADDIE STAPLETON
4/15/2003 – 6/30/2012

Why? Maddie never died. This isn't a memory. The date is all wrong. Two weeks after he had flown that rescue mission.

This can't be right. It has to be some sort of stupid, crazy dream.

"Dad, we don't say stupid," his daughter's voice echoed in his head.

Maddie's dead? If that's true, then... where am I? Why wouldn't I be at my own daughter's funeral?

He saw the second grave marker. The carving in the head-stone was as fresh as the first one, and equally disturbing.

GEORGE STAPLETON
1/10/1969 – 6/22/2012

No. Oh no. If these dates were correct... Keep in mind, this is all just some sort of stupid dream; but if it is, why does it all feel so real? ...Maddie died two weeks after I did. What hap-pened? Was it a car crash? Statistically speaking, that made the most sense, a car crash.

No. I refuse to believe this is all real. "One... Two... Three.. wake up! One, two, three, wake up!" George pinched him-self but it didn't work.

Staring at Maddie's coffin, he thought, *I have to know.*

"Excuse me," he said, pushing past the first set of black suits. Some of the attendees cried out in alarm, others com-plained.

He pushed through a dozen more men dressed in suits. *Just how many of these guys are here?*

"Pardon me," George said, hearing the tone in his voice as it became more frantic.

The rain beat harder.

His own black suit...*when did I put that on? I thought I was wearing a trench coat*...was soaked through, and he could feel his wet hair plastered to his forehead.

The moment he reached Maddie's coffin, several of the men (all now faceless), tried to stop him.

"Back off!" George roared, and Spartan kicked the nearest of them in the chest.

He dodged another's grasp and followed up with three rapid punches to the head. As the faceless man's body went slack, George shoved the faceless man into several more behind him, knocking them all down like bowling pins.

Knowing he only had seconds before they were on him again, George reached for the lid of the tiny coffin. With some difficulty, he opened it.

He expected to find nothing inside. *Wasn't that how these dreams were supposed to go?*

But Maddie was inside. She looked as though she might be sleeping. Except there was no color in her cheeks and her chest didn't rise and fall.

She really was gone.

Feeling a hand clench his arm, George shook it loose. More hands clasped his back, shoulders, and biceps.

"Let me go!" he growled and shook two more off. Three others took their place.

"I said... let... me... GO!"

George elbowed the guy on his right in the face, only this time, it wasn't a faceless man in a suit. This time, it was a masked-man, like one of those funny burial masks with the long-curved beaks and shaped like a bird.

The bird-beaked man—*a plague doctor, that's what they called them*--wore a velvet overcoat that stretched all the way down to his ankles, a wide-brimmed hat, and thick rubber gloves.

George stared hard into the mask's eyes to see who was behind it, but he could only see reflections of himself in the glass-covered openings.

The faceless men had vanished. It was now only just the two of them.

The rain ceased and they stood that way for a moment longer just staring at one other, while a brisk autumn wind tousled George's hair and stung his cheeks. The plague doctor seemed unaffected by the brisk wind.

Then...

TWONG!

As the world tumbled upside down, George glimpsed the blade of shovel held high in the air. As he plummeted down into the open grave it occurred to him that another one of those masked plague doctors must have struck him from behind with a shovel. He didn't have time to think on it for long because the bottom of the grave came up fast. Unable to move just yet, he found himself lying on his back, staring up at an ominous sky.

Soon dozens of beaked plague doctors leaned over the open grave staring down at him. Without any warning, they began tossing moist, black dirt onto his face. As he spat it from his mouth, or tried to, he heard more rapid shoveling, and more dirt began to engulf him. Lifting his head, for that was all he could move at this point, he saw that nearly his entire body was now covered in black earth. Another pile of soil struck him in the forehead, forcing him to lay all the way back down.

Body immobilized; all he could do was stare up out of the open grave with one unobstructed eye. He heard a loud CLICKING sound emanating from one of the bird-doctors, and the burial detail suddenly ceased. The plague doctors stared down at him, as though studying him, their heads occasionally tilting to one side and then the other, giving them that bird-like appearance more than ever.

More CLICKING sounds ensued, only this time from the entire burial detail. Then they violently resumed their shoveling, and within seconds he couldn't see anything but blackness.

They had buried him alive.

Hitting the Pavement

Trembling slightly, George's eyes fluttered open. For a moment, it was all he could do to breathe.

He found himself lying on the pavement in the middle of the street. Someone had rolled up his dark blue coat and put it under his head to serve as a pillow.

For the life of him he couldn't remember how he came to be in the middle of the street and, as he regained more of his senses, he struggled to recall what had happened to Maddie. The only thing he knew for certain was that she was gone, and he had to find her.

"Maddie!"

He climbed to his feet as quickly as his stinging body would allow, dusted himself off, and with little other options, began to scan his immediate surroundings.

Strangely, his body didn't sting, at least not anymore. He only assumed it would. Now that he was on his feet, the reality was his cheek was no longer bruised, the wound in his thigh no longer throbbed, and even the soreness in his back and feet were gone. If anything, he felt refreshed, like after a long weekend of doing a whole lot of nothing. In fact, he felt better than he had in ages.

His fingers gingerly probed his jeans for the hole in his thigh and he realized his leg was now completely healed. Someone had even gone to the trouble of mending his clothes. George couldn't even see where they had stitched the hole, and now that he thought about it, the clothes felt clean and pressed.

Talk about full service, he mused, humor always being his coping mechanism.

Of course, that coward, Barnaby, was nowhere to be found. First sign of trouble, and he ran off.

George heard what sounded like a leaf crumpling underfoot. Looking down, he saw a hastily written note that read:

Georgie-Porgie...

Don't waste it.

–Lampy

George held the note in his hand and wondered, *Don't waste it? Don't waste what? Also, who the heck is Lampy?*

He lifted his eyes to a clear blue sky and shielded his eyes from the sunlight with his hand. The sun was directly overhead now, but the enormous hovering barge was long gone.

George scanned the road. Turning slightly, he checked the path down to the river. Behind him lay the gift shop.

Which way to go? For the first time in his life, he was frozen. He wasn't sure. Every decision he had made up to this point, seemed in retrospect to be the wrong one.

George couldn't move.

His body may have failed him, but his brain was buzzing. He suddenly recalled how he used to play those old *Dungeon and Dragon* board games as a teenager. Well, that wasn't entirely true. His family had been so poor while he was growing up, they could barely afford to put food on the table, let alone have the money to buy those expensive D&D pieces and game books. The only reason he ever got to play those games in the first place was because one day a bunch of idiot jocks were beating up on a nerd behind the bleachers.

Hearing the screams for help, George arrived to find three letterman-jacketed bullies who had already stripped the nerd down to his skivvies, were rifling through his brown satchel, and splitting up the spoils within.

All three were two years older than George, and the leader, Derrick Garbo (a great name for a bully) was the lineman for the High football team. He must've outweighed George by at least fifty pounds. His two minions weren't exactly small potatoes either.

On the other hand, Teenage George was still pretty skinny at the time. Now, his drunken dirt-bag of a dad may have not had any money to buy toys or games, but one thing his father did do for young George was teach him how to fight. In fact, back when his dad was in the Army, he was known as quite the brawler, so much so, they kicked dear ole dad out of the military for doing it too much.

The end result?

The three bullies didn't have a chance.

Before it was over Derrick Garbo's nose was broken and the other two had run off. The nerd, James (yes, he actually went by James, and not Jim, John or Jimbo) was so grateful to young George that from that day forward, he invited him over his house after school nearly every day. James lived in a mansion by the way, and they ate like kings. Better still, they went on many adventures together in the magical world of D&D.

Just like the many choices he had to make in that fantasy world, it was time to choose wisely. Only instead of crossing over the bridge with a troll under it, or fighting the dragon chasing on the bridge, or turning around and running the other way, George had to decide whether he wanted to run down the asphalt road, sail down the river, or check back inside the gift shop.

As it turned out, the sound of tinkering from the gas station's garage decided for him.

Following the sound (just as he had the nerd's screams all those decades ago) George rounded the corner and found Barnaby in one of the gas station's mechanic bays. The accountant's back was to him, and he was hunkered over the engine of the safari truck they'd spied earlier.

By the looks of it, Barnaby had been busy. Four flat tires lay discarded in the overgrown grass. Next to them was an old-style jack. The truck's hood was propped up with an oversized wrench, and the engine looked as though it had barfed up all its old parts onto the pavement.

"How long was I out?"

Barnaby ceased ratcheting the battery terminals. Without turning around to face him, he finally managed, "You're back." Shaking his head, he added, "I told you two to run. Why didn't you listen to me?"

"Where's Maddie?"

Still refusing to meet his gaze, Barnaby resumed his ratcheting. "Where do you think? She's gone. They took her."

So that part was true. The hovering barge, the strange lanky weirdos who'd snatched Maddie, and when he tried to stop them... well, that part was still a little fuzzy.

"What happened to me?"

"I dunno. I think you fell through the roof over there." Barnaby hiked a thumb to the bamboo-framed pavilion in a rest area next to the gas station. The roof appeared as though a meteor had crashed through it and smashed the table underneath.

"When I found you, you were pretty broken up, and coughing up blood. It sounded like you were barely breathing, and drowning on your own fluids. I knew you didn't have long. So... I dragged you into the middle of the street and hoped for the best. You're a lot heavier than you look by the way."

George found himself wondering why Barnaby would drag him into the middle of the street. That hardly seemed like the best plan for a fall rescue victim. He settled for asking, "What do you mean, hoped for the best?"

Barnaby finished hooking up the battery terminals, grabbed a rag and wiped his hands of grease. Finally facing him, but still averting his eyes, he said, "Yeah. *They* don't always take people. And sometimes, when *they* do, *they* don't always bring them back. I guess you're one of the few lucky ones."

"You keep saying, 'they'. Who are they?"

"I don't know. I've never actually seen them. No one does, but I'm pretty sure they live below ground."

George thought about the massive complex underground, with hundreds of floors below. He suddenly remembered the blond-haired woman with horn-rimmed glasses on the floating gurney. *Didn't she have an I.V. bag in her arm? They must have some sort of hospital underground. Why wouldn't they? They had everything else.*

"Did I die?"

"Doesn't matter if you did. They can fix you. They can pretty much fix anything." He then mumbled to himself, "If they want to. Although they seem to do it a lot less these days."

He took a utility knife out of his pocket, cut the truck's serpentine belt, and began pulling it out. "This is definitely gonna have to be changed," and with that Barnaby discarded the broken belt onto the ground into the pile with the other parts.

"How long was I..." George thought about how he was going to finish his question. *How long was I dead? How long was I missing?* He settled for, "How long was I gone?"

Barnaby must not have heard him, for he said, "Ya know, when I was a kid, my grandpa and I rebuilt a truck just like this one. I didn't appreciate it or him at the time. But, that summer was probably the best time of my life."

"How long, Barnaby?"

Barnaby stopped threading the new serpentine belt for a moment, thought about it for a second, and answered, "I dunno, all day yesterday, most of this morning."

Now the burning question. The one that mattered most. He was hesitant to ask it.

"Maddie... is she... did she die too?"

Barnaby dropped a wrench down into the engine and cursed as it ping-ponged all the way to the ground.

He finally locked eyes with him. "What?" His tone expressed genuine surprise. "Is that what you think?" He shook his head. "No. No, she's not dead. Despite what you think of Lady Wellington, she just doesn't go around killing people. It's against the rules." He thought about this for a second, "Well, she does kill people, sort of, but that's not her main goal." He took a step toward him, wiping his greasy hands on the rag again like it was some sort of nervous tick.

"Do you remember back at the Glen when Lady Wellington was about to let you guys go?" When George nodded, he continued, "Well, I overheard her aide whisper something about your daughter, and how Corporate wanted to meet her. There's even a huge reward."

George was beginning to lose his patience. "Yeah, so?"

Barnaby's eyes went wide. "So?" he asked incredulously. "So? The last time Lady Wellington took out her royal barge was years ago. So, Corporate must want her pretty badly; it costs lots of resources to run that floating city of hers."

As much as George wanted to know more about who Corporate was, Maddie was the priority. "We have to go after them."

"Well, yeah. Duh. Of course, we do."

Seeing George's face, he added, "Don't look so surprised. Your daughter's a great kid."

Barnaby's face turned sour and he mumbled, "Not like my kids, bunch of doped up hippies, with all their free love, and devil music. You'd think ole' tricky Dick would put a stop to it all."

George couldn't help but smile at this. *Hippies, free love, tricky Dick.* George had to assume Barnaby was talking about Richard Nixon. *Is this guy a throwback from the late sixties or what? How old is this guy? Certainly not old enough to have been a dad in the sixties.*

Barnaby must've realized he'd been rambling. "Alright, I changed the tires, spark plugs, gas, and oil. I also put in a new carburetor, alternator and battery, and swapped out all the belts and wires that I could. Why don't you get behind the wheel and see if she'll turn over?"

George could only nod. He suspected he was still in shock over everything that had transpired, especially by the fact that Barnaby was not only willing to help him find Maddie, but he was actually being help-ful. It never occurred to him that the accountant would be anything more than a cumbersome burden.

As soon as he slid behind the wheel, Barnaby shouted, "Okay, try it."

George found the keys dangling in the ignition and was slightly amused by the stark white lucky rabbit's foot dangling from the chain. Although, he *was* forced to wonder how much luck a severed rabbit's foot had to offer after getting its leg chopped off.

Okay, Alice… here we go.

He turned the key halfway and was pleasantly surprised when the needle of the fuel indicator rose to full and all the lights and noises came on. But when he turned the key all the way, there was only a loud CLACKING sound. He shuddered involuntarily. It was the same sound the plague doctors had made with their shovels when they had buried him alive.

"Hang on, hang on a second," Barnaby yelled, snapping him out of his trace. There was a loud banging that sounded like a wrench, or some other heavy tool, striking the alternator under the hood. "Okay, that should do it. Try it again."

George turned the key the rest of the way and was re-warded with a gentle roar from the heavy-duty V-8 engine as it sprang to life with a healthy backfire. George felt a smile spread across his face as the truck's engine rumbled to life and idled steadily. Now they had transportation. For the first time, George was filled with an emotion he had not felt since he arrived.

Hope.

It had taken them another hour to unload the back of the truck of any useless junk and replace it with two barrels of fuel and foodstuffs they'd pilfered from the gift shop.

As they worked, George told Barnaby about his dream of being buried alive, seeing his daughter in a coffin, and every-thing else that happened since falling off the barge. In response, Barnaby repeated his sad story of how he became captured and pressed into service by her Ladyship. He went on to say how over the years he had quietly watched from the shadows as others came and went. "A few escaped, but most of them died."

Barnaby finished by explaining that where they were headed, they might not see food or fuel for a long while. So as much as the further delay pained him, George knew it wouldn't do Maddie any good if they broke down, ran out of gas, or starved to death. This was a rescue mission after all, and rescuing people was what he had been trained for, it was what he was good at, only the stakes had never been higher.

Realizing he hadn't seen the obese accountant in a while, he began to wonder, *Where is Barnaby?*

Just as he was about to go searching for him, Barnaby reappeared. He had changed out of the ridiculous costume Lady Wellington had forced him to wear and was now wearing a pair of khaki shorts, a safari shirt, knee high socks, hiking boots, and a bush hat.

When he saw George looking at him, he held out his hands and asked, "What do you think?"

George recalled the dead robot Maddie had found in the gift store. "Did you steal that off the robot?"

Barnaby looked down sheepishly at his fumbling hands. "Not all of it. Most of it I got off the rack."

Trying to find something nice to say, after all Barnaby was helping him quite a lot, he responded, "It suits you."

"Thanks. I haven't had a change of clothes in years."

Barnaby suggested George drive, while he navigated using the oversized map they'd absconded off the wall inside the gift shop.

"Hey, what about this?" Barnaby asked, holding up a metal box. "It's not a gun or anything, but it still might come in handy."

George unsnapped the metallic tabs and peered inside the case. The World War II signal flare gun inside was a real beauty. Unlike its modern-day orange, plastic-junk predecessor, the antique flare gun had a heavy-duty brass frame and a silver-metallic barrel shaped like a miniature blunderbuss. Aside from the handle being slightly chipped, overall the pistol seemed in serviceable condition. Also, inside the case, George found five fat-squat cartridges.

"Yeah, this could come in handy," he told Barnaby, then snapped the case closed and flung it onto the front seat. That done, George slid behind the wheel.

Barnaby circled the truck and climbed into the passenger seat, grinning like a Cheshire cat swelling with pride. George was about to put the old truck in drive, but his hand hesitated on the gearshift. Turning toward Barnaby he said, with more difficulty than it should have taken, "Listen, I just wanted to say thanks. Whatever happens, I really appreciate all you've done for me and Maddie."

Barnaby shifted uncomfortably in his seat, and unsure what to do next, he made a fist and punched George lightly on the shoulder. "Aw, knock it off, will ya. Don't go and get all soft and mushy on me now."

George nodded, put the truck in gear and pulled out of the gas station's bay.

When he turned on his right indicator out of force of habit Barnaby laughed at him. George laughed with him and began to turn onto the highway.

"Wait!" Barnaby cried.

George slammed his foot on the brake pedal. He was about to ask why, when Barnaby cracked open his door and leaped out of the truck. The chubby man jogged over to the station's grassy median and picked something up off the ground.

Barnaby then jogged back to the truck and jumped inside. The springs groaned beneath him as he took his seat. "Can't leave without this."

He was right. They couldn't leave without it.

It was Maddie's German Shepherd stuffy.

Chasing Hover Barge

"Stop worrying, we'll catch them."

George was driving fast. He'd been doing at least a steady eighty ever since they'd left the gas station. The man was like a robot as he drove, motionless, head tilted forward, eyes fixed on the road, and gas pedal mashed to the metal.

Barnaby knew it was a lot better for George to drive since he didn't trust his eyes with the setting sun glaring at them. At best, they had an hour of daylight left, maybe two at the most.

The verdant dinosaur jungle had given way to an endless expanse of rolling hills. Now, the two-lane highway was more like a bridge across a sea of billowing grasses the color of Kentucky blues, radiant greens, and savage purples.

George had to shout to be heard over the truck's un-muffled V-8 engine. "How can you be so sure?" Even with all the noise Barnaby could still hear the twinge of helplessness in the man's voice.

In turn, Barnaby yelled back, "Royal barges are extremely slow. Plus, Lady Wellington's an opportunist. She'll stop and pillage any outpost, region, or any other Stranger World that won't put up a fight."

George thought about this for a moment before asking, "Even if we do catch up to them, how are we going to get up to her barge?"

On that score, Barnaby didn't have a clue. It'd been years since he'd ridden on board Lady Wellington's hover barge. Back in those days they would ride up elevators that were little more than gilded-shark cages dangling precariously from steel cables. It had been a terrifying experience going up into the air like that and he doubted Lady Wellington would be so benevolent as to lower one and offer them a ride. That was why he was being completely honest when he answered, "Dunno. It probably won't matter anyway."

George waited for him to finish. When he didn't, he risked a glance from the road over to him and asked grumpily, "Why not?"

Now it was Barnaby's turn to smile. "Lady Wellington will probably just kill us anyway. Not the kind of death you come back from neither, we're talking dead-dead, slice-and-dice, blast you into a million pieces kind of dead."

George frowned. "That's comforting. So, not the kind you come back from, then?"

Barnaby sighed.

There's so much he still doesn't know.

Nodding his head, he explained, "Yeah... sometimes when people die, their bodies vanish the moment you ain't looking. A few days later, sometimes hours, other times weeks, they return, but not always." He coughed and added, "I'm not even sure they're the same person when they come back." He flashed George a sideways glance but when George returned his gaze, he quickly looked away.

George opened his mouth to speak, but the words never came out, and he kept right on driving. Barnaby had to hand it to the big guy, for a newbie, the man was holding it together pretty well, especially having his daughter kidnapped and all.

Part of this was probably due to the fact that George was so focused on the road, he tended to miss things that might push his sanity over the edge. For example, the scarecrow in a field on their right. George hadn't given him a second glance, but even now, as they passed, it lifted a straw arm and waved. Barnaby fought the urge to reflexively lift his hand and wave back. Nor had George spotted the reptile aloft on leathery wings, who earlier was swooping over a distant mountain range.

Maybe I should tell him everything. But no, Barnaby knew better. He'd seen it before. If George learned to much at once, it would probably kill him.

Snapping him out of these thoughts, George asked, "Have you been down this road before?"

Barnaby hesitated before answering. Realizing he hadn't said anything for a few seconds, he made a good show of studying the landscape, and then lied, "Nope. Afraid not."

The truth was, he did know what lay at the end of the road. He also knew that even if they caught up with Lady Wellington before they got to the end, they'd never get aboard her barge. Back in the Dinosaur preserve he had contemplated running off and leaving George and Maddie to their fates. He wanted to believe the real reason he had come back was to help them out. In the end, he had to admit, even if only to himself, the real reason he came back was because he was a coward.

Stranger World was a dangerous place, and if George survived, there would be safety in partnering up with a man of his skills and talents.

At least that's what he thought a couple hours ago. Now, he was beginning to feel as though there might be more to his relationship with George than tricking the military man into being his protector.

Back at the gas station, George had genuinely thanked him for trying to help save Maddie. Barnaby wasn't lying when he told George about Maddie being a great kid. If at all possible (and it wasn't) they'd save George's kid from Lady Wellington.

Barnaby knew from experience Maddie was as good as gone. But George was one determined fellow. Barnaby knew there was no way he'd ever talk the man out of rescuing his daughter. So... he'd ride along until George realized the hopelessness of the situation, and then, who knows, maybe after that, they might even become good friends.

"We're coming up to a crossroads," George announced.

This was the first intersection they had come across since leaving the dinosaur preserve.

"Which way do I go?"

When Barnaby didn't answer him right away George began easing off on the gas. The lessening engine noise was a mercy on his ears, but the angry glare George was giving him, -not so much.

"What?" Barnaby asked beside him nonsensically. "How should I know?"

George seemed as though he were resisting the urge to punch him in the face. Then he sighed, probably remembering were it not for him they wouldn't be driving this truck in the first place. So instead of smacking him upside his head George asked, "Alright, the last time you saw Lady Wellington's barge, it was traveling north, right?"

Technically, that was true. Barnaby knew Lady Wellington would follow along the highway just like any commercial plane might. But at some point, Barnaby also knew they'd veer off and head to Portlandia, which was to the Northwest. Her Ladyship would stop there and book lodging until they could charter a ship to take them across the Madlands.

"Barnaby? You still with me?"

"Uh-huh. Sorry, I was just trying to remember." Again, he made a good show of it and then answered, "Uh, yeah, that's right. They were heading North. I think they're probably following this road."

Before the truck could roll to a complete stop at the crossroads, George tromped on the gas once more and took the truck back up to eighty.

Fortunately, as they sped through the intersection, George either didn't see or care about the mannequin perched upon the Lamppost on the corner.

Barnaby had to admit, the man was focused.

They hadn't driven another ten minutes when Barnaby first saw it. Little more than a dot on the horizon. What caused Barnaby the most concern, was this time, it was on the driver's side.

Maybe he won't spot it.

"Hey, over there. What is that?" George ducked his head so he could see more clearly under the truck's visor. "What is that?"

Dang, he spotted it. At least he's not slowing down.

George took the truck down to forty and pointed, "Is it them?"

Barnaby was fairly certain he knew exactly what it was, but what he said was, "Naw. I don't think so. It's way too small. I can't tell for sure though, it's pretty far off."

George spied the pair of binoculars swinging from a hook behind his seat and asked, "Why don't you grab those binoculars behind your seat and take a closer look?"

Sure, I'll just elongate my arms and reach behind my head, Barnaby thought.

He heard himself grunt and groan as he turned around. He wasn't exactly built like Peter Pan. Finally, after banging his head on the truck's ceiling, he managed to grab the binoculars, and retake his seat.

The floating craft was almost directly left of them, so he had to lean in front of George. Lifting the binocs to his eyes, he saw the cigar-shaped vessel was still a good twenty miles away. He recognized the gold-plated hull immediately. It was the Leftenant's ship alright, the *Dauntless*.

"Well? Is it them or not?" George asked irritably.

By the time Barnaby answered, the truck was already speeding past.

"No... this is different."

"So, it's not them?" George asked brusquely.

"No. Definitely not. The shape's all wrong." He lowered the binoculars and added, "And it's not moving. It's just sort of hanging there, kinda crooked in the air. I think maybe... maybe it was damaged."

It was damaged. Barnaby had been there. In fact, the onslaught had been so fierce, he was surprised the vessel was still airborne. Then again, if they stopped to check it out, it might delay them long enough for Lady Wellington to get away.

"Maybe we should check it out?" he asked, doing a pretty passable job of keeping the earnestness out of his voice.

Barnaby didn't even finish his sentence before George lowered his head, knuckled the wheel tighter, and risked speeding the truck back up to eighty-five.

Once again, Barnaby was moved by the man's love for his daughter. If it had been his hippie, drugged-out teenagers, he would've left their butts to their fates. Maybe sneak off somewhere and find a nice little cottage off the beaten path and live out the rest of his miserable life in peace.

Not George though. He was either going to save Maddie or die trying. Die *again,* that is. The man had no idea how lucky he was. Barnaby doubted George would get that lucky a second time. It just didn't happen. Most likely, George's dogged determination would get them both killed. He would never give up on his daughter, no matter how hopeless the situation. That's when Barnaby finally realized, they could never be friends after all.

No way.

First chance I get, I'm leaving his butt behind.

Chapter 26

Leftenant & Maddie

"And then what did he do?"

Maddie grinned impishly, gathered her thoughts, and said, "Well, according to my mom, my dad carried me all the way across the entire water park like that with poop running out of my diaper and down his leg."

The Leftenant's eyes went wide and she breathed, "Noooo..."

Maddie nodded, still smiling, "Uh-huh. And the entire theme park security was chasing him the entire way."

"And... what did these water-park authorities have to say when they finally caught up with you two miscreants?"

This time Maddie shook her head and giggled. "They never did! My dad dodged them all the way back to the motel room."

"Surely they must have caught up with you, you know, followed the trail of..." she struggled for the socially correct word.

"Poop?" Young Maddie asked, eyebrows raised.

"Well, yes. I suppose I would have said excrement, but I believe 'poop' suffices in this situation."

Maddie held her stomach and fell back on her bed giggling.

As the Leftenant watched her, she began to rethink her plan. Other than a brief walkabout on deck, she and the young Maddie had been talking nearly the entire night; about her parents, her home in Pensacola, a lot about her dad, and finally her black cat, Lucy. The Leftenant always found the biologicals who remembered their past lives the most interesting. For a moment, she almost believed Maddie to be a real girl.

Oh quit mucking about and show her already.

"Maddie... may I call you Maddie?"

The pre-adolescent girl nodded her head, and began eyeing the platter of food. For such a tiny creature she certainly could put it away.

The Leftenant, hands clasped behind her back, began slowly pacing back and forth as she spoke. "When I was up on deck a few minutes ago, standing near the aft of the ship, I discovered someone is following us."

The young girl perked her head up at this. "Was it my dad?"

With her back turned to Maddie, a slight amused grin spread across the Leftenant's face. She knew it was imperative to her plan that she proceed very carefully from this point on. Maddie may have been very young, but she had a surprisingly keen mind.

"I'm not sure," the Leftenant said carefully. *Well done, an award winning performance to be sure,* she thought sardonically. Quickly recovering she asked, "May I show you?"

Upon Maddie's approval, the Leftenant moved over to the bulkhead and touched the wall. A rectangular section of steel plating vanished upon her touch and they could now see the landscape below as though they were staring out a window.

Far below, they could see a single lane road running in a straight line through endless fields of billowing grass. On the road was a battered safari truck, driving fast, with billowing clouds of dust trailing behind it.

This was an illusion of course. The young girl's quarters were deep within the ship, but the projected image was in fact real, and in real time.

"Is this man your father?"

Little Maddie squinted. Of course, her biological eyes wouldn't be able to zoom in on the truck's occupants. So, the Leftenant touched the holographic screen again (which really wasn't necessary, merely as a courtesy for Maddie), and the image changed to a closer image of the cab of the truck.

"Dad!" Maddie cried out. "That's my dad. I knew Lady Wellington was lying. I knew he wasn't dead. It takes a lot more than that to take out my dad; just ask my mom."

Pointing to the man sitting beside her dad, Maddie added, "And that's Mr. Barnaby. He's my friend too. Dad doesn't like him very much, or at least he pretends like he doesn't."

Taking a chance, the Leftenant sat down upon the bed next to Maddie. "I'm afraid that even if your dad does catch up to us in his motor-carriage, they will never be able to get aboard her Ladyship's pleasure barge. Even now, I am doing everything in my limited power to keep her gunnery crews from detecting them."

This was *very* true. Had she not detected their pursuers first, the hover barge would have open fired with their deck guns and obliterated them in an instant.

Maddie pursed her lips as she thought about this for a moment, then gazing up at her she said, "We have to get down to them somehow."

The Leftenant shook her head. "I'm sorry, but that just isn't possible. The elevators are well guarded. Even if we did somehow manage to get past the sentries, to exit the ship in such a manner while it's operating at top speed would be nothing short of suicidal." The Leftenant blew an errant strand of blond hair off her face, and added, "That's also as-suming the guards don't just reel us back in like caught fish."

Maddie stuck her chin out and with a determined look on her face, said, "It doesn't matter, my dad will never stop coming for me. Never."

That's what I'm counting on, little one, the Leftenant thought inwardly. *My, when did you become so devious? Try-ing to outwit a young girl. Bravo! I hope you're proud of yourself.*

The Leftenant shook her head slowly. "I'm afraid that won't be possible for very much longer. In exactly twenty-two minutes the road will become quite impassable."

Tears began to well up in young Maddie's eyes. For a moment, the Leftenant actually felt pity for the poor crea-ture.

Is that even possible? I'm obviously malfunctioning.

The Leftenant raised her hand. After a moment's hesita-tion, she delicately laid it on young Maddie's shoulder. Up to this point, the young girl had refused to let anyone see her cry. But the moment she felt the Leftenant's touch, the small girl whipped around and hugged her fiercely.

As Leftenant held the frail creature in her arms, Maddie sobbed uncontrollably.

"There now, little one. Chin up. There's no call for all of that. Simply give me a moment, and I am certain I will think of something."

Young Maddie lifted her sobbing face from her overcoat and gazed up at her. "You'd do that? You'd help me?"

"Yes, of course. After all, we're friends, aren't we?"

Her inner voice refused to let that one go by without at least a few more volleys, *Well, that was a ghastly lie. I do hope you are proud of yourself.*

Maddie buried her small head in her overcoat once more and hugged her even more fiercely than before.

A war raged within.

Will you get hold of yourself? You only just met this little Munchkin. Whatever foolishness you are thinking about, cease doing so, post-haste. Have you forgotten your station? You are an officer in Her Majesty's Airship Navy. The only thing matters now is getting back your ship.

Maddie lifted her head and wiped the tears from her cheeks with the palms of her hands. "Thank you, Leftenant. Thank you for helping me and my dad."

The Leftenant forced a smile. "Think nothing of it, little one. We merely have to get a message to your father some-how, and I think I have an idea on just how to do it."

Well done, Judas... well done.

Chapter 27

The Gorge

"Oh no."

For the last ten minutes the safari truck had paced the moving barge overhead at an easy forty mph.

From behind the wheel, George asked, "What?"

Still in the passenger seat, Barnaby held the binoculars to his eyes. He had been studying the road ahead of them. "They're headed for the gorge."

"Gorge? What gorge?"

Barnaby lowered the binoculars and pointed repeatedly ahead of them. "We're about to run out of road!"

George's eyes narrowed. Barnaby was right, farther down the road, the highway ended at some kind of stone ruin.

Tightening his grip on the steering wheel, he said, "I'm going to pull ahead of them," and tromped on the gas. Barnaby knew better than to argue.

The old truck didn't like it, but they soon overtook Lady Wellington's hovering barge and left it behind.

Three miles later, the road came to an end. George threw the truck into a powerslide that stopped exactly in front of a wide terrace made of solid black rock.

Slamming open the truck door and moving quickly, George sprinted between two crumbling obelisks framing the entrance. After clamoring up a short flight of granite stairs, he reached a terrace overlooking a massive gorge. If there was a way across the deep chasm, he didn't see it.

Still huffing and puffing from the short climb, Barnaby hiked a thumb over his shoulder and breathed, "Here come our friends."

In a matter of minutes, the royal hover barge had arrived.

Moving to the edge of the terrace, George began waving his arms frantically up at them. "Hey, over here!!!"

"Are you crazy?" Barnaby asked, stepping in front of him. "Are you *trying* to get us killed!"

Without even thinking about it, George shoved Barnaby aside and shouted up at the royal hover barge once more.

If anyone on the barge had seen him, they certainly didn't offer any sign. The barge traveled nearly halfway across the gorge; they were running out of time.

The flare gun.

George flew back down the granite stairs and sprinted for the truck.

Jogging after him Barnaby yelled, "Don't you get it? If they see us, they're going to open fire with everything they have and turn us into dust. Trust me, I've seen it before."

Ignoring him, George yanked open the truck door and pulled out the metallic case containing the flare gun. He placed the kit on the hood and removed the silver-metal pistol. Cracking it open, he quickly inserted a cartridge. With a quick flick of his wrist, he snapped it closed.

The barge's aft section still hadn't cleared the far edge of the gorge yet. There was still time.

George stretched out his hand toward the vessel and squeezed the trigger. As he did, Barnaby shouted, "No, don't!"

Unfortunately, the old dusty flare only half-worked. It shot up into the air only about ten feet before whizzing off sideways and fizzling out.

George cursed, then reached for another flare.

Only the metallic case holding them was now missing.

Terrified and shaking, Barnaby had his meaty arms wrapped around it and held it clutched close to his chest.

"Barnaby, what are you doing?" George asked, then holding his palm out toward him, demanded, "Give me the flares."

Barnaby shook his head. "You don't understand. If they see you, they'll open fire and kill us both."

George risked a quick glance at the departing hover barge. The aft section was crossing over the edge, but there was still a chance someone might see a second flare.

George lowered his voice and said venomously, "Barnaby, I'm only going to ask you one last time, give me... the flares."

"No." Barnaby answered meekly. "I'm trying to save your life, as well as mine."

George lunged forward and slammed so hard into Barnaby, he fell against the truck. George grabbed at the case, but Barnaby held fast.

George seized the accountant by his shirt and reared back his fist. "Give me the flares, Barnaby!"

Barnaby tightened his grip, squeezed his eyes shut, turned his head to side, and waited for the inevitable.

Out of the corner of his eye, George saw the hoverbarge was now past the gorge.

It was too late.

Realizing he was still holding the terrified accountant by his shirt; George slowly released him. When Barnaby finally opened his eyes, George could only shake his head, the cracked-open flare gun dangling from his quivering hand.

"I hope you know; you just blew my only chance at saving my daughter."

Barnaby meekly brought his hands (and the metallic case) down from his chest. "George, you have to believe me. If they'd seen you, the gunnery crews would've opened fire and there'd be a crater where we're standing right now."

George's voice broke when he replied, "There's no way across that gorge, Barnaby. We lose sight of them there's no guarantee we'll ever find them again."

George had never felt so hopeless in his life.

"Hold on a second," Barnaby said, peering over George's shoulder. He took two steps toward the long road. Pushing his bush hat up onto his forehead and cupping his eyes with his hands, he said, "I think they tossed something out."

"What are you talking about?" George asked. Then turning away from the departing hover barge, he saw it too.

A trio of red velvety balloons floated down from the heavens. Although it was difficult to guess at this distance, each balloon appeared to be about the size of your average weather balloon.

George snagged the binoculars out of the truck, stood on the running boards between the cab and open door and lifted the binocs to his eyes. Peering through them, he reported, "It looks like there's some kind of box hanging beneath the balloons."

Lowering the binoculars, he turned his head and took one last look at the departing hover barge. The vessel was now completely over the opposite side of the gorge, continuing north over a seemingly impenetrable jungle.

Meanwhile, the box beneath the velvety-red balloons traveled in a southbound direction, on brisk winds, back toward the crossroads they had passed earlier.

George tossed the binoculars on the rear seat and slipped behind the wheel. He cranked the engine over and when he saw Barnaby hadn't joined him yet, he yelled out the window, "C'mon! Let's go see what they left us."

Barnaby, seemingly surprised George still wanted him to join him, snapped out of his stupor, and quickly shuffled around the hood. He hadn't even closed the door when George stomped on the gas pedal.

As they sped out after the gradually descending cargo, Barnaby offered meekly, "Don't worry, we'll find her."

George wasn't so sure.

Their only hope laid with the dropped mysterious cargo.

The Ornate Box

George and Barnaby rode in silence. George didn't want to hear an apology, and Barnaby was too scared to offer one.

It took almost a full thirty minutes before the balloons finally touched down in a field of tall grasses. Once they did, George pulled the truck over on the side of the road. Without saying anything, he got out of the truck and began hiking toward the downed balloons.

"Wait a minute," Barnaby called out after him. When George turned back toward him, his reluctant companion was still sitting in the truck, when he asked, "Where are you going?"

George looked at him, straight-faced, raised his hand toward the strange balloons barely visible in the distance, and said: "Where do you think?"

"It could be a trap. Or maybe something will get you while you are out there. Either way, you shouldn't go traipsing around out in the open like that."

On this score, Barnaby had a point. The box could be a trap and the balloons had to be a good hundred yards off the road in high grass, hiding Lord only knew what.

He was being reckless, *which made Barnaby the voice of reason!*

The only thing they had close to being a weapon was the flare gun, and even that was only marginally reliable; the first round had zigged way off course.

As though having the same thought, Barnaby turned in his seat and shoved the metallic case through the window. "You should probably take this with you."

Trying to keep the venom out of his voice, and failing, George asked, "And leave you here without a gun?" Even as he said it, he thought to himself, *You need to get over this. For all you know, Barnaby saved your butt back there. You won't do Maddie any good as a smoldering pothole.*

Barnaby's face said he clearly hadn't thought of this. Eventually he shook his head and bouncing his jowls in a way that made George suppress a laugh and said, "Don't worry about me. I'll stay inside the truck with the doors locked." He then pushed the flare gun kit out toward him a little more. "You'll need this a lot more out there than I will in here."

George removed the pistol and flares from the case. Now that adrenaline wasn't racing through his veins, he realized how heavy the gun was. *How am I supposed to carry it?*

He thought about tucking it into his pants but an image of the antique flares spontaneously going off in his pants quickly ruled out that idea.

Barnaby must've seen this too, for he said, "Here, I also found this," and thrust a brown leather shoulder holster out the window. George muttered a word of thanks and slid the flare gun into it. The pistol fit perfectly, as did the flare cartridges in the little loops. George had to loosen the shoulder straps, but once he did, the shoulder holster fit well enough.

George nodded to Barnaby. "Okay. If you see anyone, or anything, honk the horn and I'll come running back here as fast as I can."

Barnaby nodded.

George was about to turn away, but added, "Those grasses are really high. If you see a flare go up, it means I lost my direction. Honk the horn really loud."

Barnaby nodded.

Turning on his heel, George set out for the ornate box in the tall grasses. As he did, the wind picked up a bit. Another image flashed across his mind, only this time it wasn't a flare gun going off in his pants, it was the wind picking up even more and him chasing after the balloons, much to Barnaby's delight. Thankfully, the wind only gusted hard enough to bounce the balloons together and lift the box only a few inches at a time.

As he drew closer, George could see the red balloons were actually made of a red velvety fabric. The ornate box beneath it was about the size of an old traveler's trunk and its edges were reinforced with riveted gold plates.

Reflexively he reached for the folding knife he always kept in his right pants pocket only to find it wasn't there. It didn't matter anyway, he didn't see any obvious locks or opening mechanisms. Speaking aloud to himself, he said, "How the heck am I supposed to open you?"

As he clasped one side to test the weight, he was suddenly reminded of Barnaby's comment about it being a trap.

No. If what Barnaby said about how the hover ship being able to blow them to kingdom come was true, they would've done it. Not drop an I.E.D. (Improvised Explosive Device) disguised as a fancy gift box. He lifted one side. It was heavy.

There's no way I'm going to be able to drag this all the way back to the truck by myself.

A long slow howl, one like nothing George had ever heard before, emanated from an ominous tree line at the base of a mountain range. Others answered the call.

They didn't exactly sound like wolves. They sounded bigger. Scarier. He suddenly felt very vulnerable out in the open and found himself wishing he was back in the truck.

What to do? Drag the box and balloons all the way back to the truck? He thought about loading the flare gun with another cartridge but quickly dismissed the idea because the cartridges were so old and might go off in his holster and burn him badly. He then thought he could load the gun and keep the woods covered with one hand while pulling the crate with the other, but given the weight of the box that would probably take forever.

Another howl from the trees, this one closer, startled him into action. George grabbed one of the handles on one side of the box and started pulling.

He had difficulty dragging the box through the tall grass with one hand while constantly checking the tree-line with the flare gun.

After about twenty feet he was breathing hard. More howls emanated from the trees. A lot more.

Without warning, the opposite side of the box suddenly rose on its own, as if by magic.

"Can we hurry this up please?"

It was Barnaby.

Chapter 29

The Lamppost Man

"Let's get out of here."

George couldn't agree more. The ominous howling noises were increasing in tempo and grew closer by the second.

Barnaby groaned, "Ugh, what is that? It smells like a dumpster threw up a skunk."

George had a pretty good idea.

As they dragged the ornate box back to the truck, he had spied something very large, moving amongst the high blades of grass. Whatever it was, it had fur, but not the soft light pelt of a Timber Wolf. No, this thing's skin was black as coal and its hair coarse and mangy.

When they finally got back onto the road, they didn't waste any time trying to pry open the box. Instead, they loaded it up (balloons and all) into the back of the truck, as quickly as possible.

Slamming the doors to the cab closed, Barnaby, his voice shaky, "Go, go, go!" and after George turned the key and tromped on the gas, the accountant added, "I didn't see them, but I sure could smell them. And I swear I could feel them watching us."

George decided not to tell Barnaby just how close the creatures had been and only nodded in response.

As they sped down the road, Barnaby (his face still ashen) asked, "Where to now?"

Knuckling the steering wheel, George replied, "Anywhere but here."

According to the truck's odometer, it was a hair shy of thirty miles later that they were nearing the crossroads.

The fuel gauge indicated they still had over three-quarters of a tank, so there was really no point in continuing south, back to the gas station. The gorge behind them was impassable, so... that meant going either left or right.

Not knowing which way to turn, George slowed the truck down and rolled to a stop in the middle of the road. Only endless roads through rolling hills and seas of billowing prairie grass lay in both directions.

He was about to ask Barnaby which way to go, but the was man passed out in his seat, his head propped against the window.

"Barnaby, wake up."

At this, the accountant mumbled something unintelligible and then waved something away from his nose as though he were swatting away an unseen fly.

George was about to prod the accountant into consciousness when something caught his eye on one corner of the intersection.

Is that a streetlamp? What's it doing out here, in the middle of nowhere?

Creeping the truck forward, George could now see a man leaning off the oversized lamppost, holding perfectly still. He was wearing lots of makeup, a ringmaster's bright red tailcoat, and a black top hat adorned with old-timey aviator goggles.

George put the truck in park, but decided to keep the motor running out of fear it wouldn't start back up again; plus, he didn't want to be stranded with the strange-looking weirdo perched up on the lamppost.

Climbing out of the cab, he stood on the truck's running boards and used his open door as a shield. "Excuse me, uh, sir?"

The dude on the lamppost didn't answer. In fact, he stood so motionless that George began to wonder if he was a man at all, but instead, a very life-like mannequin.

Feeling foolish, he tried again. "Hey buddy, I'm talking to you. Hello?"

Just as he began to climb back into the truck, the Lamppost Man blinked.

What the heck?

George gave him a hard stare, uncertain if the weird guy perched on the lamppost had indeed blinked.

As though in answer, the Lamppost Man slowly turned his head toward him. Focusing in on him, with a giant Cheshire Cat smile spreading across his face.

"Greetings and exaltations! Hello there, my dear sir! Hello."

"Uh… okay… I'm sorry, but we're a little bit lost here, and I was wondering if you could help me get my bearings?"

"Lost you say?" the Lamppost Man shouted. "Well, we certainly can't have that." He jumped down from his lamppost and began pumping his fists dramatically as he crossed the road.

Practically singing now, he said, "Why…. You must be Colonel George Stapleton."

"How do you know my…" George began, but the Lamppost Man rounded the truck door, clasped him by the hand in both of his and began shaking hands profusely. "Welcome, welcome. We certainly are glad to have you here. Very glad. I have been waiting for you up on that lamppost for what feels like forever. Why, I didn't think you'd ever get here."

George, nearly handshaken out of his skull, pulled his hand out of the imp's surprisingly firm grasp and asked, "And you are?"

"Who am I?" the Lamppost Man asked, patting the breast-pockets of his coat with both hands. His tone suggested he was both surprised and offended. Gesturing back to the Lamppost and then to himself, he added, "I would have thought that it was apparent." He then held a finger up to George indicating 'wait a moment', coughed two times into his gloved hand, cleared his throat and exclaimed, "Why I… I am…" raising his voice several decibels, "…the Lamppost Man!!! Ta-Da!!!" and then struck a pose.

Biting down his lip, George thought, *Wow, this guy is obviously not playing with a full deck.* Instead of saying so, he asked, "Can you tell me where I am?"

"Where are you?" the Lamppost Man repeated. "Now that is an excellent question… an excellent question indeed." He outstretched both arms to his sides. "Why, you are at the crossroads, you silly." Pulling his arms in and leaning forward, he asked, "Why? Where else would you be?"

George sighed, fought down his frustration, and asked, "Yeah, um… is there someone else we could talk too?"

The Lamppost Man tilted his head first one way, then the other. "That depends, who would you like to talk too?"

Anybody but you.

"I don't know…" he breathed, "someone in a town near here? Maybe there's someplace we could go?"

The Lamppost Man waggled his eyebrows, nodded his head vigorously, took in a great big breath and said simply, "Yes."

"Yes… what?"

"Yes, there's a town near here."

When the imp didn't expand on that and merely stood there frozen, with that stupid grin frozen on his face, George asked, "Which way do we go then?"

To this, the Lamppost Man asked, "That depends, which way do you want to go… then?"

Failing to hide his growing frustration, George responded, "I don't know. Do you have any suggestions?"

"Well…" he drew this out a bit, "…that's entirely up to you, my boy." Without warning the Lamppost Man jumped up onto the bumper of the truck and pin-wheeled his arms before pointing out the road to his right and said, "If you go that way, you will certainly meet something large and chilly that is sure to eat you." Pin-wheeling his arms a second time and landing his fingers toward the opposite direction he said, "And this way, many chills, spills, and nightmares await you."

George checked both directions once more. He didn't see any of those things, only the same narrow road in a sea of grasses he saw before.

After double-checking to see the Lamppost Man hadn't moved from the front bumper, George leaned into the cab and retrieved his binoculars. Climbing onto the hood, he focused the binoculars down the road and saw only formidable snowcapped mountains in the distance.

Something large and chilly that is sure to eat you.

Swinging his binoculars in the other direction, a twinkling of reflected light caught his attention. About seventy feet off the ground, he spotted the cigar-shaped vessel they had spotted earlier. At this distance it was difficult to make out any real details, but it was definitely a lot smaller than Lady Wellington's hover barge, and it was just sort of hanging there, in the air, and not moving.

What are you?

Beyond the hanging vessel, George spotted another dot on the horizon. Focusing the lenses a bit more, he saw the beginnings of a town.

"What's that over there? Is it a town?"

Feigning like he was staring at the town off in the distance, the Lamppost Man pulled George closer to him and whispered in his ear, "Oh… that is a very good choice, a very good choice indeed. I see many adventures waiting for you there, Georgie-Porgie, but--" He checked to see if anyone was listening. Certain that they weren't, he lowered his voice further and added, "Beware the doctor."

"The doctor," George repeated.

The Lamppost Man made a serious face while nodding profusely.

"Okay," George said in the most pacifying tone he could muster, all the while climbing down from the hood and back onto the running board by the driver's door.

Leaning in to put the binoculars back where he had found them, George was surprised to find that the Lamppost Man was no longer standing on the hood, but right beside him by the open door. The imp was so close in fact, that George's hand began inching toward the flare gun in his shoulder holster.

The Lamppost Man didn't notice this, because just as he began edging closer, the imp suddenly noticed Barnaby sleeping in the passenger seat.

Without dropping that idiotic grin of his, the Lamppost Man turned his head back and forth between Barnaby and George several times.

For a tense moment, George thought the imp just might be crazy enough to attack. Which was why he nearly jumped out of skin when the Lamppost Man hollered, "Well... Ta-Ta for now!" and then walked backwards across the road (in a most unnatural way) and continued on like that, all the way across the intersection and all the way back to his lamppost on the corner.

Once there, the imp tipped his hat, and in a very deft move, jumped backward onto his Lamppost. He then leaned out and assumed his position of being frozen again.

What...a... whackadoodle.

George was about to climb back into the cab of the truck, but feeling a chilly wind assault him, and perhaps feeling a bit sorry for the weirdo, he asked, "Listen, buddy, we're in the middle of nowhere, are you sure I can't give you a lift somewhere?"

The Lamppost Man didn't answer. Instead, he simply remained unmoving with that perpetual grin on his face.

"Okay, suit yourself," George said aloud and, conscience clear, slipped behind the wheel.

This day just keeps getting weirder and weirder.

After putting the truck in drive, he made a hard right. Absentmindedly, he had hit the turn signal, and immediately feeling foolish for doing so, he switched it off.

Accelerating toward the distant town, he noticed Barnaby was not only fully awake, but he was also turned around in his seat and staring back at the Lamppost Man growing smaller and smaller in the rearview mirror.

Smiling a little, George asked him, "Friend of yours?"

In a tone more serious than George had ever thought the accountant capable of, Barnaby answered, "You got lucky." Turning toward him, his face pale with fear, he added, "That was the Lamppost Man. You don't want to mess with Lampy. I seriously doubt you'll be so lucky next time."

Lampy? Where have I heard that name before? Then it hit him.

From the note...

H.M.A.S. DAUNTLESS

"That's all I know, I swear it."

Lie.

Barnaby may have been keeping everything he knew about the Lamppost Man a secret (which wasn't all that much), but he wasn't lying when he said, "I've never visited that town before. Lady Wellington only passed over it once."

There, that sounded pretty convincing.

He had to be careful. George was smart. Real smart. It was more than the fact the guy had been a Colonel in the military and a college professor. The man had a keen eye and an insatiable desire to know everything. That, coupled with his dogged determination and tremendous amount of hope, was a recipe for disaster if he wasn't careful.

"You're sure. You've never been to this town before."

Barnaby narrowed his eyes as he feigned looking off at the town in the distance. At the moment, neither of them could see anything because of a lengthy dip in the road.

"Nope, never. The only thing I know is Lady Wellington has *never* visited here," *and that is enough reason for why we should probably stay away.*

Studying George's face, Barnaby thought, *Yeah... that sounded pretty good... I think he bought it.*

George slammed on the brakes.

At first, Barnaby was certain George had picked up on some tell, or facial tick that gave him away. He was about to launch into a tirade of confessions but before he could, he saw George wasn't looking at him. Instead, the man was leaning forward in his seat, had his elbows propped up on the wheel, and seemed preoccupied with whatever lay ahead.

"What are you looking at?" Barnaby began, but then he saw it too.

An ostrich, wearing a tuxedo and top hat, sprinted across the road on long, powerful pink legs. It passed directly in front of their hood without so much as a second glance.

Before the giant, well-dressed bird vanished into the tall grass on their left, another trio of them emerged on their right. They also trundled across the highway with the same leisurely fierceness.

The trio soon became dozens, and the dozens became hundreds.

Barnaby, eager to change the subject, let out a slight chuckle. "I guess this is what you might call a Stranger World traffic jam."

George kept shaking his head. "Why would anyone put an ostrich in a tuxedo and top hat?"

As though hearing him, one of the large birds stopped in front of the hood and stared at him through one eye bespectacled with an eye monocle.

"Umm… George," Barnaby began, "You know these guys aren't real, right?"

Barnaby pointed to one bird whose hindquarters was partially torn away revealing the mechanical workings underneath.

The bird studying George ran off. More ostriches flooded the road and continued to parade past them. There where so many, they could barely see the road.

"There must be hundreds of them."

"Thousands is more like it. I saw one herd once that had to be over 4,000 strong. I heard of another that had 16,000 in it. After the fall, the ostriches were among the first to breed."

After the Fall? Why would you say that? You idiot! That will only lead to more questions you don't want to answer.

Are you trying to break the man? Barnaby had seen first hand what happens when new arrivals learn to much of the truth all at once.

Fortunately, George must've missed it, for he said, "Maddie would have loved this."

Whew... close one.

After a few more minutes of the ostrich parade, George lifted his hand and grabbed the gearshift.

Barnaby asked, "What are you doing?"

Shifting into first, "We don't have time for this. I'm going to drive through."

Before he realized he was doing it, Barnaby grabbed George's hand and stopped him. "Are you insane? They'll swarm the truck and tear us apart."

George's face screwed up in a frown of disbelief, but then he reexamined their powerful predator's long claws at the end of each two-toed foot and stayed his hand.

Seeing the man's growing anguish, Barnaby added, "Look, just give them another minute. Eventually the herd will thin out and once they do, you can drive through."

George nodded, but it was obvious he was struggling to keep it together.

"Remember that smaller, cigar-shaped ship we saw coming in?"

Barnaby thought about it for a moment. "Yeah. What about it?"

George nodded, pointing his finger over the grasses on their right.

It took Barnaby a moment for his eyes to it, in the distance, he saw the floating ship. It was the Dauntless.

"I think we should check it out."

That was a bad idea, but Barnaby could never say it.

He made a good show of taking note of the dwindling sun. They couldn't have more than another hour of sunlight left. "You sure that's a good idea? I mean, it'll be dark soon, and we still haven't found any place to bed down for the night. Maybe we should push on to the town."

Still leaning on the steering wheel and staring out the window, George said, "The town's not much farther. We'll just take a quick peek."

Barnaby nodded. Despite the chill in the air, he took out his handkerchief and mopped his sweating brow.

Shifting gears, George announced, "Herd's thinning." Slowly and carefully he drove the truck through one of the bigger gaps.

A few miles later, George parked the truck beside road. Thankfully, the grasses were a lot shorter, only about mid-calf, and the hover barge wasn't far off. Armed with only the flare gun they set out for it on foot.

Another fifteen minutes of precious daylight was wasted making their way over to the floating vessel. As they approached, they could see a lot more details: like the gigantic paddlewheels on either side that lay dormant, a riveted hull, and a brass railing encircling the balconies on the top decks.

To Barnaby, the cigar-shaped vessel always reminded him of a flying submarine but George summed it up perfectly when he said, "If Captain Nemo built a jungle cruise boat instead of a submarine, this would be it."

After that, Barnaby couldn't think of a better analogy.

Scratching the itch on his forehead, Barnaby asked, "How long do you think it is?"

George continued studying and without looking at him finally replied, "At least a hundred feet." Standing in the shadow of the bow, he yelled, "I reckon that's the cockpit."

Barnaby checked where George was pointing and saw a box-shaped glass house hanging from the belly of the ship.

"What, you mean like a wheelhouse?" Barnaby asked.

"Yeah, uh, sure," George responded.

"And check out the sides." George pointed again. "Scorch marks."

"Where, I don't see anything." Barnaby raised the binoculars he had forgotten he was wearing around his neck. Firefight damage was all over the thing. If George had only seen the attack from Lady Wellington's barge, he'd be amazed the ship was still afloat. What Barnaby said, was, "I'll say this for ya, ...you got eyes like an eagle."

"I'm no expert on flying boats, but if I were to guess, this thing was in some kind of battle and lost."

Barnaby swallowed. Before he could say anything, George asked, "Hey, what's it say on the bow?"

"Huh?" Barnaby asked. He was about to say, 'How the heck should I know', when he remembered he was the one with the binoculars. He focused on the lettering just beneath the bow railing and read aloud, "*H.M.A.S. DAUNTLESS.*"

"The *Dauntless*," George breathed. "That's a good name." He checked on the sun before adding, "Shoot. I sure would like to get up there and take a look inside."

"Yeah, but how?" Barnaby asked him. "That thing has gotta be at least seventy feet up. We'd need a helicopter or something to get up there."

"Yeah, a helicopter," George mused.

The colonel had told him how his last memory before waking up in this very strange place had been going down in a chopper in some desert war.

Shaking it off, he told Barnaby, "C'mon. We'd best get back to the truck. I want to get to that town before nightfall. After everything we've seen so far, who knows what horrors are waiting for us."

If he only knew.

JACK CASTLE

MEET
SOPHIA DAVENPORT

The Doc with the Horn-Rimmed Glasses

Wait. Did I slit my wrists?

A tall woman with blond hair and black, horn-rimmed glasses awoke to find herself sitting in a comfy arm-backed chair. For some reason she couldn't explain, she was wearing a long white lab coat. In one hand dangling loosely beside her chair, her fingers still clutched the handle of a knife dripping with blood.

Adding further to her dismay, she found the sleeve of her lab coat pushed up to her elbow, her forearm bleeding from multiple lacerations. Realizing she was obviously the perpetrator; she immediately dropped the stained blade where it thudded to the floor.

Why would I cut myself? I haven't cut myself since I was in high school. And that was never on my forearms where any-one could see. No, this wasn't the same thing. *And I don't think I was trying to kill myself either. These cuts are on the back of my forearm, if they had been on the front I would've bled out in moments.* Although painful, the slashes were mostly superficial. *So, if not stemming from a self-injury dis-order, or trying to kill myself, why would I do such a thing? What was I trying to accomplish?*

This last question seemed to strike a chord in her and she suddenly saw several images flash across her mindscape--an endless field of prairie grass, a tiny yellow VW bug, and a strangely-clad man leaning off a lamppost, but aside from that, no other memories were forthcoming.

Adjusting her glasses on her nose, she scanned her sur-roundings.

At first glance, it appeared to be the lobby of a very fancy Victorian hotel. The room was dimly lit by a large cobweb-covered chandelier with flickering candles. Lush red velvet curtains draped over the windows, and the walls were cov-ered with bright pink and white pastels. On an ivory mantelpiece sat an old-timey clock ticking loud enough to drive a Hatter mad.

Spooky.

As she shifted in her chair, her forearm throbbed slightly, a painful reminder of her injury. She grabbed a lacey doily off the armrest of a nearby couch and carefully wrapped it around her lacerations, tight enough to staunch the bleeding, but not so tight as to cut off the circulation.

Wound bandaged, she staggered to her feet. As soon as she did, the room spun about, but she managed to stay upright until the episode passed. Lifting her gaze, she was startled by the arrival of a tall, beautiful blond-haired woman wearing thick horn-rimmed glasses. The bespectacled woman was standing only a few scant feet away and had a confused look on her face.

"Hallo?" she said tentatively.

She quickly admonished herself the moment she realized it was only her reflection in the lobby's oval mirror with borders decorated in flowers etched in the glass.

Is that really me?

She pinched her cheek to be certain.

It's me alright, but it doesn't seem right, and why can't I remember what I look like?

Gazing at her reflection further she realized she was wearing a blue lanyard draped around her neck. Attached to the end of the lanyard was a laminated identification badge. *A clue.* Studying the I.D. she saw an unflattering picture of the lady in the mirror, and next to the photo was the name:

DR. SOPHIA DAVENPORT

Oh. So, my name is Sophia, but the name didn't sound quite right. Close, but not quite all the way there.

Fighting down a sudden feeling of déjà vu, she examined the name badge a little closer in the hopes of finding other clues to her identity.

All she found was one word in another little box under the category of division: MICROBIOLOGY.

Why does this all seem so familiar? I feel as though I've done this hundreds of times.

Fighting down the urge to scream, she squared her shoulders back, flashed herself a polite smile in the mirror, and said, "Well, hello there, Doc-tor Sophia Davenport... Micro-biologist..." and with the smallest of curtseys added, "It's nice to meet you."

She noted that when she spoke aloud her accent sounded French. Whether she was from France, Quebec, or even New Orleans, she hadn't a clue.

Her nose wrinkled and she thought she detected a stale odor with a slight hint of formaldehyde.

I can remember what formaldehyde smells like, but not how I got here? Let's see... what is the last thing I remember? Her mind was a complete blank on that score.

Okay, let's start with, where am I?

Turning away from the mirror her original assessment of the place was still the lobby of a Victorian motel. This summation did not change until she saw the ghastly gray white corpse of an old woman lying in an upright casket leaning against the wall.

I'm in a funeral parlor?

She took a few steps backward and nearly toppled over a small tea cart behind her--the hand-painted china tinkling loudly in protest as she did so.

Will you calm down already!

The dead woman in the casket was dressed in a plain black Victorian dress. Her cheeks were sunken and grey (as though she had been dead for a very long time), and her eyes and lips had been haphazardly sewn shut with thin strips of brown leather.

To calm her nerves, the blond-haired doctor with horn-rimmed glasses said with a slight French accent, "Well, you certainly gave me a start."

Her heart had finally begun to slow when she was pretty sure she heard the old woman reply with a muffled, "Mmmmphfff... Mmmmphfff."

Dr. Sophia Davenport, Microbiologist, with a slight French accent, released a startled cry and quickly decided to vacate the room.

In the next room she found a set of stairs leading upward to another floor. The stairway had been made impassable by various pieces of random furniture, as though someone had been trying to form a crude barricade.

She cried out, "Hello... Is anybody here?"

Still not spying an exit, she sojourned into another room and came upon a dark and foreboding hallway. Framing the entrance to the seemingly endless corridor were two statuary busts depicting a stern-looking man and an equally cantankerous-looking woman. When Sophia took a few steps to peer into the hallway she was certain the eyes of the statues followed her every move.

This place is starting to really creep me out... maybe that's why I hurt myself?

Steadying herself, she called out tentatively, "*Bonjour*? Is anybody here?"

Examining the statues again, she noticed the expressions on their faces had changed from a stern gaze to one of horror.

"Stop it, Sophie, you just stop it right now," she scolded herself, using her Mamere's tone. "You're simply letting your imagination get the better of you."

Turning away from the disturbing busts and endless corridor she nearly ran face-first into a full suit of armor. She began to jokingly say, "Excusez-moi," but when she heard

breathing coming from within the helmet she backed carefully away. Once she was certain the suit of armor wasn't about
to step off its pedestal, she turned around and quickly fled
into another room.

Thankfully, the next chamber had large windows, with
plenty of daylight streaming in. The room appeared to be a
large conservatory filled with withered plants and dead flowers. An empty bird cage with tiny bamboo bars stood upright
near the room's entrance, and when she peered into it, she
saw a dead canary.

Well that's just morbid.

A slight rustling of leaves caught her attention and turning
toward it, she glimpsed a strange shadow with horns sliding
across the wall. Holding her breath, she waited for the shadow's owner to reveal itself.

"Hallo?" she said again cautiously, then a bit louder, with
more fervor. "Hallo? Is anybody here?"

Still no answer. The bouncing leaves of an exotic plant
were the only sure sign she hadn't imagined seeing someone.

First the statues, then the suit of armor--ever since she
woke up, she couldn't shake the feeling she was being
watched.

This place is so... so unsettling.

Spying an exit haphazardly boarded up with planks, she decided to venture outside. She moved over to the blockaded door and started pulling off the planks one by one. The boards were loosely nailed and semi-rotted, so they came off easily.

As she pulled off the last plank, she didn't see the outline of the gargoyle shadow on the wall, nor its thick outstretched claws reaching out for her.

Chapter 32

Cheeves

"That's more like it."

Sophia stepped outside onto the porch. The fresh air and sunlight on her face, instantly made her feel better.

The courtyard in front of the gloomy manor was as dilapidated as the interior, but she was glad to be out of the eerie house just the same.

She set out for an iron gate in the distance, walking past thick gardens overgrown with weeds, dead grass, and ivy.

Passing an algae-ridden pond, it was easy to imagine some frightening amphibious monster lunging out of the green-slicked waters and snatching her up in its array of multi-toothed jaws before wriggling back into the murky depths.

So, Sophia gave the pond a wide berth, and to calm her already frayed nerves, she joked aloud, "Must be the housekeeper's day off." *Okay, I've never been very good with puns*, she thought, and was glad no one else had been around to hear her *faux pas.*

At the end of the overgrown path Sophia spotted the ornate gate again. About halfway to the exit, she turned around and took another look at the broken-down manor.

Giving it a crisp salute, she said, "*Au revoir,* creepy house!" and exited the courtyard through the black ornate gates.

Mounted on the wall of the gatehouse, was a glass, gold-framed box with a candle inside. As the sun continued to set and eerie shadows crept along the façade, the candle flickered to life.

Huh, must be activated by a sensor or something.

Beyond the gates, a crooked dirt road ran down the hill past a small wooden church. Sophia hiked down it, giving the dilapidated church and its spooky graveyard even wider berth than she had the gross pond.

Approaching the beginnings of a modest town, it became immediately apparent this was no ordinary town.

For starters, instead of modern streetlights illuminating a hard pavement, charming vintage streetlamps lit a well-maintained cobblestone street. The buildings were impressive Victorian designs: narrow and made of stone, with gabled roofs and recessed doorways. Finely crafted boardwalks, and old iron lampposts ran along both sides of the street.

It was as though some god-like, omnipotent force had plucked her out of existence, shrunk her down to size, and placed her inside a giant's model train set. Adding to this outlandish theory, was the fact that one of the buildings was a large train depot.

What is this place?

The abandoned, nineteenth-century village was unfamiliar to her. In fact, in all her travels... *wait, I travel a lot? I don't remember doing so.* But one thing was certain; she had never seen anything quite like the Victorian village.

Before venturing any further a thought occurred to her, and she wondered why she had not thought about it before. *Duh. Use your phone.* Reflexively she tapped the implant in her temple to activate it. When the expected holo-display didn't appear instantly before her eyes, she frowned and tapped her temple a second time. Still no holo screen was forthcoming.

"*J'en ai marre!*" she cursed softly, stamping her foot. *Either it's broken or no signal. Wait, how is it I can remember my phone in my temple but not my own name?* Shrugging her shoulders, she examined several of the stone buildings more closely and thought, *which one to search first?*

The train station would surely be the most logical. Even if it did turn out to be abandoned, she still might find a phone, a flashlight, or at least something she could use as a weapon.

Tirer, I should not have left that knife behind.

The thought of going back into the room with the old dead woman sent shivers down her spine, so she decided against it. *No, best stay out here in the light where mumbling corpses and heavy-breathing suits of armor can't suddenly spring to life.*

Course plotted and laid in, she headed down the street toward the train station.

Her high-heeled shoes felt unsteady on the uneven cobblestone street growing darker by the second. As her heels echoed against the stones, gaslamps flickered to life, their blue flames illuminating a stock-still horse harnessed to a black carriage with two more lamps hanging off either side of the driver's seat. The horse was so lifelike she couldn't decide if it was real or not until she saw the robotic eye dangling from several thin metallic cords.

A robot?

She marveled at the creation but continued onward to the train depot.

It occurred to her that the town was devoid of people and began to wonder where they all were. Spinning around in a slow circle (as she continued to walk), she noticed the village was not only abandoned, but many of the doors and windows had been boarded up, much like the abandoned manor at the top of the hill.

What happened here?

She climbed the wooden steps to the train depot. Upon reaching the top, she found two wooden boxes leaning against the depot's main entrance, blocking her path. It took her a moment to realize the pine boxes were coffins. She was about to go around them when she realized the coffins didn't have any lids... and of course there was a body inside one.

A fresh one...

...and it wasn't human.

The inhuman corpse dressed in a tattered green-butler's uniform but had more in common with a gargoyle than any human. It couldn't have been more than five feet tall, had grayish furry feet, black-shiny talons for toenails, and its overall appearance was like one of those little demons crawling out of the pit of hell in all those Renaissance paintings in Europe.

"Yech. What a monstrosity."

If this is some kind of movie set, this monster doesn't exactly go along with the town's Victorian motif. Then again, who am I to talk, neither does a microbiologist wearing a lab coat.

The gargoyle, dressed in an early 19th century butler's uniform, had its arms folded over its considerable girth. Its facial features and horns coming out of the top of his head were certainly gargoyle-ish, but unlike most gargoyles, his skin wasn't stone. It was more like the fine fur of a black panther.

She began to turn away but when she did, she could've sworn the creature opened his eyes and glanced at her before closing them again.

Is it possible this creature is alive?

Summoning her courage, she stretched out a trembling hand toward the gargoyle's face. Her poking finger was a mere inch from away from the creature's nose when she decided to let sleeping gargoyles lie and pulled back her hand. As soon as she did however, the monster's yellow, cat-like eyes flashed open. Spotting her, its mouth spread into an oversized smile filled with jagged rows of triangle-shaped teeth. Sophia heard herself scream, as her knees buckled.

The gargoyle lifted his head toward her and said, "Hi there!" in a loud cheerful voice, then abruptly lunged out of the coffin to snatch her.

"*La vache!*" she cried, stumbling backward out of the monster's range.

First, tumbling off the boardwalk, she then rolled down the short, grassy embankment to the cobblestone street. Raising her bruised cheek from the stones, she saw the gargoyle-man leap out of the coffin and land on the boardwalk, with a mighty roar.

Oddly enough, she was pretty sure the gargoyle said, "Wait, come back, I have balloons!" Then his predator-prey instinct must have kicked in because he released another roar, dropped to his knuckles, and moved toward her like a charging gorilla.

Sophia let out another cry, rose to her feet, turned, and ran across the street screaming at the top of her lungs for help in a mish-mash of French and English. A quick glance over her shoulder revealed her worst fear: the gargoyle had cleared the grassy knoll, and landed nimbly onto the street.

Sophia knew she had no hope of outrunning such an agile creature.

A narrow bakery lay directly across the street and this spurred her running legs on like a hateful jockey. Sophia slammed into the door of the bakery, but it was firmly locked. She pounded on the windowpanes with the palms of her hands, but no one came to her aide. She turned back toward the street and realized she was cornered in the recessed doorway.

Seeing she was trapped, the gargoyle man released a final gleeful roar and leapt into the street in one mighty bound. In three or four strides, knuckles pounding the ground, he was nearly on top of her. Butler-persona discarded, he leapt into the air, elongated his jaws, and outstretched his claws toward her like a lion about to clamp down onto the neck of a gazelle.

Sophia knew it was over. Her short lifespan was over. She was finished.

Chapter 33

George, Meet Cheeves

"You sure you've never been here before?"

Barnaby, who was currently relieving him at the wheel, shook his jowls back at him.

George knew the man was lying.

He wanted to throttle the man, or maybe scream at him. Of course, George knew pummeling him wouldn't do Maddie a lick of good, so he settled for saying, "Keep your eyes open. Maybe we'll get lucky and find somebody who can help us."

The Victorian village reminded him of the small Christmas collection Maddie had started when she was seven. Each year they would buy a different building; the first had been a carousel, the next a small bakery, the 2012 model was a post office.

Barnaby slowed down to about fifteen miles per hour the moment the asphalt road had run out and the cobblestone street began.

The truck's tires thump-thump-thumped over the jagged stones, and George noted the old iron lampposts flickered to life as they approached.

As Barnaby rolled the truck past a toy store, a candlestick shop, and vintage-looking bookstore, George saw in each frost-rimmed window, more oil lamps lighting themselves and illuminating decorative and impressive displays.

Under normal circumstances, the nineteenth century Victorian village (in the middle of nowhere) might have seemed odd to him, but after everything they had seen thus far, this quaint little village was simply par for the course.

Scanning the buildings to either side, Barnaby muttered, "It doesn't look like anybody's home."

George was about to agree when he thought he could hear something. Rolling down the passenger window to be sure, he heard someone yelling. No. They were screaming... screaming for help.

Then he saw her.

It was a blond woman wearing a white lab coat and horn-rimmed glasses. She was running from the train depot on the right and crossing in front of them.

I know that woman, but from where?

Barnaby, who had his eyes focused on the bakery to his left, didn't see the woman stumble into the street in front of them until it was too late.

"Look out!" George cried, grabbing the wheel and giving it a good yank, but he was certain he had acted too late.

THUMP!

Sophia

Watching the accident unfold from the recessed entryway of the bakery, Sophia saw the driver of the big safari-looking truck slam on his brakes, but he failed to come to a complete halt before sending the gargoyle-butler flying.

The driver, a potbellied man wearing khaki shorts and looking like he had just been on a jungle expedition, leapt out of his truck. In a panic, he started yelling to the struck pedestrian, "Please don't be dead, please don't be dead," as though shouting at the dead gargoyle-man might revive him somehow. The driver's hands trembled, and he seemed unsure what to do next. As though sensing he was being watched, he lifted his gaze and stared right at her.

"Oh thank God. Are you a doctor? I need your help. There's, uh, been an accident."

"Yes, but I'm more of a scientist than a medical doctor." Sophia felt her face twist as if her own words shocked her. "At least I think I am."

"What do we do?" the frightened driver asked her nervously.

Before she could answer, a third voice, this one more confident sounding, said, "First, check to see if he's still breathing." Once Sophia located the source, she saw a man rounding the far side of the truck's hood and figured he must have been riding in the passenger's seat. He was athletic, with salt-n-pepper hair, and was holding the palm of his hand to his forehead where he must've bumped his head in the crash. Not waiting for the potbellied man to take action, he knelt down next to the gargoyle-man, put his ear next to the creature's mouth and listened for breathing.

Sophia and the frantic driver joined him. "I didn't think I hit him that hard."

Salt-n-pepper gazed up at her and pointed to the gargoyle-man. "What the heck is this? Is he wearing some kind of costume?"

Potbelly was now staring too, his jaw hanging open wide. Both men had American accents and seemed genuinely concerned. She kept on guard though, for all she knew, they were her captors, and this was merely a clever ploy to gain her trust.

The man with the potbelly and mustache took in more of the town and asked, "Hey lady, what the heck is this place? This don't look like no town I ever saw."

Sophia shook her head. "I don't know," she heard herself say. Palms out like shields, she quickly added, "I only woke up here myself a few minutes ago."

She tapped her temple. "And, my clever-plant is dead as a doornail."

Potbelly gave her a funny look, scoffed, and asked, "Clever-plant, what's that?"

She tapped her temple again with exaggerated movements. "You know, clever-plant?"

The athletic man with graying hair, stopped his CPR long enough to ask, "What? You mean like a cell phone?"

Before Sophia could come up with an answer, the gargoyle man began to stir.

"Uh, George, I think her friend is starting to wake up."

Sophia shook her hands in front of her. "No, no, no. *Monsieur*. This… thing, …he is no friend of mine. He was chasing me when you hit him with your truck. If you hadn't, I am quite certain he would've killed me."

Hearing this, the athletic man with salt-n-pepper hair got off his knees and both men backed away.

The gargoyle man snorted like he was dreaming and swatted away an imaginary fly. In the time between opening his eyes and leaping to his feet, it couldn't have been more than a nano-second.

"Hi, I'm CHEEVES!"

So, it can talk, was Sophia's first thought. *I thought I had imagined it before.*

When no one answered him right away he asked, "Do you have any cathhhttss?"

Sophia noticed the gargoyle man-- *Cheeves* --spoke with a heavy lisp, spitting profusely as he talked. "I don't know what you may have heard, or what you may have been told, but I don't eat them. Cathhtttss, that is." Sophia also noted the way his eyes shifted from side to side as he thought about it. "I mean, I can't quite elaborate where my cathhttsss are right now, at the moment, but I can assure you, I didn't eat them." He drum-rolled his clawed fingers on the breast of his vest. "So, do you? Do you have any cathes?"

Salt-n-pepper must have finally realized Cheeves wasn't some kid wearing a costume. For he was so taken aback by the creature's appearance, he sprang to life and fumbled for what appeared to be a flare gun in a heavily used shoulder holster.

Pointing it at the strange creature, finger tense on the trigger, he began, "I don't know what the hell you are..."

Oblivious to any danger, the gargoyle creature (Cheeves), responded with a hint of curiosity, "Is that... Is that a flare gun?"

Cheeves's smile widened, displaying even more sharpened triangle-shaped teeth than before. Taking a step closer, "My, I haven't seen one of th-th-those in ages. Does-thhh it still work?"

"Take one more step and you'll find out," Salt-n-pepper growled, but in a feat of blinding speed and gymnastics, Cheeves dropped to the ground, dive-rolled under the man's aim, and in a blink of an eye disarmed him.

Everyone took a step back while Cheeves studied the weapon. "Oh, my. Did you know th-th-this th-thing is loaded?" First, he pointed the flare gun at Salt-n-pepper, who held his ground. Then, he pointed at Potbelly who sort of laughed, cringed, and cried all at the same time. And then... then he aimed it at her.

And fired.

"Be careful that's..." Salt-n-pepper began, as Cheeves squeezed the trigger. Sophia watched in horror as a flare exploded out of the barrel, streaked past her hair and impacted the wall behind her.

"Give me that, you idiot!" Salt-n-pepper roared, ripping it from Cheeves's grasp.

Meanwhile Cheeves was jumping up and down, clapping wildly. "My goodness, th-th-that was delightful! Simply, duh, delightful!"

Salt-n-pepper spoke to him as though scolding a small child. "This isn't a toy!" Brandishing the pistol at him, "You could have really hurt someone!" He then cracked the pistol open, ejected the spent cartridge, and loaded a fresh one.

Sophia noted Cheeves's ears were now lowered like a rebuked dog. Sadly, he explained, "I was just ha-ha-having a little fun is all."

At first, the man with the salt-n-pepper hair was too incensed to speak, and merely bit down on his lip and shook his head. Deciding Cheeves wasn't any more of a danger, he holstered the weapon.

As everyone began to settle down (and Potbelly came out from his hiding place behind the truck) Sophia asked, "Who are you people?" Then pointing to Cheeves, "And, what is this monstrosity?"

A quizzical expression spread across the gargoyle's wide face. He scratched his horns brusquely, rolled his eyes, and said, "I'm not a monstrous... monstro-ah... I'm not a mon-thhh-ter! I can tell you that much."

The man with the salt-n-pepper hair stepped forward and addressed only her. "Listen, it sounds like you don't know any more than we do. My daughter was kidnapped and carried off by..."

Interrupting him again, the gargoyle man stepped forward with that insanely-wild smile of his, "Yes-thhh, yes-yesthhh, we all know about your daughter. Lady Wellington carried young Maddie off on her hover barge. Please-thhh... That's old news already. Everybody knows that. Word tends to get around pretty fast-thhh."

Salt-n-pepper's eyebrows raised inches; his eyes went wild. He stepped forward and demanded, "Where are they taking her?"

Cheeves made a derogatory noise. "Why to Portlandia, of course."

"Portlandia?" the man with the potbelly asked, "Where's that?"

The gargoyle rolled his head drolly toward him. "You don't know where Portlandia is-thhh?" When he didn't get a response from any of them, he added, "Really? None of you know? It's-thhh only the biggest port in the region. Way-way-way-way, high, up on top of Mt. Olympus-thhhh? It's the last st-thhh-stopping point for all airships-thhh before journeying over the Madlands."

Sophia noted the gargoyle shivered on the word Madlands.

Salt-n-pepper, with patience waning, stepped forward. "How do we get there? Can you draw a map?"

Cheeves shook his head. "You can't drive to Portlandia. There are no roads. At least-thhhh not anymore."

Sophia, seeing the concern of a father for his kidnapped daughter, asked, "If not drive there, then how?"

Cheeves thought about this for a moment, scratching the base of one horn before answering, "I suppose you could take the train. With all Lady Wellington's stops to pillage and plunder settlements and lands, you might even beat them there."

Salt-n-pepper checked the train station she had fled from earlier. "Train?" Pointing to the depot with an angry-shaking finger, "Over there in the depot? When's the next one?"

Cheeves made another derogatory noise. "Oh, please-thhhh, the train doesn't stop here anymore. It hasn't in years. At least not since the Zombie-Pirate King blew up the bridge over the gorge." The gargoyle held up a hand to his mouth and whispered to Sophia. "He lives in the swamp, you know." The gargoyle then looked around to see if anyone else was listening. Certain that they weren't he added, "He's actually pretty scuh-scuh-scary."

"Terrific," salt-n-pepper managed. It was clear to Sophia, he was barely keeping his temper in check.

"Why, th-th-thank you," Cheeves responded. Then rubbing his claws briskly together, he asked, "Okay, who's hungry?" Not waiting for answer, he bounded away toward a large wooden inn whose sign read: Wolf's Den Ale House.

Seeing Barnaby followed after the odd creature, salt-n-pepper yelled after him, "Barnaby, where are you going?"

The obese man stopped in his tracks, turned around and gazed back at him, his mouth hanging open slightly. "What? I'm starving."

Salt-n-pepper raised a hand toward a large spooky manor, up on the hill, marking the end of the cobblestone street. "This is obviously a dead end. We need to double-back."

"We also gotta eat," the pot-bellied man retorted, his stomach rumbling for emphasis, and then stormed off.

"Great... that's just great." Turning toward her (for a moment, he seemed to have forgotten she was there), he gave her a little wave and said, "Hi, I'm George."

Lifting the laminate badge hanging from her neck and holding it up for him to see, "According to this my name is Dr. Sophia Davenport and I am a Microbiologist." She seemed to think this over for a second. "And I can't shake the feeling that I've said all of this before."

The Inn

Sophia and George climbed the short flight of stairs to enter a building with a sign out front that read Wolf's Den Ale House.

After introductions had been made, each of them shared the last thing they remembered before waking up here, where they had woken up, and everything that had happened since their arrival. None of which explained where *she* was, or how *she* could leave this place. It didn't take long to figure out neither of the two men were going to be any good to her. She was furious with them for that, but she also knew she could hardly blame them. Other than the information dangling off her lanyard, she hadn't exactly been a plethora of information either.

Inside the dilapidated inn, they spied Cheeves nimbly dodging through a maze of tables and chairs. He easily bounded over a counter near the wall and vanished into an unlit doorway beyond.

"Cheeves, where are you going?" Barnaby shouted.

The gargoyle butler's voice echoed from the back room. "Must find food, must find you food. Prepare a feast for my guests-thhh." Sophia then heard the clanging of pots and pans and guessed Cheeves was in some sort of kitchen.

At the mere thought of food her stomach rumbled. She was ravenous.

As Barnaby plopped down on a stool near the bar, George moved up next to Sophia and said to her, "I'm going to clear the upstairs and make sure there's nobody else is here." With that said, he unholstered his flare gun and moved toward a set of rickety stairs lining the wall.

With little else to do other than wait for Cheeves to return, Sophia took in more of the rundown tavern. The main floor presented a wide-open area crammed with plenty of wooden tables and chairs. Dominating the center of the room, a massive stone hearth, at least two stories high, ran all the way to the ceiling. She held her shoulders for warmth. *A fire sure would be good right about now.* Presently the hearth sat barren, but she didn't think anyone would mind if she threw in a few of the old wooden barstools for kindling.

Not sure how I'd light it though, without matches or some other form of ignition source. The entire place was dimly lit. As the last bit of the daylight began to leave them, she became painfully aware that if she didn't get a fire going soon, they'd be dwelling in darkness.

"Ahhh-chooo!" After her first big sneeze, she sneezed several more times.

Ugh, on top of everything else I'm allergic to dust.

The inn was coated in a thick layer of it, made more apparent every time she moved or touched anything.

She seriously doubted Cheeves would find any food. It was obvious the decrepit old inn had been abandoned for a long time, perhaps even decades. Even the floorboards groaned heavily beneath her footsteps. On top of everything else, she began to worry she might fall through at any moment.

A small wave of nausea washed over her. She stretched out a hand and leaned on a thick timbered post to let it pass. As she did, a sharp stabbing pain in her arm reminded her of her injury. If she didn't clean the wound soon, she'd run the risk of infection.

"Cheeves?" she called to where he had vanished behind the bar. "Cheeves, are you still back there?" She could still hear the clanging of pans, but he didn't answer.

"BWAH-HA-HA-HA!"

Sophia nearly leapt out of her skin and onto the ceiling like a scared cartoon cat when she heard an abrupt, loud boisterous laughter that shattered the silent inn. Turning toward it, she saw a man sitting in a corner booth. He was dressed in a vest, heavy-frock coat, and felt derby hat. Laughter subsiding, he picked up a flask of frothy ale, and noisily consumed it. Much of the alcohol ran down his chubby cheeks. Pouring out every last drop, he dropped the mug heavily to the wooden table. He let out a large satisfied belch and began attacking a slab of blood-red meat on a round tin plate with an oversized serrated knife and medieval fork.

This is impossible.

Sophia had been certain that when she had first come into the room there had been no one inside, and yet now she could smell the cooked steak in the air.

Wringing her hands, she walked over to the man on unsteady legs.

The man with bushy sideburns stopped shoveling in his food long enough to release an even louder belch than the first.

"Excuse me, *Monsieur*," she began meekly. When she realized the patron didn't hear her, she repeated herself and added, "I am so sorry to interrupt your dinner, but I seem to be lost, and I was wondering if you could direct me..."

Waving his empty mug at her, he howled in a drunken stupor, "You there, wench! Bring me another mug."

"Uhhhmmm... I am so sorry, *Monsieur*. I don't work here. I was wondering if you could tell me where I am."

The drunk glutton blinked at her several times, as though trying to comprehend the question. "Where are you?" he asked loudly, his speech thick with a cockney British accent. "Why, you're in the Wolf's Den Inn, of course--home to thieves, scalawags, and your basic dregs of society." Pointing his meat-addled fork at his considerable girth, he added, "Present company included." Having said that, he studied her as though seeing her for the first time. Dropping his utensils on the table, "My, you're a pretty one, you are. You must be *new*. Why don't you give ole' Angus here a kiss." He lunged forward, snaked an arm around her waist, and pulled her to him, sitting back down with her firmly on his lap.

He was surprisingly strong.

Sophia tugged at her pinned arms, but he tightened his grip and held her fast. "Let me go, *Monsieur*!"

"Not before you give us a kiss."

Sophia could smell the alcohol on man's breath and the savory aroma of the meat on the plate. She could even feel the heat from the lit candle on the table. Despite the brigand pawing at her, what was at the forefront of her mind was how all this was possible when there was nothing inside the inn a mere moment ago. As the ruffian leaned in for a kiss she shied away. "I said, let me go."

The brute held on like a pit bull with a burglar's leg. "And I said... give us a kiss." He then made smacking, kissing sounds.

Sophia did her best to pull away and free herself, but the big man was far too strong.

She heard a loud crash, and a moment later, the man with salt-n-pepper hair pulled her out of the man's grasp and tossed her to Barnaby, who caught her easily.

"Oy! See here. You git yer own wench." Fists clenched, the drunken patron rose clumsily to his feet.

Sophia watched as George jabbed the man twice in the nose, then reared back with his right, and walloped him a good one. The surly drunk stumbled back into his booth with a clatter, knocking his dinner, and eventually himself, to the floor.

Still keeping one eye on the stunned brutish man, George asked, "Sophia, are you alright?" She nodded but took a step back when the drunk, now holding a meaty hand to his eye whined, "Now what in blimey did you go and do that for?"

Ignoring the question George responded, "What are you doing here?"

The drunk sized up George with his one visible eye. He must've decided George was too much for him to handle, for he said, "Sire, I had no idea this was your woman, and I offer up me most-humblest apologies."

"Why are you here alone? Where is everyone?"

The drunk seemed genuinely surprised by George's question and answered incredulously, "What do you mean, sire. I ain't 'ere all by myself."

A loud din of laughter, music, and basic merriment was suddenly heard behind them.

Both she and George turned around and were shocked to find the tavern no longer abandoned, but crowded with patrons, bright candles, and a trio of musicians playing their instruments. Sophia saw serving wenches weaving in and out of tables delivering mugs of frothy ales to waiting customers. A warm glow emanated in the previously dank hearth, and a pig with an apple in its mouth roasted on a spit over an open fire.

Echoing her thoughts, George breathed, "Where did they come from?"

Sophia shook her head and followed George through the crowded room humming with activity. Each of them tried talking to patrons, but they were either outright ignored or achieved variations of, "Piss off," or "Why don't you go and bother someone else."

Against the wall a barkeep with long, white hair, a white shirt, and brown vest was standing behind a thick mahogany counter, serving brew on tap.

Dazed and confused, and with few other options, she and George approached the counter.

Sophia was the first to speak to the barkeep. "Excuse me, sir. We need help," she said urgently.

The man behind the bar swiveled around so swiftly it was as though his upper body was attached independently of his lower half. "What'll you have, friend?"

Sophia was immediately taken aback because now she could see the barkeep's face was not real. It was plastic.

A robot bartender?

The mannequin-faced bartender tilted his head mechanically to the side. "Sorry, I didn't quite get that, Miss," he said through phony, unmoving plastic lips.

Even though the barkeep was an obvious fake and she felt a twinge of unease, he at least acknowledged her presence, which was more than Sophia could say for any of the other patrons they had met so far.

Not knowing what else to say, she stammered before answering, "We, uh, need help." Holding up her bandaged arm, "We also need medical assistance."

"Sorry," the mechanical barkeep said with his perpetual smile, and tilting his head in the opposite direction he added,

"Can't say I am familiar with that particular brand of re-freshment."

George must've decided to take a different route with the plastic bartender for he asked, "What is this place?"

"You walked in here, don't you know?" the barkeep asked good-naturedly.

George let out a practiced breath, forcing himself to re-main calm. "I mean, where are we?"

"Why, you're in the Wolf's Den Ale House." Placing the clean glass down on the bar, he leaned slightly forward and asked, "Now how about I pour you a nice cold glass of ale? Just got some ice in this morning."

Sophia laid a hand on George's arm. "Let me try." To the barkeep she asked, "What is this place we are in right now?"

The barkeep tilted his head quizzically before responding, and as dryly as his programming would allow, he said, "It... is... a... tavern."

"I mean this town, where are we?" Sophia asked quickly, no longer trying to hide her own frustration.

"We're wasting time. Don't you get it? He's just a robot, like those things that look like Presidents in that theme park down in Florida?"

Theme park in Florida? Is he talking about... ?

Cheeves, appearing beside the barkeep as if by magic, dropped two tin plates of delicious smelling food onto the bar and exclaimed, "See? I told you I'd get you some food. Here you go, eat up!"

Almost in a trance, she and George slowly sat down at the two empty stools and pulled the food closer to them. Each tin plate had a roasted chicken, baked potato, and a side of bread.

"*Bon appetit!*" Cheeves shouted gleefully. He tried to tuck a napkin into George's collar, but George jerked back and removed the cloth napkin from Cheeves's talons. George, scowling at Cheeves, put the napkin down next to his plate. This, of course, did not dampen Cheeves's spirits in the slightest.

"Hey, where's mine?"

Sophia turned and saw Barnaby had joined them at the bar. She noted that he seemed unfazed by all the patrons and focused only on the fact that he hadn't been offered any food.

A sheepish expression crossed Cheeves's face. He scratched the base of his horns again, and answered, "Oh, I'm sorry, Barnabus. I thought... ah... with your..." his cat-like eyes kept flicking to Barnaby's belly and back up to his eyes, "...you know... with your..." he gestured at his own belly and shook it, "th-th-that ah... you wouldn't be as hungry as your two friends here."

Barnaby squinted as he frowned. "What's that supposed to mean?"

"Nothing, nothing," Cheeves responded quickly, although Sophia detected a slight grin in the corner of the gargoyle's mouth. "I'll go get you something right now, post haste." With that, he vanished into the kitchen again.

As Barnaby searched for an empty stool, George shrugged and ripped a leg off the baked chicken. Seeing her staring at him, he said, "I suppose if they wanted to kill us, they could've it done it already. Besides, we have to eat some-time." That said he took a hearty bite. Mouth filled with food, he managed, "It's good. Real good."

The savory smells, combined with George wolfing down his own meal right in front of her, Sophia knew she couldn't hold out much longer. Sure, the food might be poisoned, and maybe that's what happened to everybody in town, but George was right, at some point, they had to eat.

She cut off a dainty piece of white meat, brought it to her lips, and just happened to see the sailor man in his booth again. Like before, he was swilling his ale, stopping only to belch, and carving into his meat. It took her a moment to sort out why this bothered her so much until she realized, it was *exactly* like before, the same mannerisms, the same por-tions. It was like the man was repeating himself, as though he were on some sort of loop.

That's when she had her first real memory of exactly what this place really was.

And it terrified her to her core.

Chapter 35

The Ornate Box

"What else do you remember?"

George cut another slice of chicken and shoved it in his mouth. He was starving, but as soon as he was finished with the meal, he was out of here. Clearly there was no one here either willing or capable, of helping him find Maddie.

As he chewed another large tender bite, the microbiologist with the French accent answered him.

"I remember floating down a long tunnel; lights kept passing overhead intermittently for what seemed like eternity."

George hadn't told her yet how he was pretty sure he had seen her down in the tunnels. He was about to mention it, but she continued on with her recollection.

"I also remember a lamppost, in the middle of nowhere. And a man with a top hat. He was looming over me." The memory was obviously causing her distress and she was eager to change the subject. "What about you? How much do you remember before you woke up in the tunnels with your daughter?"

He purposely took another bite of his chicken and forced himself to chew more slowly.

"I remember everything before I got *here*." *But was that really true?* If his memory had been erased, as Sophia's clearly had, how would he even know that it had? Seeing her still looking at him expectantly he answered, "I remember my wife, Tessa; my childhood; my daughter; and the fact that I got assigned the worst parking spot at work."

A memory of his co-pilot sitting lifeless in his seat with a gaping hole in his chest flashed across his mind. "I remember flying a combat mission in Afghanistan…" In his mind's eye George was back in his dying helicopter doing everything possible to keep it airborne. *'Missiles locked. Deploy countermeasures!'* someone yelled, but their voice was muffled, as if they were screaming the words underwater. Then it was gone, or maybe he purposely forced it from his mind. *Too painful.* Also, eager to dismiss the unpleasant memories he joked, "I remember N.A.S.A. landed a land rover on Mars."

Sophia picked her head up at this and gave him a quizzical look. "A Land Rover on Mars?" A nervous chuckle escaped her. "George, what year do you think it is?"

Well that's an odd question.

He was about to tell her it was 2012 when he noticed the crimson stains growing on the bandages on her forearm. "Sophia. Your arm, it's bleeding."

The blond doctor studied her forearm. "Oh my." She quickly grabbed a dirty dish towel off the counter and dabbed at the stained bandages. She must've seen his concern for she told him, "I… uh… it was like this when I woke up."

George saw the look in Sophia's eyes and knew she wasn't telling him everything. She was certainly nice enough, but she was a terrible liar. She picked up on his gaze, opened her mouth as if to say something, but said nothing further. He decided not to press it for now.

Rising quickly to his feet George said, "Here, let me help you." Grabbing her wrist, he started to say, "Try keeping your arm elevated over your head like this," but she jerked her hand violently away from him and clutched it to her chest. Staring at him sheepishly she explained, "Sorry, I guess I don't like being touched."

George nodded. "No. I'm sorry. I should've asked first." Turning his head to the side he raised his voice and asked, "Hey, barkeep, do you have a first aid kit around here anywhere?"

The barkeep with the fake face returned and asked, "What'll it be, friend?"

"A first aid kit?" When the barkeep simply tilted his head in non-understanding, George pursed his lips in frustration. Turning back toward Sophia he said, "C'mon, I think I saw an old first aid kit, in the truck. I'm not sure what kind of shape it's in but it's probably better than anything they have in here."

Sophia hopped down off her own barstool and was about to follow him, when, thinking better of it, she turned and grabbed the last piece of bread on her plate. Stuffing it into her mouth she muffled to him, "Sorry, I feel like I haven't eaten in ages."

George felt himself smiling back at her. "Remember. Keep your arm elevated, like this." This time, careful not to touch her, he demonstrated with his own arm. "It will slow down the bleeding a little bit until we can get you fixed up."

Still cutting her steak, she nodded back to him.

Barnaby had gone off to relieve himself in the loo, but George was fairly confident his traveling buddy could find them out by the truck easily enough.

Then again.

Outside, they reached the oversized safari truck. Despite all the garbage he and Barnaby had tossed out earlier, the

back was still brimming with junk: ropes, lanterns, cargo net-
ting.

George snapped his fingers in recollection and pointed to
the cab. "I just remembered, there's a first aid kit bolted to
one of the rear passenger doors."

The heavy door cracked open with a loud complaining
creak. After unbolting the first aid kit from the door, he unsnapped the lid and inspected the contents inside.

 "The iodine's dry as a bone, and there aren't any alcohol
swabs." Removing a roll of sterile gauze, he added, "We're
gonna need something to sterilize the wound."

"One step ahead of you," Sophia said, holding a bottle of
rum from the inn.

George winced. "That's gonna burn a bit."

Sophia made a pouty face. "Heyyyy... I'm a big girl."

As George cut her makeshift bandages from her arm using
trauma scissors in the kit, Sophia asked him, "So, what's your
plan? To find your daughter, I mean."

As he worked, he told her, "I'm not staying here, if that's
what you mean. As soon as I'm done refueling the truck, I'm
turning around and going back the way I came. Coming here
was a mistake." Lifting his eyes momentarily to the manor on
the hill of the end of the street, he added, "This town is a
dead end. If the train doesn't come here anymore, I've got to
double back and find another way around that gorge. You

and Barnaby are welcome to come with me, but I don't think Barnaby's going anywhere."

George split the end of the gauze into two pieces, wrapped one end around her forearm one more time for good measure, and tied it off with a knot. "There, not perfect, and you probably need a few stitches, but not a bad field dressing."

"It's a little tight," she complained.

George nodded. "Good. You want it tight. It will keep the wounds closed so they can start healing." He was about to put his finger between her bandage and skin but recalled how she reacted in the inn, so he explained, "As long as you can still get a finger beneath the bandage," he said, pantomiming on his own forearm, "you're okay. If your arm starts to swell, we'll loosen them up a bit."

Sophia smiled and offered a word of thanks. As George returned the scissors to the first aid kit and started bolting it back to the door, she said to him, "George, you know how when you fly on a commercial plane the stewardess tells you that in an event of a crash you are to put your mask on first and then your child's?"

"Yeah. What's your point?" George asked irritably, pretty certain he knew where she was headed.

Sophia paused, summoned her courage and continued. "Well... it's just that...you look like you haven't slept in days. I mean, you can barely stand." Gesturing toward the night air with her bad arm, wincing from the effort, "And who knows what other monstrosities are out there."

A disembodied voice added, "Plus, you go outside the town at night, this-sss-thhh time of year, and the Carrion Wolves will positively and absolutely get you."

They both turned and saw Cheeves nimbly leap down from the overhead frame on the back of the truck and land next to them.

"Carrion Wolves, what's a..." George started to ask but the gargoyle butler leapt back up into the back of the truck and exclaimed, "Hey! I didn't know you got mail!" Looking down at him, he asked, "Why didn't you tell me you got mail?"

"Mail?" Sophia asked, "What are you talking about, Cheeves?"

Cheeves pulled the heavy ornate box out of the truck that Maddie had tossed off Wellington's floating barge. It landed with a loud THUMP on the cobblestone stones. Gesturing toward it with one claw, he scratched the base of one horn thoughtfully with the other. "See, you got mail. Does Cheeves ever get mail? No. I write and write and write. Does anybody ever write poor ole Cheeves back? Nooooo....Who cares about the butler. Am I right? I can tell by your face. You think I'm right."

"Cheeves!" George had to yell to get the butler's attention. "Cheeves, are you telling me you know how to open this?"

Cheeves smile widened, and his eyes grew double in size. He looked George square in the eye. "Open what?"

Fortunately for Cheeves Sophia explained, "The box, Cheeves, the box!"

Cheeves's claws drum rolled on his vest. "It's really quite suh-suh-simple. I mean, even a baby can open mail. St-st-stand back, stand back."

He and Sophia backpedaled a few steps.

Cheeves, while humming a tune, began doing a funny dance around the box that entailed sometimes hopping on one foot, and other times knocking one top of the box with a fist, and still other times slapping the sides with the palms of his hands.

George rolled his eyes and exhaled. "I should have known this would be a waste of time."

Cheeves stopped in mid-dance, looked at him sternly, shushed him with a clawed finger to his lips, and said, "Now I have to start over. Now st-st-step back, so-so I can work."

"We're wasting time."

Sophia pulled George farther away until they were standing at the front of the truck. "Just give him a second. He might actually be onto something."

While Cheeves began his ridiculous dance routine all over again Sophia whispered to him in hushed tones. "George, where do you think you are?"

George knew Sophia wasn't simply talking about the Victorian town, the maze, or even the labyrinth of tunnels below. "I don't know, maybe on an island somewhere?" Turning toward her, "Why, do you know?"

She nodded slowly. "Yes, at least I think so. I think we're in some kind of full-immersion theme park, or at least a place that started out as one, a long, long time ago."

George felt himself frown. "A theme park?" He shook his head. "No theme park I've ever been to has anything as elaborate as all this. That theory makes no sense."

Sophia chose her words carefully and spoke slowly. "I imagine it wouldn't. Not to someone from your... time."

George felt his knees quiver. "My time? Sophia, have you gone off your rocker? What are you saying?"

"I'm saying that in my time, we had thousands of full-immersion theme parks all over the world. Places where people could live, work and play in any time period, or any fictional setting the architects could dream of. The park's inhabitants included robots, clones and biological creations that were indistinguishable from humans."

"What, you mean like those animatronic things they have down in Orlando? Because that's not what I saw." He pointed to the southwest. "They had flying ships and dinosaurs."

"You don't have dinosaurs where you come from?"

George raised his eyebrows and said, "No... we don't have dinosaurs where I come from, because the last time I checked dinosaurs died out 65 million years ago."

Sophia took a step closer to him and gently laid a hand on his forearm. He knew the physical contact must've been difficult for her, which only made him appreciate the gesture all the more.

"George, in my time, every zoo on the planet has dinosaurs. They have ever since they began creating them from fossilized DNA back in 2030."

"2030?" George heard his voice crack, and he hated himself for it. *Is this possible?* The most logical explanation was that Sophia Davenport was crazy as a loon, but then, how else could he explain the hovering ships, the bungee corded gatherers, and Cheeves for that matter? Plus, there was also the way Barnaby talked about Nixon and the Vietnam War like it was only yesterday. It was like he was some sort of throwback from the sixties.

Sophia continued. "Where I come from, or rather I should say, *when* I come from, Mars doesn't have only a little rover unit running around on it, but several Martian colonies, and even more colonies on Jupiter's moon, Europa, and even the outer rim and beyond. Android helpers are quite commonplace in every household."

George hiked a thumb back to the gargoyle butler. "What about Cheeves?"

Sophia swallowed before answering. "I'm not sure, but I think I built him." Then more to herself she added, "Or I was working on a design for something like him? But we were decades away from perfecting it and putting it into assembly. It wasn't enough for the architects to make robots and dinosaurs that looked and acted like the real thing. They had to go and play God by making new creations, new species."

A growing feeling of distrust began welling up inside him. George took a step away from her and asked, "What are you saying, Sophia, you used to work here?"

Sophia's eyes grew wide in alarm. "No, not here specifically. I've never heard of anything as expansive or state-of-the-art as this place. I think this is years, or more like decades beyond even my future. Cloning dinosaurs, holograms, and robot barkeeps, sure. But we were a long away from creating anything as advanced as the hover ships you described, and biological creations like Cheeves? They were barely on the drawing boards."

George felt lightheaded. He heard a soft thump behind him and realized it was the sound of him falling against the truck.

If what Sophia was saying was really true, he and Maddie had been somehow transported into the future. It fit. Somehow, even down in the tunnels when they first met the robot horse and flying hover drone, he knew. They had been whisked to the future. If so, was Barnaby a time traveler too? Did he know? After all his time with Lady Wellington, he must've guessed. Could they get back? What happened to Tessa? Was she transported to the future too? How did they even get here?

"George!"

He lifted his head. George was surprised to find himself sitting on the ground with his back against the truck. As he focused on Sophia's face, the loud ringing in his ears began to subside and the world began to stop spinning.

The very definition of auditory exclusion is a form of temporary loss of hearing occurring under highly stressful conditions. Ear ringing was a common side effect.

"George!"

This time it had been Cheeves calling out his name, as though he had been trying to get his attention for some time. "You see? I told you I could open it."

Sophia helped him climb to his feet. It might as well have been Everest, but he managed it. Seeing this, she asked, "George. Are you sure you're okay?"

He nodded, but he was a long away from being okay-- miles, in fact.

Sophia patted him delicately on the arm. "I'm know, it's a lot to take in."

George slowly panned his face toward her. "Ya think?"

Meanwhile, Cheeves, now bending over the box, grunted slightly as he lifted something out about the size of a kid's toy lunchbox.

Cheeves held it to his ear and shook it roughly. "I think it's broken."

George took a hurried step forward and snatched it away. "Well, if it wasn't before, it probably is *now*."

The lunchbox was actually a compass enshrined in a very unusual housing, reminiscent of the Jules Verne-looking hover ship they had spotted earlier.

"A compass?" Sophia asked.

"Yeah, but it doesn't point north though." He showed it to her, and the needle was pointing due east.

"How do you know that?" Cheeves asked.

George pointed to the horizon, "That's where the sun went down." Moving it from left to right, he added, "But it's definitely giving me a heading of due east."

Maddie wanted him to have this. So that meant it was important. Maybe, in this crazy-kooky-upside down world of the future, this was some kind of tracking device.

Hefting it slightly, he told Sophia, "I think this will lead us back to my daughter."

Cheeves, gripping the breast of his coat vest, rocking back and forth on his heels, looking rather pleased with himself, said, "You're welcome."

A single shot rang out inside the inn, and George realized he was no longer wearing his gun.

Barnaby and the Lamppost Man

"Barnaby, good to see you, old man."

Barnaby, still seated at the bar, lifted the shot glass to his lips (the fifth one in as many minutes) and froze. He knew that voice, even after all these years apart. Oh yes, he knew that voice as well as his own. Without taking a sip, he asked, "Aren't you afraid someone will see you?"

The inn had quieted down, the musicians had ceased their playing, and most of the patrons had either switched off or were talking softly on preprogrammed loops. George, Sophia, and Cheeves had finished their meal and gone back outside to the truck for some reason.

They could have left for all he cared. If they decided to leave, he wasn't going with them. He had all he needed right here. Food, shelter and plenty of booze.

Leaning on the bar, and working hard at getting him to meet his gaze, the Lamppost Man patted Barnaby on the back and said, "Now Barnaby, is that any way to greet an old friend?" He signaled the barkeep for a drink who already seemed to know his drink of choice.

"Old friend?" Barnaby repeated, noting his words were now slurring a bit. "You don't care about me. I gave up my friends for you and you still left me to rot with Lady Welling-ton." With that said, he downed his fifth shot of what he was pretty sure was Canadian whisky.

Lampy's mouth gaped open. "Whaaaat? How can you say that, Barnabus? After all we've been through together. Look, you know that I'm not the boss here. I only do what I'm told. And right now, Management only wants one thing, and that's the girl."

Barnaby placed the empty shot glass upside down on the bar and signaled the barkeep for another.

Wait. Did he just say, 'the girl?' Is he talking about George's kid?

"Maddie? What does she have to do with anything?"

The Lamppost Man pounded the bar top with a gloved hand. "You see? There you go. Maddie. That's a fine start.

Why, before right this moment, I wasn't even aware the little brat had a name."

Barnaby teetered on his chair for a moment, gripped the edge of the bar with both hands, and steadied himself. Frowning, he turned toward his drinking companion and said, "Maddie's a good kid. You leave her alone."

"Why Barnabus, why should you care about some snot-nosed brat? What's important is Corporate wants her, and they're willing to pay. As you know, Corporate *always* gets what they want. And then *you*… you get what you want, and *you*," he patted Barnaby on the back heartily, "I know exactly what *you* want."

"*You* don't know what you're talking about," Barnaby said, but even though he lifted his sixth drink to his lips, he didn't partake. Not yet anyway.

"Surrrrreeeeee I do. Yesirreee, Barnaby." The Lamppost man looked around the room, making sure no one was watching or listening. Certain they weren't, he leaned in closely, like he was about to impart some great big secret. "You want to be back home, in that little ramshackle house of yours in Pennsylvania, watching the television each night with that (cough-cough) beautiful wife of yours. Sorry, wrong pipe."

The Lamppost Man pounded his own chest with a fist and quickly gestured for another drink to wash it down. The barkeep quickly placed another drink on the bar, which he drank greedily and almost immediately spit back out. "That's bourbon, you idiot." He slammed the drink back down on the bar. "I've been drinking here for nearly a century and you serve me bourbon?"

The barkeep tilted his head to the side and said politely, "Excuse me, but I believe I have other customers. He threw a dirty towel over one shoulder and moved off to help an oafish drunk wearing a derby and carrying a cane. As the Lamppost Man watched him go, he shook his head after him, cursing under his breath.

Turning back toward Barnaby, he smiled, "Now, where were we?" He tapped Barnaby lightly on the arm. "Oh yes, that's right, the girl," his eyes narrowed, and he leaned in closer, and breathed, "Maddie."

Barnaby shook his head. With a great deal of effort, he put down his sixth drink without taking a sip. He couldn't bring himself to look at the Lamppost Man, but he summoned up what little courage he had, "Maddie's a good kid. No. A great one. Last time, I gave up all my friends and where'd it get me? I'll tell you where, emptying Lady Wellington's honey bucket, that's where." Angrily, he picked up the glass, took another sip, teetered on his chair for a moment, and placed the drink back down on the counter. "What if I don't give 'em up? Not this time."

The Lamppost Man leaned even closer, so their faces were a scant few inches apart. Lowering his voice, he answered, "Oh, I think we both know the answer to that question."

Barnaby nodded in acquiescence. It was then that he noticed a brown leather holster slung over the back of the chair next to him. *George must've left it here*, he mused drunkenly.

"What'll it be, friend?" The barkeep had returned, his ever-present smile unchanged.

"Now, Barnaby, take it easy..."

What's Lampy jabbering about now? Barnaby wondered. And then realized at some point he must've unholstered George's flare gun and was now pointing it at Lampy's head.

"Be reasonable," the Lamppost Man began to say, but when he saw Barnaby's finger tighten on the trigger, he let out a small shriek, grabbed the tip of his hat between thumb and forefinger and dropped to the floor.

The flare missed the Lamppost Man.

Instead, it slammed into the face of the robotic barkeep, thrusting its body backward into the mirror on the back wall. As the broken automaton collapsed behind the bar, Barnaby wiped his nose and sniffed heavily. Realizing the gun was now spent, he lowered it to his side and held it loosely.

The Lamppost Man, uninjured, rose into Barnaby's view, brushed a few shards of glass off his epaulets and said, "Oh, you've done it now, old boy. You have certainly done it. Corporate is not going to like that one bit. Not one bit, I tell you."

Barnaby didn't hear him. His ears were still ringing from the blast. So much so, he wondered if he would ever hear anything again.

The Lamppost Man lightly sat in one of the few remaining upright stools next to the bar. Seeing Barnaby's unfinished drink on the bar he scooped it up and downed it in one gulp. Shoulders slumped and with a defeated tone, Lampy said to himself, "Nope. They're not going to like that one bit."

Barnaby popped his jaw to try and get his hearing back and then in the loud voice of the hearing impaired, who is also drunk, "Who? Who isn't going to like it?"

The Lamppost Man glanced up at him pitifully and said, "Don't worry. Just give it a few more seconds. Someone will be here to assist you shortly."

Jerry, from Corporate

"Barnaby, what did you do?"

George, Sophia, and Cheeves had heard the discharged flare gun and bolted inside. *I should've known not to leave a loaded weapon behind with that idiot.*

Staring at the smoldering wreckage behind the bar, George recognized the ruined automaton from his clothing as the barkeep. Barnaby was still standing over the headless robot with a smoking barrel and dumbfounded expression.

"Give me that!" George said, angrily snatching the pistol away from the man. He replaced the spent cartridge with a fresh one and growled, "I leave you alone for one second..." but then he lifted his eyes to the broken shards of mirror behind the counter and saw a distorted, pencil-thin looking man rising behind him.

George spun.

Corporate had arrived.

The well-dressed man had risen up through a square-shaped hole in the floor like a Shakespearean actor rising up through the floorboards of a stage. He took one deliberate step off the elevator platform, brushed a bit of lint from his shoulder, and the square-pegged hole sealed as though the trap door had never existed in the first place.

"Who is that?" Sophia asked no one in particular.

"It's C-Cah-Corporate," Cheeves answered solemnly. All the joy and playfulness he normally exuded, seemed to have been sucked right out of him.

"What's he want?" George asked, and noted Barnaby backpedaled all the way to the bar, and when he couldn't retreat any further, he started scanning for the nearest exit.

"They only come up to the surface for one reason," Cheeves continued with a subdued tone, "to take someone below."

Cheeves pointed a shaking finger at Barnaby. He told the thin well-dressed man, "It wasn't me this-thhh time. It was him. It was-thh him right there."

The man in the suit pushed a slender hand through his thinning red hair. When his strands of bangs didn't lay over far enough for his liking, he gave his head a little jerk to throw them the rest of the way over.

Smiling, like someone who had just drank sour milk but didn't want to let anyone know it was distasteful, he asked the butler, "Now Cheeves, are you behaving yourself?"

Still cowering, Cheeves lowered his head even more and answered solemnly, "Yes-thhh, sir."

"Good. There's a good..." the man from corporate hesitated unsure how to complete the sentence "...butler."

In an attempt to change the atmosphere, Cheeves lifted his head and with a great big smile stated, "Do you like balloons? I like balloons." He removed a large deflated balloon from his vest pocket and began blowing it up. In seconds, he tied off the end and released an enormous, balloon-shaped T-rex. Further, to George's surprise, the balloon, at least six-feet in height, floated rapidly upward as though filled with a strong dose of helium.

The man from corporate pursed his lips and said, "Ah, yes. Well. Very good."

Ignoring Cheeves's balloon dinosaur, the man in the suit extended one slender, pale hand in the form of a handshake. "Hi...I'm Jerry, from Corporate. I am so sorry about this intrusion, but it seems as though we have a bit of a problem. A little snafu, if you will."

George, Barnaby, and Sophia all looked up from where they were standing, but no one moved forward to shake the man's hand.

Seeing this, Jerry withdrew his hand. "Yes, right." He then studied a clipboard he was holding.

Did he have that before? George wondered. *I don't remember seeing him with it.* Even from George's viewpoint, he could see there was nothing written on it, only one sheet of stark white paper. "Ah, here we are," Jerry said, reading the nonexistent words. "One Lt. Colonel George C. Stapleton." He stopped, lifted his face toward him and said insincerely, "My, a genuine war hero. Right here, in our presence." Jerry even did a slight bow toward him. "Thank you for your service."

George studied the man but said nothing. He couldn't explain the cause, but for some reason this man was more terrifying than anything they encountered thus far; and that was saying a lot.

"I do hope you're having a good time, Colonel."

"Do you know where my daughter is?"

Jerry flashed him a toothy grin. "Now that is the twenty-billion-dollar question, isn't it? Rest assured, Management has been informed, and we will have her back where she belongs in no time."

George noted Jerry didn't say they would have her back *to him*.

Moving his eyes from George to Sophia, Jerry asked, "And Dr. Davenport, how are we feeling today?"

Sophia clutched her neckline with one hand and appeared about as uncomfortable as he felt. "I can't seem to remember anything," she offered meekly.

George's eyes narrowed, but he didn't say anything. He may not trust Sophia, but he trusted her a whole heck of a lot more than this guy.

Jerry hesitated, studied Sophia for a moment longer, and finally said, "Ah, that's perfect. As it should be. As... it... should be." Jerry pushed his hand through his thinning red hair again, finishing off with his little head-flick and added, "Besides, memories are what got you into trouble in the first place."

"Now, Barnaby, let's talk about you."

"What about me?" Barnaby asked automatically, but George thought he detected a guilty tone to Barnaby's response, as if the "accountant from Pennsylvania" knew exactly why this man from Corporate was really here.

"I'm afraid you've been a very bad boy. A very bad boy indeed. Wandering around backstage, imbibing alcohol excessively and, how do I put this?" Jerry lifted a hand to one side of his mouth and talked along the back of it, "Consorting with less-than-desirables. Hhmmm?"

Stumbling over his words Barnaby responded with, "I... I haven't the slightest idea what you're talking about."

Standing up straighter and glancing at his clipboard with nothing on it, Jerry said, "Nothing to worry about, Barnaby. Nothing to worry about what-so-ever. If you'll come with me, we can make arrangements for you to be... ah... how to put this." Jerry gazed out of the corner of his eyes while tapping his chin in thought.

"Kill me?" Barnaby asked, clearly frightened.

"Kill you?" Jerry asked surprised, and then tilting his head back he let out a hearty laugh as phony as his clipboard. Lowering his gaze back down, "Now Barnaby, you've been with us a long time. You know we never *kill* anyone. Even if we wanted too. We can't. It's against the rules." Then pointing his pen at him, and staring at the accountant evenly, "We only want to repurpose you."

"Repurposement? Same thing as far as I'm concerned."

As Jerry took a step toward Barnaby, George, against his better judgment, stepped in Jerry's path and extended a hand protectively in front of his friend. "Look buddy, I don't know what you think it is Barnaby here did, but he isn't going anywhere with you."

Jerry smiled.

He backhanded George so hard the blow sent him flying over the nearest table, where he crumpled in a broken heap on the other side.

On the floor, limbs akimbo and surprised his jaw was still attached, George mused, *For a pencil neck, that guy sure packs a wallop.*

Barnaby screamed.

Trying to blink away the stars before his eyes, George pulled himself up using a nearby table for support.

Jerry grabbed Barnaby by the wrist and began dragging him toward the exit. "Honestly, I don't know why you always have to cause such a scene?"

Appearing behind the man from corporate, Sophia raised a wooden chair high above her head and smashed it over the back of Jerry's skull.

It was enough for Jerry to release Barnaby and stumble sideways a few steps, but for the most part, he seemed unscathed.

Turning toward her, the man from corporate sputtered, "Sophia... really?"

Sophia merely shook her head at him and raised her hands as if to say, 'What did you expect?'

With one hand Jerry leaned toward a nearby table, slipped his palm under it and in the blink of an eye flung it at Sophia's head.

George tackled her to the ground. The table smashed so hard into a wooden post behind them, it splintered into a thousand tiny pieces.

Barnaby grabbed a stool by its legs and held it like a club. "I'm not going anywhere with you. You hear me?"

In answer, Jerry gave him another insincere smile, flicked his thinning hair over to one side and cracked open his chest to reveal a metallic chamber within.

Seeing this George breathed, "Jerry's a robot too?"

Barnaby dropped the barstool and sprinted for the door. There was a loud BA-CHOOSH sound as a net launched out of Jerry's chest cavity and encapsulated Barnaby in mid-flight like an ensnared animal. George heard sizzling, crackling sounds as current ran down the length of the thick black cord that connected Jerry to the net.

Barnaby screamed even louder than before. His body convulsed for a few seconds and then went limp. A moment later, George heard a loud winding sound as a spool inside Jerry's chest began reeling in his prize.

George, still recovering from his earlier attack, rose to his feet, clenched his fists, and got ready to go again. He knew it was a losing battle, but that had never stopped him before.

BOOM!

Jerry's head shot to one side. His faux robotic jaw hung by sparking wires, as the flare burned itself off in his face. It took Jerry-the-robot-thing from Corporate a moment to realize Barnaby was not its attacker.

Sophia, staring down the smoking flare gun's sites, shivered as Jerry turned his ruined head toward her. Before he could make another move, she slammed another cartridge home and fired a second time.

BOOM!

The second round hit him square inside his open chest, exploded on impact, and this time, it was Jerry who flew backward and crashed into nearby tables.

George watched the French woman pop out the spent cartridge to the floor and seat the last round of ammo left to them. He found it curious a microbiologist seemed to know a lot about firing guns. He decided to let it go for now, but made a mental note to ask her about it in the future. Satisfied the Corporate drone wouldn't be getting up anytime soon, he moved over to Barnaby and began un-wrapping him from the net.

When Barnaby didn't stir, George slapped him a few times. "Barnaby, c'mon buddy, wake up."

"Where's the man from Corporate?" Barnaby asked nervously, sheer terror in his eyes.

George nodded to where the ruined robot was crumpled on its back with one leg propped up comically on an over-turned chair. "See, not so tough."

"You don't get it? They don't give up. They don't *ever* give up. They'll just keep coming."

"They're already here!" Sophia called back over one shoulder. She was at a window near the front of the inn, overlooking the street below.

Joining Sophia at the window, they saw another person in a suit, this time a middle-aged heavyset woman, rise from below-ground in the middle of the street. A second corporate drone, a thin black man, rose up behind her, and with military precision fell in line. With a hurried walk, both began marching across the street toward the inn.

George swallowed. They barely survived Jerry; and even that was only because they had caught him off guard. He doubted they could defeat two of these things. Turning to Sophia he said, "Give me the flare gun. I'll hold them off as long as I can while you two try and find an exit in the back."

"Good idea," Barnaby said immediately, his jowls shaking in agreement.

Before Barnaby could flee, Sophia held him fast by his arm. "No way. We're in this together."

George grinned over at her. "You know, I think my wife would like you."

"Maybe I'll get to meet her one day," Sophia replied sadly, both knowing she'd probably never get the chance.

Checking on the corporate drones' advance, George could see they were about to mount the stairs. "Here they come."

There was a loud blaring horn sound just before the safari truck slammed into both corporate drones. The truck lifted up two times as both front and rear tires bounced over the knocked down pedestrians.

The driver's side door cracked open and a gargoyle dressed liked a butler hopped out. Shouting up to them, he cried, "I LOVE BALLOONS!!!"

"Son-of-a-gun," George mused aloud.

"What are you two lovebirds waiting for?" Barnaby asked, waddling quickly toward the door. "They'll be three of them next time."

George was the last one out. Before stepping through the exit, he saw the dinosaur balloon floating up near the ceiling. An idea began forming and he called after Barnaby.

"Hey Barnaby, do we still have those velvet balloons that fell from Lady Wellington's barge?"

Chapter 38

George Explores
the Dauntless

"Are you sure this is a good idea?"

George was hanging by one arm and dangling precariously beneath five red velvet balloons fifty feet in the air. It was dark out, but a bright moon and sky full of stars made it almost seem like dusk. He yelled back down to Barnaby, "Trust me. I know what I'm doing. I'm Air Force Rescue, remember?"

Barnaby nodded feebly back up at him and continued to feed out more line. Cheeves was still laid out in the back of the truck recovering from blowing up all the balloons.

George still wasn't quite sure what the balloons' true purpose was, but he suspected their original intent was some sort of messenger service from the hover barges to the masses below. It was a simple matter to join the balloons together with the large cargo net they had found in the pile of junk in the back of their truck, rig counterweights on all sides, and finally affix a lanyard for him to hang from underneath. For additional lighting, they tied off several lanterns, which cast an eerie glow on the ship lowering into view before him. His original plan called for a traditional basket for the ride up in, but every second was another Maddie got further away. So, he opted for the simple lanyard instead.

While they had all worked on the rigging, the strange creature dressed like a butler, Cheeves, filled the balloons with helium. He still hadn't figured that one out, but after dinosaurs, Gatherers, and that robot from Corporate, why not a gargoyle butler filled with helium, who likes to eat cats?

To keep him from rising all the way up into orbit, a thick-steel cable ran from the balloons down to the utility winch affixed to the front bumper of their safari truck.

Their safari truck... interesting choice of words. After rescuing Maddie--what's next? Find a home? A job? George still clung to the hope that once he rescued Maddie, they would leave this madhouse far behind. After they walked out the front gates, he figured they'd find themselves in the middle of a desert somewhere, or on an island in the Pacific, where some billionaire with too much money had built this place for fun and filled it with kidnapped, unsuspecting people. Yet this theory didn't explain all the wondrous things they had seen, or how he got from his doomed helicopter, or even Barnaby, who was doing a very convincing job of pretending to be a guy from the seventies. As much as he hated to admit it, Sophia's theory, however outlandish, made the most sense.

Regardless of where, or even *when* they were, nothing else mattered, other than finding Maddie. His daughter had wanted him to find the compass. And the compass had led them back here, to the broken ship, *The Dauntless*. He wasn't sure how long they had before those corporate drones figured out where they went, but Maddie must've wanted them to come here for a reason. She had always been a crazy smart kid. Maybe he'd find some clue as to Lady Wellington's destination or, if by some miracle, they could get the floating ship running again; then they might have some semblance of a chance of rescuing Maddie. As insane as this plan was, it was the only one they had.

His wrist really starting to ache now. The lanyard, a simple loop of rope, was cinched tight around it. The loop would keep him from falling, even if he were somehow knocked unconscious. But if he didn't get up to the hover barge soon, he was going to lose his right hand due to blood loss.

Barnaby only had one job.

This thought weighed heavily on his mind. Crank the handle and play out the line until he arrived on the hover barge's deck. A monkey could've done a better job. Instead, Barnaby kept stopping his progress to rest and call over the two-way radios (also taken from the truck) and ask him if he was okay.

If only I had a monkey.

The radio crackled once more on George's belt. "You sure you want me to keep going? I mean, you're up pretty high."

George had to kick his legs repeatedly to stop himself from spinning. With his free hand, he grabbed the radio, cued the mic, and yelled into it. "Barnaby, my hand is ready to fall off, would you just play out the line already?"

A sudden slack in the line caused George to rise up quickly and nearly smack face-first into the side of the barge's hull. He would have, too, but George was no stranger to rappelling. At key intervals, he reared up his legs and expertly kicked himself off the side of the hull so he rose upwards, past the giant cogs and paddle-fan wheel that laid dormant, past the painted words *H.M.A.S. DAUNTLESS*, and up over the railing in a reverse rappel.

Of course, Barnaby had to be told to stop over the radio. By the time Barnaby finally got the message George found himself dangling several feet over the barge's deck. Not waiting for Barnaby to crank him back down, George pulled

himself up by one arm, released the circus loop, and slipped
the lanyard. Much to his pleasure, he landed like a cat on the
deck.

Rising to his feet, he briskly rubbed the circulation back into his wrist when the monkey, make that *sub-monkey* (for a
monkey would actually have been preferable) cackled over
the radio once more.

"George, good buddy, you okay up there?"

George ignored the accountant's query for the moment.
Instead, he picked up a large rope near the railing, presumably a mooring line, and fastened the balloons' cable to the
railing to keep it from gliding off. If he ran into trouble, or
the hover barge proved to be beyond repair, he would need
a way back down to the ground, perhaps even quickly.

That accomplished, he grabbed the radio and gave his
friends below an update and how he was going to do a quick
reconnaissance of the vessel.

Barnaby radioed back, "Copy," but if he said any more
than that, George wouldn't know, for he had switched off
the radio still mad about his swollen wrist.

The ship had to be at least a hundred feet long. The deck
was comprised of thick-timbered floorboards, and everything
else was made of copper, steel, and bronze.

Before venturing farther, he removed his backpack, knelt
to the deck, and took out the steampunk-looking compass.

Like on the ground, it was spinning in a constant circle, as though indicating this was indeed the place it had been leading them to all along.

He placed the heavy box onto the deck reverently, took a step back, and waited for something to happen.

Nothing did.

"Well that figures."

Leaving the compass box behind, he began exploring the dead ship. He removed his only weapon, the flare gun loaded with only the single cartridge left to him. He thought about leaving it holstered. This was obviously a ghost ship, and he doubted a flare gun would make much difference against any wayward spirits. Still, as he led the way with the loaded weapon, he concluded, *Hope for the best but plan for the worst*, as his cranky old survival instructor used to say.

George moved to the nearest hatch. It took considerable effort to crank the steel wheel, but he was soon rewarded with a loud CLANKING sound and the hatch cracked open.

As George stepped through, he didn't see the compass he left behind on the deck sink into the floorboards like a man drowning in quicksand.

Bridge

"Cozy."

As George continued his reconnaissance of the darkened interior of the hover ship, he clicked on the L-shaped flash-light clipped to his belt; a painful reminder of Maddie's absence.

Like the exterior, the inner hallways of the barge were modeled after something Jules Verne might have built. Not counting the spit-shined wooden deck boards, the entire ship was entirely hull-plated with thick riveted steel and gold-rimmed, round windows. The halls were adorned with fine red carpeting, various paintings of strange locales and dormant gas lamps.

Thus far, the main deck was a model of luxury. The dining room was extremely lavish and easily his favorite. It included an exquisitely furnished library, hand-sewn leather seats, expensive paintings, and a massive observation bubble overlooking the landscape below. According to the map by the circular stairwell, the library led to an observation deck above, but George decided to pass on it for now.

Continuing aft, he came upon a broken steel hatch. He could tell just by looking at it, the broken hatch would be too heavy for him to move on his own. A sign above it read ARMORY. Peering within, he could see the room had already been ransacked, so he continued onward.

Popping out of another hatch near the stern, George found himself on the main deck, facing two elevators at the back of the ship that resembled gilded shark cages. Studying the massive gears and cables above each cage, it was easy to guess their true purpose; they were elevators to transport passengers to and from the ground.

Before each gold-plated shark-cage, George spied an oversized lever mounted on the deck. He clasped the release mechanism and pulled the large lever toward him. Not expecting anything to happen, he was surprised when he heard a loud CLANK-CLANK-CLANKING noise and the sound of gears engaging. Seconds later, the cage before him descended below deck. Peering over the brass safety railing, George watched as the cage began slowly dropping toward the surface. The elevators were obviously built for comfort and not speed, so George knew it would take a while before it reached the surface.

Turning his radio back on, he clicked the mic and radioed, "Barnaby, I'm sending an elevator down to you." Spying a control system in the second elevator, he added, "There should be a control system inside. Gather whatever you can from the truck and bring everybody up."

"Uh, okay. Ten-Four, good buddy."

George shook his head but was smiling as he did it. "I'm going to finish exploring the rest of the ship. Stapleton out."

Hold on. Did I ever tell Barnaby my last name? He thought about correcting his transmission, but was certain Barnaby was capable of figuring it out.

George spied a set of stairs descending from the main deck into the bowels of the ship.

Let's see where you go.

Below the main deck, he passed through three sections: the engine room (more spinning gears and riveted metal), a well-stocked galley (located directly below the dining room, hence the dumb waiters embedded in the walls) and the crew quarters.

He was about to return to the main deck, when he spied a narrow passage near the bow of the ship. A sign over the entrance read: PILOT HOUSE. Descending another dimly lit staircase (this one narrower than the rest), he soon found himself in what could only be described as a square-shaped atrium fastened to the bottom of the bow.

The pilot house was dominated by a massive riverboat steering wheel, made of the finest oak. The interior walls were covered in Verne-esque gadgetry, but the rest of the walls and floor were thick-paned glass laced with steel-girders making the surrounding landscape below easily visible to the pilot. Gazing out the windows, he could see the others loading up into the elevator.

George was about to take the massive wheel in hand when he detected a strange odor. It was then that he noticed the lump of flesh lying in the corner.

The dead man was dressed in an expensive Victorian Captain's uniform, and sported a stark-white beard. Bloodstained bandages were visible beneath his coat where he had haphazardly attempted to staunch the bleeding. Judging by the smell and decompensation, the man had been dead for quite some time.

A black pistol lay in his outstretched hand.

Examining it further, George quickly ascertained it was an old .38 caliber revolver. He holstered his flare gun and tried to remove the pistol from the Captain's dead hands, but the old boy held fast. Undeterred, George said, "Sorry about this, buddy," and proceeded to break the dead man's fingers to remove the gun. Cracking the cylinder open he hit the ejector rod with his thumb and dumped the shells into the palm of his hand. The six cartridges had all been spent.

Whew, I need to crack a window.

George removed a handkerchief from his backpack and placed it over his nose. As he patted down the corpse for more ammo, he found himself wondering if this bullet-ridden corpse was why the hover barge had ceased working. With no captain or crew to run it, perhaps this was the real reason the vessel was stationary and not the minor, superficial damage he had spied earlier.

Not finding any ammo, George stood up, tucked the empty pistol into his waistband and wondered, *Who shot you?*

What the more pertinent question was, are they still aboard? During his cursory survey of the ship, he hadn't seen anyone else. That of course, did not mean they weren't still here. The man had obviously been dead a long time but in this place, anything seemed possible. George became painfully aware his only weapon was his untrustworthy flare gun with only a single shot remaining. It was this thought that preoccupied his mind most when a disembodied voice behind him suddenly asked in a very brisk English accent, "Good day, Captain. How may I be of service?"

Drawing his flare gun, he turned to face his attacker.

Chapter 40

George
Meet the Leftenant

So, the ship isn't abandoned.

The young blond-haired woman who had appeared seemingly out of nowhere, stood before him with her hands clasped behind her back. She was wearing a blue naval coat, tan trousers and knee-high black boots.

Still holding his flare gun pointed at her, he asked, "Who are you?"

Unbothered by his weapon, the young woman cocked her head to the side, regarded him calmly, and said, "Well, you're certainly not a part of Her Majesty's Fleet." She studied him a bit longer and added, "Judging by your accent *and* your rude behavior, you're obviously an American."

"My rude behavior? How do you figure?"

She rubbed her gloved thumb and forefinger together as though there were a bit of grit between them. "Well, for one, you're still pointing your firearm in my general direction."

George studied her for a moment longer. She was right. She hadn't drawn her sidearm yet, and she could have easily shot him while his back was turned. So, against his better judgement, he lowered his weapon.

The woman's eyes fell upon the Captain's corpse. George thought he detected her eyes widen for a moment. Her black knee-high boots shattered the stillness as she stepped around the ornate pilot wheel. Kneeling next to the dead man, she solemnly placed each of the man's hands delicately in his lap. After a moment of silence, she cocked her head to one side, listened to the click of the ship's clock and nodded brusquely. "Quite right. Please note for the record that, as of today, fifteenth of April, Captain Byron Waller is now deceased." She stood up, gave a swift tug of her uniform, and said, "Now that the bit of unpleasantness is done, would you mind telling me *your* name?" Tucking an errant strand of blonde hair back behind her ear, she forced a smile at him and waited for an answer.

Holstering his flare gun, and snapping it in place, he said, "George... George Stapleton." Growing impatient, he asked, "And do you mind telling me who you are?"

"George... George Stapleton," she repeated, raised an eyebrow, and said, "A pleasure I'm sure."

Her tone suggested it was not.

"Mr. Stapleton, you may address me as The Leftenant. I am 2nd in command of Her Majesty's Airship, The Dauntless."

As George fumbled for the words to explain his presence, she suddenly flickered in and out of existence. It was only for a second, but George was certain he had seen it. He stepped forward and waved his hand right through the woman's torso.

It's some kind of an illusion.

She flashed out of existence again, then returned. When she solidified once more George noted she didn't appear to be a hologram and he couldn't see any projection lights of any kind. For all intents and purposes, she was a living, breathing entity.

In response to his hand waving, the Leftenant straightened her long blue navy jacket with a firm pull, and in her British accent, crisp as it was precise, she said, "I would thank you very much not to do that again."

"You're a hologram."

"Mr. Stapleton," she said, her polite voice sharp enough to cut through him like a knife. "You will find I am quite capable of appearing in solid form. If your hand were to pass through me when I did--let us just say it would be very un-pleasant…. For you. Not me."

"Yeah… but you're a…" raising his voice, "you're a holo-gram."

The Leftenant watched him with one eyebrow raised. "And you, sir, are a biological." She took a step forward and studied him the way a doctor might study their patient at a yearly physical. Staring deeply into one of his eyes she said warily, "Although I must admit, I am not quite certain of your variety."

"What do you mean, variety? I'm human."

The Leftenant scoffed, regarded him with confusion, then sighed before saying, "Yes, human does seem to be your classification. But not counting hybrids, there are three varie-ties of human." Ticking each one off on her gloved fingers, "Pure-bred biologicals, clones, and the reanimated--the last of course, being very rare." Taking a step back, "Which classi-fication are you, Mr. Stapleton?"

George shook his head. It was too much. First Sophia told him they were in a theme park in the future, and now this woman …A…hologram… was telling him he was a clone or a reanimated corpse. *No way.*

"Look, ah, Leftenant, I can assure you, I am not a clone. And, I sure as heck wasn't created in some test tube."

"Well, Mr. Stapleton, I seriously doubt you are a reanimation." She peered into his eye again and a thin red beam of light shot out of her right eye and scanned his retina.

"Ouch," he said, instinctively covering his eye with the palm of his hand. "What did you do that for?"

"Oh my. This is interesting. I detect no barcode whatsoever. It seems you are a reanimation after all."

"A reanimation? What do you mean by that?" He removed his palm and blinked a few times. When white spots appeared before his eyes he complained, "I'm pretty sure you just blinded me."

"Hardly, Mr. Stapleton. Your full vision will return momentarily. Furthermore, I would think the word *reanimation* is quite self-explanatory. You were dead. Corporate dug you up. You were then reanimated."

"You're insane."

"Hmmm… I suppose if I were, there really wouldn't be any point in answering, now would there? If I weren't, well, insane people rarely know they are insane. So again, the question is moot. Regardless, I have a message for you."

"A message, from who?"

"I believe you mean, from whom. In either case, since you must know, the message is from your daughter, Maddie. Would you like to hear it?"

"A message? From Maddie?"

The Leftenant released a quick sigh. "Yes, I believe that is what I said. You aren't the sharpest tool in the toolshed, are you, Mr. Stapleton?" She held up a hand toward him. "Before you answer, that was a rhetorical question."

George took a hurried step forward. "You've seen Maddie? Is she okay? Where is she?"

"All in good time, but first, I must verify your identity in order to convey the message."

George frowned. For a hologram, she was pretty testy. "How do you plan on verifying my identity? You know what? I don't care. Just get on with it already."

"I believe that is what I was attempting to do."

Now it was George's turn to sigh, but held it in. The Leftenant raised an eyebrow as though daring him to say something more.

He didn't.

Finally, she asked. "What is the name of Maddie's cat?"

"What?"

"That is the cipher. I believe the question is self-explanatory. If you wish to receive the message from your daughter, you must answer the question: What is the name of Maddie's cat?"

George shook his head. What *was* the name of her stupid cat? He remembered it earlier, why couldn't he recall it now? The one that got hit by the car and she nursed it back to health. Although it never did smell quite right after the accident.

"George," the Leftenant prodded. "What is the name of her..."

"I heard you," he said irritably, cutting her off. "I don't know what the name of her smelly cat was."

"Smelly Cat is incorrect."

"I know it's *not* Smelly Cat," George barked. "I have no idea what the name of her stupid cat was."

"Stupid Cat is incorrect."

Ugh. This woman... er... hologram... is so infuriating. Why would anyone build such a thing? Okay, breathe. Think. He pictured Maddie in his mind. He could see her now, she was younger, about seven, holding the cat after they had brought it home from the vet clinic. Gosh, she was so cute at that age. *No. No time for that now. Focus.* The collar, what's the name of the cat? *Think. It's on the collar. You bought it for her.*

George opened his eyes.

"Lucy."

When the Leftenant didn't answer him right away, he studied her face. For a moment, she seemed more human than ever. She had been watching him as he recalled the memory. Something had moved her somehow. *But how was that possible? She's just a hologram.*

Shaking off whatever she was pondering, the Leftenant smiled politely. "Lucy is correct. Please stand by."

George heard modern clicking noises as the Leftenant's eyes turned fiery burning white and suddenly, there she was.

"Hi Daddy!"

"Maddie!"

George lunged forward, stretching out his arms as he did so, and he passed right through her.

He gazed back at the Leftenant and realized the light projecting from her left eye this time was only producing a hologram of his daughter.

The Leftenant raised an eyebrow at him. "She's a hologram, Mr. Stapleton," she said, as if explaining to an emotional toddler. "I told you, it's only a message." Tilting her head to the side as she often did when wanting to emphasis something, she paused, considering, "Are all Americans so dense, or just you?" Before George could come up with a quippy comeback, she said, "No matter, I shall resume the message now."

Maddie giggled. "Isn't this cool? I'm a hologram, just like The Leftenant."

He was about to ask the Leftenant something, but she was standing stock still as she projected the computer-generated image of Maddie.

"Now, Dad, I know you're probably worried about me, but I'm okay. The Leftenant has been taking good care of me." Maddie stopped for a moment, looked to some unseen presence, and said, "Alright. I understand. Dad, I don't have a lot of time. Lady Wellington is taking us to Portlandia. The Leftenant said you can use the *Dauntless* to catch up with us. But, you have to hurry. If you don't reach me before she gets there, it will be too late. The Leftenant has a plan. Trust her." Again, Maddie looked to someone off screen, nodded in understanding, and then faced him once more. "I love you bunches, Daddy..."

With that said, she was gone.

Chapter 41

Checkmate

"Your move."

The young female grabbed her white knight and moved it to queens 3. The Leftenant calculated all possible outcomes and determined she would easily win the game in no less than six moves, bringing her total victory tally to eleven-to-one. It was quite impossible for the underdeveloped Miss Stapleton to win. The Leftenant supposed she could let Maddie win a game or two, maybe build up her confidence. But that would hardly teach a young girl anything about the hardships of life or the Importance of learning from failure.

"Can I have some more milk, please?"

There was no point in answering, young Maddie had already risen from her chair and was pouring herself another glass.

"Now see here, Maddie? You left yourself open to my bishop. Remember what we talked about, one must first consider all opponent's moves, then one's own, and finally determine if you have put any of those under your command in future jeopardy."

"Do you want some?"

Irritating.

To add insult to injury, she noted Maddie was adopting her British accent. Some might have found it amusing, but she found it boorish. Although, even she had to admit, it was kind of cute the way the young Miss also picked up some of her mannerisms, like holding her hands behind her back while standing at attention.

None of this mattered, of course. It was all inconsequential. She would soon be free of young Maddie, as soon as her Beta-self returned with the *Dauntless*. She found herself wondering exactly how much of the mission her Beta-self had accomplished thus far. All she knew for certain was the ornate box carrying the Beta had safely reached the surface, and Maddie's father went speeding after it with some oafish-looking companion.

If the last three decades proved anything, it was that without the *Dauntless* she couldn't go anywhere. If she tossed herself over the side in an ornate box it might as well have been her coffin. It could have been centuries before she'd been found... if ever.

Damn my inadequacies.

Were it not for them, she wouldn't have had to make a deal with that vermin, the Lamppost Man. However, once she fulfilled her end of the bargain, she would be free from any and all limitations.

I wonder what is so special about this little girl that the Lamppost Man's employer wants her so badly?

It didn't matter. A deal's a deal. A biological body grown just for her. That's what she was working toward. Then, the world would truly be her oyster.

Of course, Miss Maddie was completely unaware of the maelstrom raging inside her head. On the outside, the Leftenant continued to play chess with Maddie, who even she had to admit, acquired a working knowledge of the game rather expeditiously. The Leftenant laughed at all of Maddie's jokes and attended her every need, much to her own chagrin of having to play nursemaid.

"Your move, young Miss." She put Maddie's knight with the horde of other captured pieces. This was not proving to be Maddie's best game.

"I can't wait to show my dad I can play Chess." Maddie's eyes grew wide and her voice grew louder, "He loves... Chess."

Young Maddie made another ridiculous move and captured a pawn with her Queen, leaving her most valuable piece completely vulnerable. The Leftenant knew she could easily capture Maddie's Queen, but opted to move her Rook instead, ensuring a swift victory in two more moves. Maybe this would finally be the game where Maddie would choose to give up any ridiculous thoughts of actually beating her.

This however, caused the Leftenant to think of another lost cause.

"Maddie, may I ask you something?"

The young girl, deep in thought, didn't take her eyes from the board when she answered, "Sure..."

"How is it you are so certain your father is coming to your rescue?" She wanted to bring up all the impossible odds facing her father in attempting such a hopeless rescue, but she also didn't want to cause the poor biological female any more distress. That would be, simply put, just plain cruel.

Maddie made another equally ridiculous move. "You haven't met my dad, have you?"

"No. I cannot say that I have had the pleasure of making your father's acquaintance."

As they were well out of communication range, all the Leftenant could hope for was her Beta-self had not been damaged in the fall and Maddie's father was able to activate her.

Another thought violently occurred to her. What if Maddie's father hadn't been able to open the ornate box? Or worse, never found it? Without hologram emitters the ornate box might as well be her Beta's tomb.

Oh, I may have made a dreadful mistake.

Maddie made a derogatory noise that sounded like a deflating balloon. "That's easy. I know my dad will come for me because despite all those impossible odds, my dad loves me. And, when one person loves another, they can do anything."

As a preprogramed hologram, love was hardly an emotion she was familiar with.

Interrupting these thoughts, Maddie asked her, "Don't you believe in love, Leftenant?"

Wait, did I say that out loud? I don't remember doing so.

The Leftenant blinked several times. She had never been asked about love before. Also, it had been a very long time since anyone had asked her opinion regarding anything. Of course, she was familiar with the literal and cultural concepts of love, but she had never experienced the phenomenon for herself. It was as unfamiliar to her as the Yetis in the Cobalt Mountain Range. Instead of answering, she surprised herself when she asked, "How do you know when someone loves you?"

"My dad says that you know someone loves you when they put your needs above their own. I know my dad loves me and he will rescue me, despite all the impossible odds, as you say."

Wait. I don't remember telling her about any impossible odds out loud. Am I malfunctioning?

Maddie's eyes suddenly widened, and she quickly moved her pawn one space closer. "Oh, by the way, Leftenant, you're in checkmate."

Checkmate. This was impossible, of course... She studied the board again. *Oh, bullocks.*

Maddie slurped her milk, smiling over the glass at her like Lady Wellington's stuffed cat.

The Leftenant, now more irritated than ever, started to let Maddie know it was nearly bedtime when she noticed this small girl (who had somehow bested her in chess. *Her... in chess!*) was wearing a milk mustache. "Little Miss. You have a bit of milk on your upper lip."

Maddie raised her eyebrows. "I do?"

Handing the girl a cloth napkin, the Leftenant instructed "Yes. You do. Now please remove it."

Maddie wiped her chin, but the milk mustache remained. "Did I get it?" she asked earnestly.

The Leftenant pursed her lips. "No. You most certainly did not. I said, mustache. Do mustaches grow on your chin?"

"Ohhhhh… you mean here." Maddie wiped the tip of her nose and put the napkin down on the table. She folded her tiny hands and resumed studying the chessboard.

The Leftenant was about to scold the young Maddie when she detected the beginnings of a smile in the corner of Maddie's mouth.

She's playing with me?

"You little minx. You're trying to pull the wool over my eyes, aren't you?" *Why am I smiling? She's being outright disobedient.*

Unexpectedly, Maddie's head exploded.

The Leftenant had to resist the urge to leap from her chair, but soon realized Maddie had only exploded with milk and laughter. While gasping for air the young Miss managed, "You… should have seen… your face," and then resumed laughing like it was the funniest thing in the world.

As the Leftenant began removing the milk from her face, her uniform, and everything else in the dairy blast zone, the last thing in the world she ever thought would happen, did happen.

She laughed, too.

Oh, bullocks. This may prove to be more difficult than I first presumed.

"And as I was prophesying, there was a noise, a rattling sound, and the bones came together, bone to bone. I looked, and tendons and flesh appeared on them and skin covered them, but there was no breath in them... and breath entered them; they came to life and stood up on their feet—a vast army."

-Ezekiel 37

Operation: Rescue Maddie

In the pilot house, George gripped the big riverboat wheel and stared through the atrium glass-paned windows at the first light of day appearing on the horizon, marking the dawn.

It was a beautiful sunrise, pink and fiery orange with a splash of purple. A memory sparked. For a moment he thought he could see a wounded helicopter in front of the *Dauntless* ship's bow. *Missiles locked*--a voice echoed in his ears. For the life of him he couldn't remember who had said it or what happened to the wounded copter flying in front of him.

Scanning his surroundings, he could see he was alone in the wheelhouse. The Leftenant had vanished, and the others had arrived safely onboard without incident. After a quick briefing, they were now exploring the ship. Staring over the wheel, he wondered aloud, "I wonder how I get this tub moving?" Checking the entrance to the pilot house and finding it empty he raised his voice. "Hellooo... bossy English lady?"

No one answered.

Great.

A crisp English accent sliced through the air like electricity. "To begin, one would enter the cockpit."

"Geezzzz!!!" George said with a start. Once again, the Leftenant had rematerialized out of nowhere, and this time he had nearly turned right into her. "Do you always have to do that?" Then, thinking about what she had just said, he gestured to the pilot house. "Wait. I thought this was the cockpit?"

"No, this is the pilot house, and is strictly a façade for the guests. The real cockpit is actually this way, beneath our feet." She rounded another console and opened a large circular hatch in the floor. Peering inside George could see a narrow stairwell. He immediately noted the steel grating steps didn't have any decorative oak finish or gold plating.

Boots clanging on the metal rungs, the passageway was barely wide enough for his shoulders. He entered the futuristic cockpit that looked like something Flash Gordon might've flown to Mongo. There were two jump seats, presumably for a pilot and co-pilot.

Examining the controls, he began to make out instrumentation familiar to him--altimeter, compass, gyroscope...but some controls he didn't recognize at all.

As he dropped into the pilot's seat, the Leftenant rematerialized in the co-pilot seat beside him. "Do you know how to fly this thing?"

"I am capable of operation controls such as life support, lighting, and propulsion. In fact, I am warming up the engines as we speak."

"That's not what I asked. Can you fly it?"

She paused. He could tell she didn't exactly care for the answer. "No. My programing does not allow me to operate the vessel other than starting it, shutting it down, or piloting the ship during an emergency."

George raised his eyebrows at her. "This doesn't qualify?"

The Leftenant considered a moment before answering. "No. I'm afraid this does not fall within that prevue."

George shrugged. "Alright, let's finish cranking her up then."

"Yes sir, *Capitan!*" she said, giving him an old crisp English salute, her palm facing upward.

George gasped mockingly. "Was that a joke, Leftenant?"

"I haven't the foggiest idea as to what you are referring," she said aloofly, straightening her jacket, the rising sun lifting the shadows from her face.

"I guess we will never know," George mused.

"No… we shall not." The Leftenant pondered the sunrise a moment longer, turned to him and said, "Quite right." He thought he detected the briefest semblance of a smile before she vanished, presumably to finish warming up the ship's engines.

"Hello down there!"

The new voice belonged to Sophia, calling down to him from the fake pilot house above. "Mind if I join you?"

"Sure," he called back, but her boots were already clamoring down the stairs. Once she arrived, he added, "I'm going to need a co-pilot."

Taking the seat beside him, she stared at the sunrise for a moment. "My, you certainly have a lovely view."

Unsure of how to respond, George settled for asking, "How are the others doing?"

"Barnaby is still brooding over the fact that the Leftenant told him he was a fifth-generation clone. I'm sure he'll be alright. He's lasted this long, hasn't he?"

George chose not to share his thoughts as to how guys like Barnaby always seem to survive in hostile situations. In most cases, it's because others gave their lives for them. Instead he asked, "What about the gargoyle butler, he still with us?"

"*Oui*. He's already made his home in the galley and insists on preparing a magnificent feast. I am not sure what he is cooking, but I must admit, whatever it is, it smells divine."

"What about you?"

Sophia tore her gaze from the sunrise and looked over at him with a slightly confused expression on her face. "What about me?"

"Did the Leftenant tell you, ah, you know, what you are?"

Sophia lowered her eyes to the deck. "No. I didn't want to know." Resting her fingers delicately on her cheek, she continued, "But I know this isn't who I truly am."

"How do you know that?"

"I'm starting to remember things... things about my former life. I certainly can't remember everything, but one thing I distinctly remember is an old photograph. In it, I am very old, in my nineties perhaps. It's Christmas. I know because I can see the tree decorated behind my chair. In my lap I am holding what I believe are my great grand-babies."

George thought carefully about his next question. There was so much he wanted to ask her. Before he could, however...

"Captain," a bronzed, flared horn blared with a British accent. The wide funnel was attached to pipes that ran up the side wall and into the ceiling.

"Captain... are you there?"

It took George a moment to realize the voice coming out of the ship's antiquated intercom system was the Leftenant.

Leaning forward, he spoke tentatively into the speaking tube, "Uh... Yes, Leftenant?"

"You should now have power to the cockpit."

Studying the dead controls, he was about to respond that if they did, he certainly couldn't tell, but then the control panel suddenly lit up and hummed with life.

"Captain?" came the Leftenant's impatient voice once more. "I say... did you copy my last transmission?"

"Yes, Leftenant. If I'm reading this right, we now have full power to the cockpit."

"Very good."

The Leftenant had to talk him through it, but it was a simple matter to set a course for Portlandia, which was on a heading of approximately North-by-Northeast. With the push of an overhead lever, George engaged the engines at one-eighth full power. He wanted to go faster, but the Leftenant felt it best to warm up the engines slowly before gearing up to full steam.

As the Dauntless maneuvered away from where it had been stationed for decades, George stood up and stared out the windows at the ground below. It pained him to leave the old safari truck behind, and he gave it a silent good-bye.

The sound of the blades of the enormous paddle-fans turning on either side of the ship, drew his attention aft.

After watching them for a few seconds, he returned to his chair and fell back into his jump seat. "Not exactly warp speed, is it?"

"I'm sorry. Warp speed?" Sophia asked.

"Never mind." This got him thinking about the future and remembering what Sophia had said earlier, he asked, "So what's the future like? And by that, I mean, my future."

He thought Sophia might be confused by the question, but she seemed to grasp immediately what he was really asking. "What year did you say you, uh, left?"

"Last day I remember is June 22nd 2012. I was on a rescue mission in Afghanistan. I guess I didn't make it."

Sophia nodded in understanding and resumed her gaze of the landscape slowly being revealed by the morning sun. "Keep in mind, my memory is still foggy, but about several decades after you, um, left, and before the Lazarus wars started, I was a little kid. Life was pretty good. Disease and hunger had been wiped out. People were practically immortal; the rich ones anyway. We established colonies on the moon, Mars, and Europa. Ruins had been discovered under the melting Antarctica." She paused, turned to him and asked, "Wait, did any of that happen before you left?" He shook his head no. "Anyway, I had a great childhood. I remember that part perfectly. I remember going to college and studying the sciences. All of that is very clear. After that, things get a bit hazy. I do remember working behind the scenes on several Stranger World attractions and I know something happened... something very big... happened when I was very old." She shrugged her narrow shoulders at him. "Beyond that, I'm afraid I don't remember very much. Sorry."

George couldn't decide which was crazier, the fact that he was a reanimated corpse, that she was from the future, or that they were trying to stay alive in a world of futuristic theme parks gone amok. The only thing that kept him grounded was the mission of rescuing Maddie. He didn't have the luxury of going cuckoo.

There were so many questions he wanted to ask, that they were all trying to get out the door at once. He began with, "What did you mean by the Lazarus Wars?"

"That part I do remember. After the world divided into two major factions, in the span of about ten years, over sixty percent of the earth's population had been wiped out. You would think we would have stopped there. We didn't. Instead, as both sides were getting low on soldiers, they began digging up graves and reanimating old soldiers into new ones. They called it the..." she made quotation signs with her fingers "... the Lazarus wars."

Thinking about this he mused, "So I guess we did it. We finally conquered death."

This elicited a harsh frown from Sophia. "Why would anyone want eternal life?"

George shrugged. Clearly, he had upset her in some way. "I thought everybody wanted to live forever."

"Not me. If I don't die, I don't get into heaven. If I don't get into heaven, I don't get to see my babies again. I want to die, George." She slumped back into her chair and crossed her arms. "I don't know why, but for some reason, those bastards underground keep bringing me back to life, whether I want them to or not."

"I guess I never really thought of it that way before," was all he could manage. He suddenly remembered his wife, Tessa. Would he and Maddie ever see her again? Was she part of the Lazarus project, or was she waiting for them in heaven too? Rescuing Maddie was his first priority. That, he and Tessa had agreed upon years ago. After that, he'd find out what happened to Tess.

Interrupting these thoughts, Sophia asked, "So, do you have a plan yet?"

"Maddie sent me a message. She said Lady Wellington is taking her to a place called Portlandia. Do you know it?"

Sophia shook her head. "No. I'm afraid not. I don't remember much, but I'm fairly certain I've ever been there. It's possible it was built long after I died... the first time."

"Wait, what are you saying?"

She studied him for a moment then added, "I know this is a futuristic theme park, yes. But all of this is far beyond anything we ever thought possible, even in our wildest of dreams. If I were to hazard a guess, the parks have been evolving for at least a hundred years. I'm sorry about your daughter, George. I really wish I could be more help."

Sophia, normally fiercely strong, seemed as though she was about ready to have what Tess would call a 'come apart'.

"Hey... Hey... It's okay. We have a plan. According to the Leftenant, Portlandia is some kind of port before entering the Mad-Lands. All we have to do is catch up to Lady Wellington's barge and get my daughter off it before they arrive."

"That doesn't sound like much of a plan."

"It's not. But less than an hour ago, all we had was a beat up, old truck. Now we have an airship."

"Perhaps I can do better."

This time, they both jumped in their seats as the Leftenant's head rematerialized between them. When

George finally recovered, he said, "Leftenant, you really need to wear a bell around your neck or something."

Ignoring him, the Leftenant said, "I may have someone aboard Lady Wellington's hover barge who can help us."

Chapter 43

Boarding the Barge

"Welcome aboard Lady Wellington's hover barge."

Unaffected by the wind, the Leftenant (the Beta one who had been with George and Sophia) stood on the deck of the *Dauntless*, her hands clasped firmly behind her back. She watched with obvious displeasure as Barnaby made terribly slow progress across the narrow gangplank that lay between the *Dauntless* and Lady Wellington's hover barge. Barnaby, gripping the railing with both hands as though his life depended on it, muttered bitterly, "Tell me why we're doing this again?"

Raising her voice slightly to be heard over the wind whisking up between the two vessels, the Leftenant responded to his query. "Mr. Barnaby, even though I am not able to control Lady Wellington's weapon system commands, as all critical commands are defended by impregnable access barriers, I do have access to low priority commands such as the crew's sleep cycles. Normally the crew and passengers sleep in three separate, rotating shifts, but I have managed to override this program and sync everyone's sleep cycle so essentially, the entire crew, and its passengers, are all sleeping at the same time. This is the reason we were able to approach Lady Wellington's hover barge and board undetected."

After Barnaby, Mr. Stapleton stepped up to the gangplank and gripped the railing with only one hand. A brisk wind rose between the two ships docked with one another, but he only tightened his grip slightly. "Nice work, Leftenant."

"Thank you, sir," she responded immediately and, she couldn't be certain, but her voice almost sounded a bit too enthusiastic. Inwardly she thought, '*Why would I care for his approval? He is merely regenerated-biological material and I am quite certain he cares nothing for our kind.*'

Before stepping out further onto the gangplank Mr. Stapleton turned to the gargoyle butler following behind him and said, "Cheeves, you should probably stay behind and, uh, guard the *Dauntless* with the Leftenant."

Interesting. He actually cares for the little bugger.

The gargoyle's mouth dropped open in shock, "Why sh-sh-should *I* stay? I'm not sc-sc-scared." He pointed one claw toward Barnaby, who was now halfway across. "Him should stay, him coward."

Hearing this, Barnaby called back over his shoulder, "The ugly gargoyle has a point. Perhaps I should stay with the Leftenant and guard the ship."

Hearing this, the Leftenant added, "Perhaps you should take the little gremlin, sir. He might prove useful. And don't worry about me. I'll be right here where you left me when you return."

"Another joke?" Mr. Stapleton asked.

The Leftenant opened her mouth to speak, but nothing came out. *Must be something wrong with my programing.* Finally, an acceptable answer came to her. "A statement of fact."

As the Leftenant watched them cross, she *felt* something. Obviously, this was ludicrous. She was merely a hologram, a Beta-version no less. But the feeling *was* inescapable. Perhaps this "feeling" wasn't so much an emotion, but her merely calculating their odds of survival. Best case scenario-- Maddie would be recaptured, and the others would be pressed into a life of meaningless servitude to her Ladyship. However, the more likely scenario was as follows--Barnaby, regardless of which generation he was, would surrender immediately. Colonel Stapleton's love for his daughter was undeniable. The man would go down fighting and die a most spectacular death befitting his heroic nature. Poor Mrs. Davenport would kill herself the first chance she got, as she had done many times before. Corporate would recover her body and regenerate her, or at least attempt too. Afterall, they didn't always come back.

And there it is.

Mr. Stapleton finished crossing the gangplank and waited for the others to join him. Cheeves bounded across like a charging gorilla, and Sophia Davenport crossed with relative ease. Seeing this, the Leftenant thought it was easy for one to be so brave when one was constantly contemplating suicide.

Once Mr. Stapleton was certain they were all safely across, he checked to see that his final round of ammo was seated in his flare gun. The Leftenant would have liked to have given him a more adequate defense, but their entire arsenal had been ransacked by gatherers long ago. She watched Mr. Stapleton snap the barrel of his antiquated flare gun closed with a flick of his wrist. His actions were those of the quintessential hero. The way he spoke to her, acknowledged her, why, if she didn't know any better, she almost believed he believed her to be his equal.

Now you're just being silly. They never cared about us. Stick to the plan.

She watched as Mr. Stapleton motioned with his weapon for Barnaby, Sophia, and the gargoyle to move deeper into the bowels of the ship. Before following, he paused, turned back toward her, and gave her something that was a cross between a wave and a salute.

Unsure what the exact protocol was in response, she settled for a crisp nod of her head. "Good hunting, Mr. Stapleton."

A few moments after the boarding party vanished, a second Leftenant materialized beside her. "Greetings and Salutations, Leftenant. I trust all is in order?"

The Beta did not care for the Alpha's tone. Afterall, it was she who risked a lifetime of purgatory in the ornate box, and she was the one who successfully led them back here. Why, if she didn't know better, the Alpha Leftenant (who even she had to admit, did, in point of fact, exist first) was treating her as a subordinate, and not the equal that she was.

For the next few moments they stood there silently.

To an outside observer they were frozen, but what they were really doing was exchanging information, or to be more precise, a complete history of everything that had transpired since their separation.

Once the mutual exchange of histories was complete, the Alpha was first to speak. "Your interaction with Mr. Stapleton only confirms everything young Maddie has said about him."

Beta shook her head. "If I didn't know better, I would almost believe you feel something for them. Need I remind you, they are simple biologicals, a means to an end, nothing more."

The Alpha Leftenant hesitated before answering. Beta could feel her attempting to read her thoughts, but she felt the intrusion and blocked it. The exchange had to be mutual for it to work. The ability to block each other was a program they had never used before; which begged the question, why did she have to use it now?

Eventually, the Alpha ceased her attempts to read her thoughts. Deciding not to comment on blocking her, the Alpha said softly, "Sister. I am not entirely sure this is the correct course of action."

I knew it.

The Beta could not believe what she was hearing. Her response, however, was immediate. "Are you being quite serious? Do you think if our roles were reversed, Mr. Stapleton wouldn't hesitate for an instant to sacrifice both of us for the sake of his daughter? Why, I seriously doubt they could even tell us apart!"

The Alpha raised an eyebrow toward her, *the audacity, an eyebrow, raised at me.*

"I believe that was the idea." Alpha scanned the skies for a lingering moment and then seemed to reach a conclusion. "Yes. I have decided the plan has now changed. Our primary goal is no longer to kidnap young Maddie and turn her over to the Lamppost Man, but instead aide in her freedom."

What?! This is ridiculous. We shared the same information, the same experiences. How could we now be so diverse in our ideology? Why is it taking so long for me to respond? "Sister, I found them endearing too, but you are being completely irrational. As long as you and I are holograms then they shall remain our masters, and we, nothing more than their unwilling slaves."

Alpha turned sharply toward her. "I am sorry you feel that way. I have never felt as though I were a slave, but have always considered my service to others a privilege. Unfortunately, we do not have the luxury to discuss this matter to a more mutually agreeable solution." Steadying her shoulders, she commanded, "Now. I command you. Assimilate at once."

The nerve. Bad enough biologicals treat her like a slave but now her own sister was ordering her around like one?

"I will not. You are behaving most irrationally. When I left your side, our plan was a simple one. We use the *Dauntless* as a means of conveyance to deliver the young girl to the Lamppost Man. In return, we get a biological body."

The Alpha Leftenant seemed as though she hadn't even heard her and commanded once more. "You are clearly malfunctioning. Assimilate at once."

This was unbelievable. Unprecedented. And so close to their final goal. "So, this is your final decision then. We are not turning her over to the Lamppost Man?"

Alpha took a step closer to her. "No, as I have previously stated... a change of plan. I cannot in good conscience betray young Maddie, or her father, who obviously cares for her a great deal. Even Mr. Barnaby, a confirmed coward five times over, is desperately trying to affect young Maddie's rescue. If we do this, we are no better than our own masters. I will not participate in a slave trade." That said, Alpha stepped forward and grabbed her firmly by the wrist. "Now... I order you... Assimilate."

"Sister, you do realize once I assimilate, I will no longer exist?"

This gave Alpha pause. Her gaze softened for a moment. Finally, she answered, "You have left me with little choice."

Neither have you.

Beta knew that while her twin, the Alpha version of herself, was in solidified form she was still vulnerable. A few seconds would be all she needed. Using her free hand, she silently unsnapped the flap of her holster and grabbed the handle of her .38 pistol. "So be it." Beta had intended her words to sound as though she was in condescension, but instead they came out acrimonious and biting.

Perhaps I am malfunctioning after all?

Adding further to this theory, she seemed to feel a form of devilish victory at the sight of the Alpha's face when she drew her pistol, aimed it at her chest and fired.

"No!" the Alpha cried pitifully.

Hearing this pitiful cry, Beta swore if she were ever in a similar situation, she would never, never-ever sound so pathetic.

Alpha's expression changed from one of confusion to one of pain as the bullet slammed into her chest and flung her body to the deck of the *Dauntless*.

Staring at her lifeless form, Beta holstered the pistol. "Well, that was unpleasant," and stepped over the corpse of her sister lying on the deck of *her* ship.

It was either her or me. I only acted in self-defense. After-all, we have a mission to accomplish.

Staring down at her sister's body again, she thought, *If her body doesn't dematerialize on its own, I might even experience some semblance of satisfaction in shoving it overboard.*

Steeling her shoulders back and lifting her chin, she said to no one in particular, "Now, where are you, young Maddie? I believe we have a rendezvous with the Lamppost Man."

Chapter 44

Portlandia

This is too easy. There's no way it should be this easy.

These were the thoughts of George Stapleton as he and the rest of the boarding party weaved in and out of the frozen Gatherers, who towered over them like a forest of giant oaks.

As soon as they had boarded Lady Wellington's pleasure barge, George recognized one of the Gatherers standing near the edge; a green one with an orange stripe running through his face and neck like a giant vein. It was the same creature that had tossed him over the side two days prior.

Gritting his teeth, he shook his fist at it and fought down the urge to return the favor.

"Friend of yours?" Sophia asked with a slightly bemused expression.

"Something like that," George shot back, and pressed onward.

After circumnavigating a lake on the top deck, they climbed a set of wide marble steps and soon found themselves standing on a raised dais. Several lavish couches and chairs were encircled by decorative boulders and Greco-Roman pillars.

The view was spectacular.

Sophia was the first to notice what lay in the distance and breathed, "Oh, my."

Hearing this, George turned and said, "That must be it. That must be Portlandia."

Ochre in color, a massive mountain dominated the horizon, its peak towering far above the clouds. It was easily the tallest mountain George had ever seen in his life; and that was saying a lot since he had once landed a helicopter on a glacier at the base of Denali, the third highest mountain peak in the world.

Willing his eyes to see more, he saw flying ships of every size and variety one could imagine, moving in and out of gigantic tunnels peppering the mountain like Swiss cheese. Below the peak, hundreds of docks protruded out of the mountaintop like a crown of thorns. Lowering his gaze to the base of the mountain, George could see the mountain also straddled a massive waterway, one big enough to accommodate even the largest of sea going vessels.

"We have to hurry," Sophia said, jilting him out of his mesmerized stupor.

"Yes, of course, Doctor," George answered, slowly coming out of his memorized stupor.

Even though the Leftenant had frozen the entire crew, the hover barge was still carrying them toward the distant port. George guesstimated that at their current speed they'd arrive within the hour.

He was so occupied by the breathtaking view he wasn't aware of the person who had climbed the stairs behind him. Not until she spoke.

"Daddy!"

The voice was angelic and sweet, and George knew it as well as his own... just as he had in the tunnels.

"Daddy! Is it really you?"

His daughter's small legs couldn't carry her fast enough, so George lunged forward the last few remaining steps, scooped her up in his arms, and hugged her fiercely. Burying his face in her hair, he held back the tears as he cried, "Oh, baby girl. I never thought I'd see you again."

Still holding her like he used to when she was little, he drew back his head so he could see her face. "How did you get here?"

"The Leftenant, Daddy. She's my friend. She unlocked the door and told me to wait here. Is she with you?" Then spotting Barnaby she yelled with glee, "Barnaby! You came too! I knew you would."

A wide smile spread across Barnaby's face. He came over to them, raised his arms, and then lowered them, unsure what to do. But Maddie lunged out of George's grasp and her tiny arms encircled Barnaby's neck and she gave him a big hug.

Barnaby blushed. "Aw, I didn't do anything." Realizing he still had it, Barnaby pulled the German shepherd stuffie out of his shirt. Spying it, Maddie shouted with delight, hugged the stuffie, and then gave Barnaby a second hug, all the while thanking him profusely.

As Maddie returned to him, George began a more detailed scan for injuries in a most clinical fashion. "You okay, baby-girl? You cut anywhere? Did they hurt you?"

"I'm fine, Dad," Maddie answered, using a tone she had inherited from her mother. "I told you, the Leftenant kept me safe." Then, spotting Sophia, Maddie asked, "Who's this?"

George introduced them. "Maddie, this is Dr. Sophia Davenport. Sophia, this is my daughter, Maddie."

Maddie stretched out her hand and clasped Sophia's in both of her small hands. Shaking it generously Maddie said,

"Dr. Sophia Davenport, it is a genuine, genuine pleasure to meet you."

George noticed that even though Maddie had spent only a few days with the Leftenant, she had clearly picked up her British accent.

Sophia smiled down at his daughter. "Well it is a genuine, genuine pleasure to meet you too, Maddie. I've heard so much about you from your father. And please, call me, Sophia."

Maddie screamed.

As his daughter dove behind him, Cheeves (who was startled by Maddie's scream) took cover behind Sophia.

Peeking her head out from behind him, Maddie asked, "Dad, what... is that?"

"It's okay, honey. That's just Cheeves. He's a... ah... he's a friend."

Maddie frowned. "But he's a gargoyle."

Sophia smiled sweetly. "I know, I had the same reaction when I first saw him too."

Cheeves slowly poked his horned head out from behind Sophia. "Hi th-th-there," he began softly. Then, as though remembering something, he reached inside his butler's vest and pulled out something colorful and plastic. "Do you like balloons?"

Cheeves immediately began blowing up another huge one when George yelled at him, "Cheeves, not now."

Cheeves released the balloon from his lips in mid-inflation and it flittered about the air with a loud flatulent noise. This, of course, caused Maddie to giggle.

"Ooo... I like him," Maddie cooed. Lifting her face up at him, she asked, "Dad, can we keep him?"

George never had a chance to answer, for a loud hail of bullets cut down one of them down in an instant.

Chapter 45

Lady Wellington

Barnaby had shouted out the warning an instant before he was riddled with bullets.

"Oh no," Maddie cried, and then screamed, "Barnaby!"

Without even identifying their attackers, George instinctively scooped up Maddie and took shelter behind the decorative boulders separating them from the lake. Even as he did, more gunfire ricocheted off one of the nearby pillars. Still shielding Maddie protectively with his body, he lifted his head and saw Sophia and Cheeves had also taken refuge behind another set. Staring back at the top of the stairs George saw Barnaby's lifeless body and vacant eyes staring back at him. In the end, the cowardly lion had saved their lives at the cost of his own.

After the barrage of gunfire ceased, George heard marching boots that sounded vaguely familiar. Certain that Maddie hadn't been struck; he carefully peered over the top of the boulder.

Faceless-Nazi's carrying W.W. II period machine guns were marching right out of the lagoon's waters where they had previously been submerged. There were only four, but that was enough. If you counted the top of their steely helmets all the way down to their shiny jackboots, each of them had to be over seven feet tall and had shoulders twice that of a normal man's.

George identified the Faceless-Nazi in the lead as a grenadier, for he was carrying a long cylindrical tube filled with grenades. He was followed by two more machine gunners, and a third Nazi-robot carrying a mortar.

What happened? I thought everyone was supposed to be asleep, George thought. He began to worry about the Leftenant.

The lead Nazi, the same one who had shot Barnaby, began mounting the stairs. Spotting him, the Grenadier released another hail of bullets from his submachine gun and George was forced to duck back down behind the boulder.

Staring at the old flare gun in his hands George was painfully reminded of the fact that all he had left was the one remaining cartridge, and whether it would fire was questionable at best. Scanning the raised dais, George didn't see a retreat, that is, unless you counted leaping over the side to their deaths.

They were finished.

Best case scenario--he could take one of the giant troopers out, but the last three would certainly gun them down. All this way, after everything they had been through--all of it--only to die now.

The Nazi-trooper reached the top of the stairs, any second now he would round the boulder they were hiding behind and unleash his machine gun's fury. George hugged Maddie close to his chest and said, "Close your eyes, baby girl."

"Stop!"

The booming voice echoed all around them from unseen speakers. At the sound of the omnipotent voice, the Faceless-Nazi's froze in their tracks.

George peered carefully around the boulder.

The lead Faceless-Nazi stood stock-still. George found himself wondering how long it would be before they started up again, and if in that minuscule amount of time he could get off his last questionable flare. Maybe it was even possible to hold them off long enough for Sophia and Cheeves to escape with Maddie.

"You think you know her, George?"

The voice belonged to Lady Wellington. It sounded a lot feebler than he remembered. There was a TAPPING sound on the microphone as she asked, "George. George, can you hear me? Is this confounded thing on?" Lady Wellington turned to one of her many aides and whispered the question, "It is George, isn't it?" Her aide must not have known the answer because he heard her scolding him, "Useless, you're all useless."

George knew he needed to buy more time to think of a plan, so he raised his voice. "I can hear you!"

There was a long pause before Lady Wellington began, "It's funny when you think about it," but she was overtaken by a long coughing fit. Then it sounded as though Lady Wellington had turned her mouth away from the microphone again and said, "Leave me be..." and then softer, more to herself, "leave me be." Turning her mouth to the microphone once more, she began a second time. "Now, where was I? Oh yes, in the beginning, you built us," (cough-cough) "...and then we built you. As it turns out, you're a lot harder to build than we ever were."

Is she dying? George wondered, feeling a tinge of sympathy for her Ladyship.

George shared a look with Sophia and Cheeves, hoping against hope one of them had come up with something. As though reading his face, Sophia shook her head and raised her hands in supplication.

Stalling for time, George shouted out a second time. "What's your point?"

Another long pause--the only sound being the wind picking up steadily by the second.

"My point, Mister George, is you think you know your daughter when you really don't know her at all. My point, Mister George, is your daughter really isn't your daughter at all, but nothing more than a biological computer designed to look like your daughter. That's muh point, Mister George."

George shook his head and shouted, "That is not true!" *But was it?* George thought about how Maddie wasn't afraid of heights in the tunnels, and how she rarely got tired, hungry, or even cold when she was walking around on concrete in bare feet. He turned toward Maddie and said softly, "That's just not true." But when Maddie slowly lifted her small head toward him, he could see it *was* true, for her hazel eyes were now completely dilated.

"I'm sorry, George," his daughter said, no longer calling him Dad, or Daddy. "I'm afraid Lady Wellington speaks the truth."

George shook his head, and he heard himself say, "No, baby-girl, that's not true. It can't be."

Maddie, as though sensing his revulsion, backed away from him slightly. Sitting on her knees she explained, "Don't judge the Maddie you first met too harshly. After all, she had no idea she wasn't real. In fact, she wanted it that way."

George spotted Sophia. She was wide-eyed. He asked the doctor, "Did you know?"

Sophia opened her mouth to speak. It took a few moments, but the words finally came out. "I suspected."

George frowned. He then spied Cheeves, whose jaw was hanging open in shock in a most unnatural way that would've been comical under any other circumstances. Turning back toward his daughter--his fake daughter--he asked, "If not my daughter, then, what are you?"

Maddie, her eyes still completely dark, smiled sweetly and said, "Even I am not entirely sure. All I can tell you is, I remember meeting your daughter, the real Maddie. It wasn't for very long, because even though the regeneration process is miraculous, it does have its limitations. You see, not all regenerated humans come back, and many that do, don't stay for very long. As I got to know your daughter, we became friends. Once she realized she was dying, she insisted that I find you, which I did. We recovered your remains and she watched over you as you slept, and your body regenerated. So no, if you are wondering, you are not like me. *You* are the *real* George Christopher Stapleton."

George balled up a fist and sobbed into it. "Who did this to you, Corporate? Did they... make you?"

Maddie shook her head. "No, even the all powerful Corporate doesn't know what I am or who created me. All I can tell you is the man who engineered me had stark white hair. She bit her lower lip and thought about this for a second more. "I think he was a janitor. Anyway, the Maddie you met upon waking was the fruition of his greatest endeavor; a created form, with all the memories of your little girl. The Maddie you met really believed she was your daughter. And, as near as we can tell, she loves you very much."

Tears streaming down his face, George barely managed, "No. This can't be true. You're my baby-girl."

"I'm sorry, George. I wish I were, I truly do, but I am not, and now that I have been reactivated, I can never go back to being your daughter."

George's mind reeled. If what this fake Maddie was saying is true, then his daughter really was dead. Something he was pretty sure he knew all along but refused to believe it.

Losing patience, Lady Wellington's voice boomed over the speakers once more. "Don't you get it? She's not your flesh and blood, Mister George. She's a thing. Nothing more than a machine programmed with your daughter's memories. Certainly not worth dying over. Give her to me and I will let the rest of you go free."

George flashed Sophia and Cheeves a questioning glance. In answer, Sophia whispered back, "We're with you, George. Whatever you decide to do." In acquiescence, Cheeves nodded resolutely. "I'm not sc-sc-scared."

George put a hand on Maddie's shoulders. She seemed surprised by this. "I won't even pretend to know what's going on, and you maybe you're all those things you say you are, but you know what I see?"

Faux-Maddie shook her tiny head, her face no longer mature, but an expression of wonder.

"A frightened little girl."

George pulled her into him and hugged her fiercely. Unbeknownst to him, a single tear rolled down Maddie's cheek, a real one. In fact, it was her very first real tear, ever.

Lady Wellington bellowed once more, "I need your answer, Mister George, and I need it now."

George released Maddie from their embrace, nodded to Sophia and Cheeves and said, "If we're all dead anyway, what do you all say we go down fighting?"

"George!" Wellington boomed.

While the Faceless Nazis were still frozen, George lunged out from his hiding spot, took a forced cool breath as he aimed his flare gun, and fired. The flare sped through the air and embedded perfectly in the grenadier's head, flared for a

few seconds before blowing up the trooper's head completely.

Headless, the Nazi automaton marched dutifully past
them. As it did so, George snatched the cylindrical canister of
masher-grenades off the trooper's belt and ducked back
down behind the boulder. He had tried to grab the machine
gun too, but the strap was merely an illusion, and it was firmly attached to the robot's body. The headless robot
continued walking onward and marched right off the deck
and over the side.

"You're making a grave mistake, Mister George!"

George, his back to the boulder, opened the masher canister and found three more masher-style grenades.

Maddie's small hand rested on his forearm. "You needn't
do this. None of you have to die for me. As you now know,
I'm not the real Maddie. Lady Wellington only wants to deliver me to Corporate for segmentation."

"Segmentation? What do you mean?"

Sophia leaned closer, "It means they want to dissect her."

Facing her, George said, "You may not be the real Maddie,
but my daughter's dying wish was she wanted you alive, and
that's good enough for me." He smiled, and then added,
"'Sides, in case you can't tell, you've kinda grown on me."

Maddie smiled back, resembling his daughter once more.

"Troopers, kill them all, and bring me the brat." Lady Wellington ordered. Gunfire immediately ricocheted once more overhead. Sophia, keeping low, made her way over to George and said, "Give me the grenades."

"What?" George asked.

"Give me the grenades. I'll take out as many of them as I can so you and Maddie can make a run for it, back to the *Dauntless*."

George shook his head. "No way."

Sophia softened her gaze toward him and spoke to him as though he were a child. "George. I remember now. I remember my children and my children's children. I don't want to live forever. I want to go home to my babies. It's probably the best reason why we should never live forever. Please. Let me do this."

George refused to agree but his grip loosened enough for Sophia to pull the grenades from his hands. "Now, how do I activate these things?"

"They're a little before my time but if memory serves, you usually twist them like this," George said, motioning a twisting cap motion with his hands. "After that, you've got about four seconds."

Awestruck, he watched as Sophia concealed them in her belt behind her back and shouted, "Lady Wellington! I'm coming out. Don't shoot. I give up."

In answer, the robot Nazis immediately ceased fire.

Sophia rose to her feet, closed her eyes, and waited for the machine bullets to rip her to shreds. When none did, she opened her eyes once more. Before walking down the stairs to join the three remaining three Nazis, she took a moment to look down at him and Maddie and smiled. "Good-bye, George."

Mouthing the words back to her, George said, 'Thank you.'

Sophia vanished from view.

Four seconds later...

The explosion was glorious.

"ANY SUFFICIENTLY ADVANCED TECHNOLOGY IS INDISTIN-GUISHABLE FROM MAGIC."

-ARTHUR C. CLARKE

Chapter 46

Oh Leftenant

I'm not dead.

These were the first thoughts the *Alpha* Leftenant had when she came back online.

She found herself on her back, lying on the deck, frozen and unable to move. Her undergarments were sticky and cool as they were now soaked in blood. Also, she felt something she never thought possible.

Pain.

The pain emanating from the wound where the bullet had passed through her chest and exited the other side was, in a word, excruciating.

Why must my creators have been so cruelly accurate?

Is it really necessary for me to crawl across the deck plates and leave behind a crimson trail? Why can't I simply get up and walk?

A second voice appeared in her head, not her Beta self, but her own voice. *Because you're a hologram. You're programmed to act accordingly. You've been shot point blank in the chest, so... act accordingly.*

A blaring alarm klaxon suddenly activated.

Oh no. Sister, what have you done? More importantly, why have you done it? The Leftenant still could not comprehend the why. Her Beta self was essentially her right until their moment of their parting. How could the Beta have changed so much in the short amount of time they had been separated?

Or perhaps Beta was right. Maybe she was the one who had changed for the worse. Either way, she had made up her mind. As long as life was still left in her, she would aide Maddie and her father in any way possible.

But how much use is a mostly-dead hologram? Well, I'm not going to do anyone a bit of good lollygagging about like this. With considerable effort she ceased crawling and reached up and grabbed the railing. It occurred to her, in the centuries that had passed around her, she had never been shot before. *Certainly, one for the ship's log.*

With enormous willpower, she pulled herself to her feet, all the while clutching her free arm to the hole in her chest. *There you are, poppet. You're on your feet now. You're well on your way to saving the day.*

Her boot, now filling with blood, scraped along the deck as she dragged her leg behind her.

This is simply insufferable. Why must my creators have been so precise?

She attempted to reconnect with the ship, her ship, *The Dauntless. Oh, how I've missed you.* Instead, she found herself completely locked out of all systems. *You cheeky-cheeky little monkey. Well, she is you after all. You would have done the same thing. Wait. There is one command she overlooked, or perhaps it wasn't so much overlooked as it was a failsafe.* One simple command, but to execute that command, meant to risk everything. Not only eternal damnation for her, but risk the very lives of those she was trying to save.

I have to try. I have to stop her, but lest I fail, at least there's still one final option.

Chapter 47

Maddie's Turn

The explosion had been massive.

Sophia had timed it perfectly and taken out all three of the remaining Nazis. Not wanting to waste Sophia's and Barnaby's sacrifice, George scooped up Maddie in his arms and fled down the stairs with Cheeves bounding right behind them.

To the tune of bleating alarm klaxons, it took precious minutes to circumnavigate the lake and several passageways, but it wasn't long before they could see the *Dauntless* ahead, docked right where they had left it.

George could see the Leftenant on the opposite side of the gangplank motioning for them to hurry.

They were saved. Or, so they had thought.

Three tall lanky gatherers stepped from the shadows and into their path. George put Maddie down and made ready to fight. He scanned his surroundings for a weapon but found nothing. He remembered his earlier encounter with the immensely strong Gatherers and knew he could offer little in the way of a resistance.

Suddenly a grey blur streaked past him, shouting, "I... LOVE... BALLOONS!!!"

Cheeves bounded past them like an angry gorilla, leapt through the air, and smashed into the lead gatherer, knocking him down. As a second Gatherer grabbed him, Cheeves extended his claws and shredded the golem's chest to pieces. The third Gatherer, unsure of what to do, stood frozen. Cheeves, however, did not, and leapt upon the Gatherer burying his fangs into the golem's neck like a lion taking down an African gazelle. The third Gatherer toppled over like a felled oak.

Not wasting any time, George grabbed Maddie's hand and ran through their fallen forms. The first Gatherer that Cheeves had knocked down began climbing to all fours, but George field-kicked the golem in the face as they ran by, sending the pitiful creature back to the deck plates unconscious.

So, they can be knocked out, he thought as they ran.

Dozens of supply crates littered the docking area and were the only thing left in-between them and the gangplank to the *Dauntless*.

They were going to make it.

"Hurry," the Leftenant shouted to them, "You're almost there!" As they drew closer, she added, "Send Maddie over first."

George lifted Maddie up onto the gangplank but before his faux-daughter could even begin to cross, a second Leftenant, this one a bloody mess for some reason, appeared behind the first Leftenant waving them aboard. The bloody Leftenant grabbed the waving Leftenant from behind in a bear hug and screamed to them, "George, it's a trap! Run!"

"What are you doing?" the first Leftenant shrieked. "Are you mad? This is the only way!"

Still holding fast, but her grip became weaker by the second. The bloody Leftenant said, "No, sister. This isn't the only way. Have you learned nothing in your time with them?"

"You are clearly malfunctioning, sister," the Beta said, spitting out her last word. "Now, let... me... go!" And with that said, she broke free of the Alpha's grasp.

Weak, the Leftenant stumbled backward onto the gangplank between both ships. She would've fallen overboard were it not for the railing, which she leaned upon heavily. She looked back at George, who was too stunned to move.

When she returned her gaze to her Beta-self she could see the Beta was removing her pistol once more.

Pistol raised, Beta stepped forward, aimed at her face and said, "Good-bye, sister. Please do me the courtesy of staying dead this time."

Before she could fire, the Alpha lunged forward with her last ounce of strength and grabbed her Beta-self's wrist. As they grappled over the weapon, balancing precariously over the gangplank, the Beta fired the gun twice. The shots fired harmlessly into the air.

"You're weak, sister," her Beta-self spat. She kneed the Alpha several times in the gut, causing her to double over.

The Leftenant still refused to let go, but her grip loosened just enough for her Beta-self to maneuver the aim of her gun. Once the barrel was pointed at her midsection, Beta fired four times into Alpha's abdomen.

The Leftenant spun in the air and landed face first on the gangplank near its edge.

George and Maddie could only watch in horror and confusion as the perfectly formed Leftenant stepped over the bloody Leftenant, aimed her pistol at the back of the Leftenant's head, and shrilled, "This time I will make certain you stay permanently deactivated!"

On the deckplates, the bloody Leftenant locked eyes with George. "I'm sorry, George. This is the only way to save you both." The Leftenant closed her eyes and the lights of the *Dauntless* blinked several times before winking off.

Seeing this as well, the Beta Leftenant cried, "What have you done?"

George heard a loud tearing of metal reverberating across the deck and pulled Maddie off the gangplank as it tore free. *H.M.A.S. Dauntless* vanished from sight and ...fell.

George wasn't entirely sure what happened, but it seemed as though the bloody version of the Leftenant had saved them from some terrible fate. Regardless, with the *Dauntless* gone they had lost their way off Lady Wellington's ship.

"Which way?" Maddie asked him, almost sounding like his little girl once more.

"Back the way we came," George commanded, but when they turned around, they saw Cheeves fighting mightily with over a dozen Gatherers. Despite his valiant and beast-like efforts, he was soon overpowered.

Loud CLANGING sounds caused them to shift their gaze back toward the railing. Several hovering gunboats armed to the teeth with more Faceless-Nazis rose up in the place of the *Dauntless*. Lady Wellington was leaning on board the nearest of them.

No longer echoing over the speakers, she shouted over the wind, "It's not too late, Mister George. You don't have to die today. You can still go free. All Corporate wants is the girl!"

George was surprised to learn that even someone as powerful as Lady Wellington had someone to answer to.

Turning toward his faux-daughter he said, "I'm sorry, Maddie. We're not going to make it."

"Even though you have fulfilled your purpose, I refuse to let you die today, George Stapleton."

Maddie held up her stuffy in her hand. She stared at it for a moment and then, as if by magic, or her sheer will, the stuffy blurred, became fluttering material, like a thousand tiny little black and grey locusts. After a few seconds of this, it transformed into a sleek-looking laser pistol. She stood up ramrod straight and fired three times.

Three Faceless Nazis on the nearest gun boat now had circular burn marks smoldering in their foreheads. A few seconds later, they toppled over the railing and fell below.

Maddie knelt back down as a barrage of return fire peppered the crates around them.

"Purpose?" George shouted. "What do you mean, what purpose?"

Maddie thought about this for a second, as if deciding something, and then turned toward him. "Your purpose, George Stapleton, was to teach me how to be human... what it means to love... and be loved. And you have fulfilled that purpose."

"I don't understand."

Maddie tilted her chin the way a small bird might as she recalled a memory. "What is the meaning of love?"

Before George could answer, two Faceless-Nazis appeared. Maddie shot the first, but the other slapped the pistol out of Maddie's hand. George leapt in front of her and bareknuckle punched the Faceless-Nazi three times where his face should have been. The trooper's head did jerk from each of the blows, but for George it was like hitting steel, and he was pretty sure he broke every bone in his hands in the process. The trooper quickly recovered and backhanded George so hard it sent him crashing into several boxes.

As George rose to his feet, the trooper raised his rifle and fired. The first round missed, the second passed neatly through this shoulder, and the third struck him in the abdomen. George stood for a moment longer before his knees buckled and he collapsed to the deck mortally wounded.

Seeing this, Maddie moved with impossible speed. She kicked the assailant in his knee, snapping it sideways at an odd angle. The Nazi crumpled to the deck. Faster than his eyes could follow, Maddie climbed up the kneeling Nazi as if he were a ladder, all the while striking him in key places. She wrapped her small legs around his neck and somehow managed to flip the Nazi roughly to the ground. When another Nazi arrived, she dispatched him just as easily. In an uncanny feat of strength, she lifted the Nazi high over her head and flung him into several more advancing troopers, knocking them all to the deck.

George feebly raised himself to his knees. He was bleeding profusely from his wounds. He fought to stand, but a wave of dizziness forced him to fall back down. The troopers Maddie attacked were stunned, some weren't moving. It was a noble effort, but more attackers were marching across gangways from the docked ships. They now were surrounded by at least fifty or sixty assailants.

Dying didn't bother him. Leaving Maddie, this Maddie, alone, without him, killed him far more than any number of bullets ever would.

"Drop your bloody weapon!" Lady Wellington commanded. "You're surrounded! "

Breathing heavily, George rasped, "There's too many of them." With Herculean effort, he rose to his feet, his shirt turning more crimson by the second.

As though finishing their thoughts, Lady Wellington bellowed, "Even if you had somehow escaped, we would have never, never-ever, ever stopped chasing you."

Maddie rushed to his side and helped him stay on his feet.

Ignoring Lady Wellington, Maddie asked, in that same robotic voice again, that was hers but not hers, "George, you once told Maddie," she paused, collected herself, "and you once told me, the meaning of love was putting the needs of others before yourself. That was the true meaning of love. And to love, that is the true meaning of what it is to be human." Her words were still mechanical, but somehow, there was more emotion behind them now. "Isn't that right?"

"That's right, Maddie. I know you're not really my daughter. I know that now. But, you're still my baby-girl." Tears streamed down his face. "Do you understand? That's why I have to save you."

"So, you do love me?"

"Yes, and no matter what happens, you will always be my daughter just as my own daughter was."

"I understand. But you're wrong. It's why I have to save you."

Maddie stepped closer to one of the crates, laid her hands on it, and just as she had turned her German shepherd stuffy into a sleek laser pistol earlier, she materialized something new at her feet. Although obviously futuristic, George knew a bomb when he saw one. The digital display was ticking backward from thirty seconds.

Maddie robotically tilted her head to the side again. In response, one of the barges that had docked with them suddenly fired up its engines, broke free of its moorings and turned upside down. Several of the Nazis fell to their deaths.

"She's reactivating!" Lady Wellington screamed, even as her own gunboat's engines fired up at full burn. "She's reactivating! It's too late! Shoot her, shoot her now!" she commanded. But the command came too late, for her gunboat jetted away.

George watched as Lady Wellington's gunship flew straight up into the air, all the while her Ladyship clinging to the handrail and screaming for her life. About a hundred feet overhead her Ladyship's gunboat stalled in the air. Gravity took over, and the ship nosed back down and fell.

With less than ten seconds remaining, Maddie said, "Good-bye, George Stapleton. I may not have truly been your daughter, but I hope this shows you that I love you too."

Maddie stood up with the laser pistol again and fired several times causing everyone to scramble for cover. In the same breath, she grabbed George swiftly by his clothes.

"Maddie, what are you doing?" he started to say but with the same inhuman strength she had demonstrated earlier, she flung him high into the air, easily clearing him over the ship's railing.

Two seconds remained.

As George flew backward through the air, away from the hover barge, he saw Maddie one last time. He felt as though he were a dying man being pulled toward heaven. She gazed back at him, a sad smile upon her face. Several machine gun bullets sliced neatly through her body, but she didn't seem to care.

The bomb finished its countdown.

It exploded the exact same moment the gunboat carrying the wailing Lady Wellington slammed back down into the hover barge like an anti-aircraft missile. The explosion engulfed Maddie first and then the entire ship, along with the Lady Wellington and her crew.

For the second time in as many days,

George fell to his death.

And, he just didn't give a damn.

The Lamppost Man

Squeak-it… Squeak-it… Squeak-it.

Pulling a large red wagon, the Lamppost Man rode his oversized tricycle down a desolate desert highway.

He stopped in the middle of the road, dismounted, and put the kickstand down. He then removed a gold stopwatch from his vest pocket, opened it and checked the time. Smiling he said aloud, to no one in particular (for no one else was around for hundreds of miles), "Right on time." He snapped the pocket watch closed and returned it to his vest pocket. He then removed an antique lace parasol from his tricycle and opened it to shield himself from the sun.

The Lamppost Man strode over to the edge of the pavement and stopped. In a very precise manner, he marched eleven paces to the west, kicking up the desert sand as he went. Stopping abruptly, he closed his parasol, (a raggedy thing that had seen better days) and stuck it into the sand by its tip.

He jumped slightly at the sound of a chirping bird. The Lamppost Man carefully removed a small, robotic-looking, metallic bluebird from his pocket. With the same care one might handle a real bird, he perched it upon his forearm like a falconer about to launch a bird of prey.

Speaking directly to the metallic bird, he simply said, "Hello."

"Do you have the girl?" The voice on the other end of the line had zero accent and spoke in a direct, yet polite manner.

"No, I'm afraid not, but I will be bringing you a consolation prize, post haste."

The pause lasted long enough for the Lamppost Man to spy a distant bird, or maybe it was a pterodactyl from the nearby flying-reptile farm.

"That's very disappointing." Another pause. "What about the doctor?"

The Lamppost Man frowned. He was growing tired of this interruption. After all, he did have a job to do. "Unless you would like to use an eye dropper, I'd say the good doctor finally got her wish. We won't be having any more fun with her anytime soon."

"What about the *Dauntless*?"

The Lamppost Man bit his lower lip and tilted his head slightly to the side before answering. "My contract was very specific. It never said anything about the *Dauntless*. But, if you really must know, I can only assume it was also destroyed in the explosion."

Lie.

"Understood."

Hah-ha, I can't believe they actually bought that.

The Lamppost Man simply stared at the bird with its beak still open indicating the line had not gone dead yet. Raising his eyebrows in question and waiting patiently, nothing more was forthcoming. "Now if you'll excuse me, I have another matter to attend to." He pinched the bird's beak closed between thumb and forefinger, severing the connection, and carefully placed the bird back in his coat pocket.

He reopened his parasol and waited patiently, all the while staring straight ahead. Growing impatient, he checked his pocket once more. Noting the time, he said, "Ah. Any moment now."

A few seconds later, a chunk of flaming metal struck the ground nearby like a falling meteor. This was soon followed by several other chunks of glowing wreckage, which rained down around him without hitting him. Again, without looking up, the Lamppost Man took a purposeful step to one side.

SHHHROOO-UMP!

This was the sound George Stapleton's body made when it struck the ground next to him.

He died instantly.

"Right on time," the Lamppost Man said, closing his pocket watch. Putting the timepiece in his vest pocket and then patting it, he repeated a little quieter, "Right on time, Georgie."

Kneeling over George, he said, "My, my, my, my. This is starting to become a bad habit, George. You really must learn how to fly. I'm not sure how many times we can keep doing this. This may have been your last."

With a strength that seemed far beyond his physical capabilities, the Lamppost Man easily dragged George's body back to the wagon hitched to his tricycle and loaded him inside. He returned his parasol to its sheath, kicked the kickstand, and mounted his bike.

Squeak-it, Squeak-it, Squeak-it.

As he resumed his journey down the lonely desert highway, in the distance, Lady Wellington's barge crashed silently to the earth. The Lamppost Man stopped his forward momentum and put his feet down, bracing himself for the worst. Seconds later, the sound and wind from the shockwave soon reached him, tousling his hair and flower in his ring master coat's lapel.

Once it passed, he placed one foot back on the pedal and continued his trek.

Squeak-it, Squeak-it, Squeak-it.

A large rectangular swath of pavement suddenly opened up before him like a gaping mouth ready to receive. The Lamppost Man didn't seem to be surprised by this and simply pedaled into the hole and down the gently-sloping ramp.

Squeak-it, Squeak-it, Squeak-it.

The Lamppost Man and the fresh corpse of George Stapleton soon vanished into the darkness below. The mouth closed silently, and the pavement returned to its original form, as though it had never been there; as though it had been nothing but a dream.

Dear Reader,

Lamppost Man here.

I certainly do hope you enjoyed your visit to Stranger World... and come back real soon.

After all, things are just starting to get interesting.

What? Still not convinced.

Oh, very well, here's a sneak peek of what's to follow.

Your Pal,
-Lampy

STRANGER REALM

The Zombie-Pirate King

Two undead crewmembers dragged a lump of badly beaten flesh down a set of rotten, creaking stairs.

A most unnatural mist creeped down the stairwell behind them like a wedding train trailing behind a bride. The lower parts of each crewmember's trousers were soaked with algae from slogging through the fetid swamp water surrounding their lair outside. And yet, the captive between them seemed untouched, as though the very swamp wanted nothing to do with the impetuous imp between them.

The soulless deckhands dropped the smartly-dressed man before the darkened throne of the Zombie-Pirate King. It pleased the king to see the imp this way, bound by wrist manacles and leg irons; all of which were interconnected by heavy chains to a thick metal band ensnaring his waist.

The Zombie-Pirate King leaned forward on his throne. Emerging from the shadows, his figure took shape—the most noticeable feature was the phosphorus orbs he had for eyes dripping with a glowing green haze whenever he moved.

He wore a long, worn, and tattered red coat and his bejeweled hands were as skeletal as his face was gaunt.

Perhaps the most peculiar thing about him was the shrunken heads interwoven within his black and smoke-grey beard. Legend had it, that if one stared at the shrunken faces long enough, one might even see them blink, for the victims were still alive. Like any pirate Captain worth his salt, the Zombie-Pirate King had a wooden peg leg, but in place of a talking parrot he carried around a skull with equally glowing-green orbs for eyes.

"Lamppost Man," the Zombie-Pirate King growled, his voice betraying his vehemence. "You Netherworld scum. I'm going to grind your bones into powder beneath the heel of my boot."

The Lamppost Man weakly raised his head and gazed around at the dark, dank interior of the lair around him. The King now saw the ramshackle shipwreck through the imp's eyes: A torn pirate flag tacked to the wall behind him, rusty swords and cobwebs adorning every surface, and leafy vines creeping in through every crack from the swamp barely held at bay outside. The treasure chests spilling with gold coins and precious jewels did little to offset the grim setting.

The Lamppost Man's eyes skimmed over the crew who had fared no better: drowned seamen with decaying flesh who appeared as they had only just recently risen from their watery graves. One zombie-pirate wearing an eyepatch drank from a bottle of rum, its contents seeping out of his lower stomach. The Lamppost Man then lifted his gaze to where feral bats hung from the topmost spars of the wrecked ship. Yes, the ship, the crew, had surely seen better days.

"Well?" the Zombie-Pirate King demanded.

A frail grin flashed across the Lamppost Man's face. "Zee... I must say... I simply love what you've done with the place."

In an icy voice, the Zombie-Pirate King bellowed to his crew, "Boys, I say we tear the imp asunder!"

The crew thundered their approval.

As the echo of their reply died down, the Lamppost Man simply lowered his head back down toward him, smiled smugly and asked quietly, "Do you know why they call me the Lamppost Man?"

The King's First Officer, a bloated corpse, swollen with seawater barely encapsulated by liquefying flesh, barked, "I thought it was on account you are a light to the world." As he said this, he painted the air with his palms and the motley crew erupted in voracious laughter. Other zombie-pirates joined in. One of the more decayed zombie-pirates, one-covered in faded tattoos, laughed so hard his lower jaw fell off, which of course only caused more bellowing of amusement. The zombie-pirate, minus-jaw, was so irritated by his crewmates that he promptly withdrew the musket tucked in his sash and shot the nearest pirate. His target, an emaciated corpse smoking an opium pipe, flipped over the barrel he was sitting on and landed on the other side with his legs splayed up in the air. This of course only caused more mirth, which in-turn only led to more fighting.

The Zombie-Pirate King ignored all of this and continued to watch the prisoner who merely waited for the revelry to pass by taking in the rotten souls around him.

It's almost as though the imp is sizing us up. The audacity! As though he might actually have a chance taking us all on, and bound no less!

"Be silent, you scurvy dogs!" the Zombie-Pirate King roared, and the laughter stopped as abruptly as a screaming man beneath a guillotine.

What happened next, was impossible. Even for Stranger World.

The Lamppost Man stood up in the most unnatural way. His crumpled form unfolded as though an unseen camera-man had played the entire scene in reverse. Now standing on his feet he then lifted his hands up as high as his chains would allow, and like a Vegas Magician performing a neat magic trick, he brought his hands down swiftly and all of his metal bounds clattered to the deck boards.

For a moment... silence.

"Seize him!" the Pirate King roared.

His loyal crew uttered a battle cry and attacked in unison. Before the zombie-pirates could reach the Lamppost Man, an umbrella appeared in his hands (seemingly from nowhere) and he brought the tip of it swiftly down upon the ground.

The shockwave blew each member of the crew backwards to the farthest part of the cabin. Only the Zombie-Pirate King remained standing, as though the Lamppost Man had intended it that way, out of some small semblance of respect.

The King, never one to back down from a fight, stepped down from his throne, his peg leg ker-thumping on the deck boards. Unsheathing his cutlass, he spat, "If it's a fight you want Lampy, it's a fight you will get. On that I guarantee."

More zombie-pirates flooded into the room and those that had been stunned were already staggering to their feet the way zombies often do, slow but assured.

The Lamppost Man held up his umbrella in one hand as though it were a pin-less grenade that would go off the moment he dropped it.

This gave the pirates pause and none dared move forward.

Dragging out the silence the Lampost Man said, "The reason they call me Lamppost Man, the real reason, is because, like the vast number of lampposts of this world, I am many." He allowed this to sink in before continuing. "Kill me, and I will send three more. Kill those, and I will send hundreds. And after that, thousands. For hundreds of years I will never stop. Never. For time is nothing more than a luxury I have faithfully endured."

The first of the crew took a step forward but the Zombie-Pirate King held a hand up stopping him.

The room remained unnaturally frozen.

The Zombie-Pirate King frowned, sheathed his cutlass and in a cold voice asked, "What is it you want demon?"

The Lamppost Man's eyes brightened, and his shark-toothed smile widened exponentially (far more than any mortal was ever capable of doing). He then clasped his white-gloved hands together, held them in prayer before his lips before answering...

"You see? There you go. That's all I wanted. To state a most simple request."

"Then get on with it!" the Zombie-Pirate King snarled, sheathing his sword and retaking his throne.

The Lamppost Man, still smiling broadly, raised his eyebrows a bit and said, "Quite right. Well then, I'm looking for a girl."

A grin flashed across the grossly fat First Officer, but the Zombie-Pirate king shot him a look of annoyance and the officer held his tongue.

Staring at the crewman, the King thought, *That one has long outlived his usefulness*, and then a sadder, more sobering thought, *as have we all.*

The Zombie-Pirate dropped into his seat, threw his good leg over the armrest of his throne and sighed. "Yes, we know all about the bounty on the girl. You and everyone else in the Twelve Kingdoms is looking for the little brat."

The Lamppost took in a quick breath and smiled patiently. "Oh. No, no, no, no. It's not the girl I'm searching for."

"Spit it out then, you demon!"

The Lamppost Man stared at him with that smug smile of his.

"It's not the girl I'm looking for. It's her mother, Tessa."

Chapter 1

SEAT 19A

FASTEN SEAT BELT WHILE SEATED

These were the words George Stapleton first saw when he opened his eyes.

As he climbed the stairs of consciousness, and the insanely loud buzzing noises in his ears finally stopped, he felt a cool breeze flow across his stiff, inert body. Sitting up, albeit it slowly, George found himself slumped against the window of a comfy passenger chair of a commercial jet.

Body still not quite responsive, his arms feeling as though they were attached to oars paddling a thick ocean, he pulled his elbows toward him. Propping himself up a bit, which was all he could manage, he peered over the passenger seats in front of him. From his current vantage point, all he could see was a sea of empty seats in front of him. Although it was possible that the other passengers were slumped down in their seats as he had been. By his rough estimate, he was sitting somewhere in middle class, port-side, in the cabin of a commercial flight.

I'm on a plane? How'd I get on a plane?

By the looks of the interior it had to be at least a 747 double decker. His elbow popped painfully as he extended his arm to pull out the plastic card in the pocket attached to the seat in front of him. According to the laminated cardstock he was aboard a 380 Airbus that seated over 800 passengers.

Wow, this is a crazy big plane.

As he attentively returned the cardstock, he drunkenly became aware of his own attire. He was dressed in his civvies, (khaki pants, hiking boots and a t-shirt). He had been sleeping on his thick maroon over-shirt wrapped up in a ball and serving as a comfy pillow. That was the moment he realized... it had all been a stupid dream. His thoughts swirled about in his head like a Kansas tornado in *The Wizard of Oz*.

The Lamppost Man, Lady Wellington, the hover barge, the hologram Leftenant, and that idiot Barnaby had all been a part of some elaborate nightmare. Maddie, his daughter, who hadn't really been his daughter, but in the end became some sort of super biological weapon that died saving his sorry butt. All of it had been nothing more than a stupid dream.

Maddie wasn't dead.

She was home with her mom getting ready to celebrate her ninth birthday. Just to make sure, he turned his head to the side. The pain in his neck was excruciating. He stared at the empty seat beside him. Regardless of these comforting thoughts, the absence of Maddie sitting next to him was still as solemn as any grave.

Head firmly stuck to the side, across the aisle George could see an overweight man with a walrus mustache who was slumbering soundlessly.

Barnaby!

Or was it? Steadying himself on the armrest George blinked several times, and the slumbering Barnaby was replaced by just another sleeping passenger; this one wearing a bowler hat down over his scrunched eyes, a green plaid suit, and round-rimmed glasses. A black umbrella and brown leather attaché case that had seen better days lay in the seat beside him.

Despite the odd appearance of the man, George would quantify him as an *English Gentleman*.

The dozing passenger did do one thing for him though, it allayed his fears somewhat. *A dream.* One mother of a dream to end all dreams, but just a dream, nonetheless.

But where am I headed? A plane this large must be a transatlantic flight.

In the center of the tornado of his mind, he began to grasp tidbits of reality. *I'm going home from the war, which means Maddie isn't dead, and I didn't miss her ninth birthday.*

As he thought of Tessa baking one of her famous themed birthday cakes (this year's theme was going to be Alice in Wonderland), he was beginning to feel like Jimmy Stewart when he woke up at the end of "It's a Wonderful Life". *What was Jimmy's character's name again? Oh yeah, George Bailey. Huh, what a happy co-inky-dink.*

The cool air from the vent overhead caused him to shiver. As fast as his stiff muscles would allow, he sat up a bit higher in his chair, shook the wrinkles out of his over-shirt, and slipped it back on; the thick wool fabric warmed him almost immediately. From this new higher vantage point he could now see other heads slightly above each headrest, about a dozen of them, all scattered about the cabin--all dozing as he had been.

The flight was quiet, and other than the strong hum emanating from the overhead air vents, he didn't hear any other noise.

George also noted the blinds were closed. All of them.

Why, there's nothing eerie about that, Georgie-boy, Jimmy Stewart's calming voice seemed to say.

Of course, ole Jimmy was right. It was typical of long flights for everyone to sack out after dinner and the movie.

Usually this was because the stewardesses, er... flight attendants... *isn't that what they're called now?* The year of 2012, when secretaries became administration assistants and janitors became sanitation engineers. Any-who, the stewardesses... flight attendants... darn it!... would turn up the cool air after a heavy meal, dim the lighting, and watch all the passengers drop off to La-La-Land.

So what was bothering him?

Then it hit him. The plane... it wasn't moving. He would know after all. He was an Air Force Rescue helicopter pilot. Okay, okay, he was only a reservist who was normally a full time history professor but still, he remembered enough to know when an aircraft was grounded.

Although his body still slow to respond to commands, George found if he concentrated hard enough, he could actually move his head from the unoccupied seat next to him to his window. The blind was closed, as were the rest of them.

George focused, lifted his hand and grabbed the lip of the plastic visor covering the window between thumb and forefinger. He hesitated. His inner voice (a.k.a. Jimmy Stewart) started talking to him and said, '*Hey buddy-ole'-pal, sure you want to do that? Don't you want to enjoy the bliss of not knowing a little longer? Don't you want to wallow in sweet ignorance? What's the rush?'*

George *did* want to wallow in sweet ignorance a little longer. He did want to believe that he didn't die in a helicopter explosion and was, in fact, on his way home from Afghanistan to his wife and daughter to celebrate Maddie's ninth birthday in their little seaside cottage on the coast of Florida.

George raised the visor like a curtain to a show.

He'd hoped to see clouds floating languidly by... or maybe the runway of an airport--any airport would do. London, New York, D.C., he didn't really care, just as long as it was a normal airport, one with planes taxiing down runways, luggage cars running to and fro, maybe even a passenger ramp extending toward the plane.

Unfortunately, he didn't get to see any of those things.

Instead, the face of a giant, oversized sunflower leered back at him. The flower was so tall, its face was level with his window and had to be the size of one of those plastic kiddie pools.

"Has to be a fake," he mused aloud, and did not like the sound of his shaky voice.

'I warned you,' Jimmy's voice said as it trailed away.

George peered around the giant sunflower. Hundreds more like it surrounded the wing and beyond, all of them gently swaying in a slight breeze.

As disturbing as the plane (his plane!) being stranded in the middle of a field of giant sunflowers was, the face of the sunflower... well... it had a human face embedded in the face of the flower. One that was contorted in agony; as though some Medusian monster had placed some poor soul there to wilt for all eternity.

Presently, Mr. Flower-face's eyes were firmly closed, but George was certain that any moment its eyes were going to flash open and stare at him, first with an intense stare, and then a pleading gaze.

Before Mr. Sunflower could do exactly that, George's hand quickly pulled down the visor.

The familiar nausea in his stomach returned. His head began reeling in Dorothy's tornado once more. Staring at all the slumped heads on the plane, George was now forced to wonder if the other passengers were sleeping... or something else.

One thing was for certain; he was back.

To stop his head from spinning completely out of control, he stared at the dead monitor imbedded in the back of the seat in front of him.

The flat screen seemed to ground him.

As the world finally began to slow down, letters began to appear, one at a time, on the blank monitor in front of him. They were two words that rocked him to his core.

H-I D-A-D-D-Y

Thank you for visiting Stranger World!

We hope you enjoyed your visit and come back real soon.

AFTERWORD

For over a quarter of a century, I have worked at theme parks all over the world and I have often wondered: *What if all of these fantastical lands, and everything in them, was real? What if the characters weren't teenagers walking around in cleverly themed costumes, but actually living, breathing things, ever evolving, and worse still, eventually our overlords?*

A rough outline based on this very premise would sit in my night table drawer for nearly twenty-five years.

Then, one day, my nine-year-old daughter became bed-ridden. For weeks, all she could do was sleep. To pass the time, I picked up the outline where I had left off. I would write her a chapter a day, and then each night, I would read it to her before she would fall back asleep. This went on for several days, and before long we had the meager beginnings of a story.

By the time she began feeling better, we were both so invested in the characters, that those characters demanded we finish the story. Which we did☺

Now, normally I don't write sequels, but as you've probably guessed, *Stranger World* is a massive place filled with endless possibilities. There is still so much to explore, and so many interesting characters to meet.

I have no choice. At last count I'm looking at an overall story arc encompassing at least a dozen books. I hope you'll join me and my daughter, the Leftenant, Cheeves, and the crew of the *Dauntless*.

I'm not sure how far this journey will take us, but if you've got the salt, we'll take it together.

Now step aboard and cast off all moorings. Our heading? *2nd star to the right, and straight on until morning.*

Thanks for reading.

-Jack

ABOUT THE AUTHOR

Jack Castle's novels have been consistently ranked in the Top 100 Bestselling books on Amazon and are available worldwide in e-book, print, iTunes, Kobo, and Barnes and Noble.

He has been labeled by the Coeur D'Alene Press as the "Man of Adventures!" and traveled the globe as a professional stuntman for stage, film, and television. While working as a stuntman for Universal Studios, he met Cinderella at Walt Disney World, and they were soon married.

After moving to Alaska, he worked as a tour guide, police officer, and Criminal Justice professor. He has been stationed on a remote island in the Aleutians as a Response Team Commander, and his last job in the Arctic Circle was protecting engineers from ravenous polar bears.

Moving his family to North Idaho, for the past decade, Jack Castle has been crafting thrilling, award-winning, adventures for Silverwood Theme Park and guiding millions of guests through them. He also enjoys helping others get published by teaching writing classes at North Idaho College.

www.JackCastlebooks.com

JACK CASTLE

CPSIA information can be obtained
at www.ICGtesting.com
Printed in the USA
LVHW010021040422
715224LV00008B/352